# THE ALIEN WAS
# TAKING CAREFUL AIM
# WITH HIS REGULATION .38.

All six of his shells struck the target, but that was the best you could say for his aim.

"That's pitiful," Sykes groaned. "Didn't they teach you anything at the Academy? Cripes, what are you gonna do if somebody draws down on you? Wave your scores on the written exam at 'em?"

Francisco listened, taking it all silently. Only when Sykes had finished did he speak up. "Why did you do it?"

"Why'd I do what?"

"Agree to work with me. You don't like me. You have nothing but contempt for my kind. I wish you would explain this to me, Matthew Sykes, because I wish to learn as much as possible about human behavior."

Sykes turned sharply. "I'll tell you why I'm ~~~~~~ ~~~ ~~ ~~~~~~~~ y partner is dead! ~~~~~~~~~~~~~~~~~ illed him before ~~~~~~~~~~~~~~~~~ n Slagtown, where ~~~~~~~~~~~~~~~~~ says nothing. You're ~~~~~~~~~~~~~~~~~ e, Francisco. You're ~~~~~~~~~~~~~~~~ g son-of-a-bitch..."

# ALIEN
# NATION

## Also by Alan Dean Foster

Alien
Aliens
The I Inside
Into the Out of
The Man Who Used the Universe
Shadowkeep
Spellsinger
Spellsinger II: The Hour of the Gate
Spellsinger III: The Day of the Dissonance
Spellsinger IV: The Moment of the Magician
Spellsinger V: The Paths of the Perambulator
Spellsinger VI: The Time of the Transference
Starman

### Published by
### WARNER BOOKS

WARNER BOOKS EDITION

Copyright © 1988 by Twentieth Century Fox Film Corporation.
All rights reserved.

Warner Books, Inc.
666 Fifth Avenue
New York, N.Y. 10103

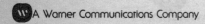A Warner Communications Company

Printed in the United States of America

First Printing: August, 1988

10 9 8 7 6 5 4 3 2 1

A novelization by
# ALAN DEAN FOSTER

# ALIEN NATION

Based on the screenplay by
# ROCKNE S. O'BANNON

**WARNER BOOKS**

A Warner Communications Company

This one's dedicated to James and Gale Anne,
Who are having a lot of fun and sharing it.

# I

Those who saw it called it spectacular, and not a one of them failed to underestimate it.

The Ship hung suspended in a cloudless sky of Mojave blue, immense beyond belief, a cityscape in metal and plastic and god knew what else. It materialized above the dry dead lake bed and hung motionless, a silvery sculpture pinned against the backdrop of the rain-deprived ribs of the southern Sierra Nevadas.

The first human beings to set eyes on the visitor were the McCoys, of Lancaster, California. They were on their way up to Bridgeport for a week of hiking and fishing when Mark McCoy leaned out the window of the family Ford and yelled "Holy Begeesus, Dad—take a look at that!" Words now as firmly set in human history as "*Veni, vidi, vici*" and "One small step for a man, one giant step for mankind." His sister Mandy was the second human to see the Ship, but her words are neither remembered nor recorded.

A trucker with a load of dead beef on his way to L.A. was the next. He was followed by a member of the California Highway Patrol who spent ten minutes staring at the apparition before remembering to respond to his radio, which by that time was going berserk. Reports were starting to come in from all over Southern California and Nevada as others noticed the intruder in their sky. Awestruck citizens in both states could see it because the desert air that morning was so clear.

Also because the Ship was six miles long.

The Army demonstrated its efficiency by completely surrounding and isolating the site within twenty-four hours of the first sighting. Unfortunately, in its haste to mobilize, three civilians and half a platoon of soldiers were killed in separate accidents. Beyond the actual touchdown site, however, there was plenty of room for sightseers. You can't hide a six-mile-long spaceship. The Army tried, though, sealing off US 395 and the secondary highways, emplacing roadblocks on dirt tracks, and keeping Apache attack helicopters on rotating patrol to discourage private pilots from approaching too close. The Air Force got into the act with flights of everything from AH-C's to F-16's. The fighter pilots got dizzy quickly from having to fly constant tight patrol patterns. Civilian air traffic was rerouted all the way south over Yuma and north no lower than Fresno. Meanwhile Soviet spy satellites altered their orbits and took all the closeups the Kremlin needed.

Nothing could prevent people from coming out to see the Ship for themselves. They arrived in cars and campers, BMW's and Jeeps, Winnebago and GM motor homes. Families set up picnic tables and boom boxes and playpens and unfurled portable satellite receiving dishes to entertain children too young to be impressed by six-mile-long spaceships. Good Sam members mingled freely with Yuppies from West Los Angeles who set up beach chairs and broke out wine coolers full of fruit juice. Blue-collar types from the Valley sipped Budweisers and munched Fritos, partied and made love and played cards.

Meanwhile the media, a second arriving army, showed up in elaborate vans and hastily aligned their Ku-band transmitters to relay pictures of the Ship all over the world.

Duncan Crais had been one of the first reporters on the scene. His report was notable for its brevity and for the feeling of excitement he managed to inject into every sentence. He was older now, gray at the temples. His work in covering the Arrival had landed him a cushy anchorman's job down in Atlanta at six figures per annum.

Presently he was narrating a documentary on the Arrival for channel six local. Those assembled in the bar recognized the familiar tense voice as it recounted the events which had forever changed their world.

"That was the scene in California's Mojave Desert three years ago today, the historic first television images of the Newcomer ship upon its dramatic and wholly unexpected arrival. As with the assassination of John F. Kennedy, who among us does not remember exactly where he was and what he was doing that October nineteenth morning when the news first broke: that people had landed. People from another star system."

Those who saw the bar called it depressing, and not a one among them failed to stay for a few minutes at least.

It was crowded and dark. Something about big-city bars makes them seem darker inside than out, even at night. The lights that lit the counter from above and behind appeared to suck the life out of the air. Small bulbs, animated beer advertisements that crawled endlessly from right to left or top to bottom, and forlorn cigarettes that danced in the hands of the still alert like fireflies in the depths of a Louisiana bayou all contributed to the feeling of frantic unease.

While the Hollowpoint Bar was grimmer than most, it was also livelier than many. Gallows humor was prevalent among the regular clientele, a reflection of their work in the profession of law enforcement. Much of the laughter that filled the air nightly was corroded with bitterness.

The single flat-plate television mounted above the far end of the bar continued to spew forth Duncan Crais's florid reminiscences of the Newcomer Arrival. Most of the patrons ignored his voice as well as the accompanying images. Only a few who actually clung to the far end of the counter like bats hanging from the roof of their cave occasionally spared a glance in the direction of those ringing tones.

Somewhere in the center of the floor, country-western clashed with hard rock, two tonal galaxies colliding without mixing. No one objected to the resulting cacophony. Most of them were too busy objecting to more important matters, like their superiors, or their mates, or their day's duty assignment.

Conversation was liberally sprinkled with four-letters words and a vile street terminology never encountered in what passed outside the Hollowpoint for "polite" society. The two men seated at the middle of the counter did not belong to polite society. It was their job to protect those who did belong from individuals only a little less disreputable than themselves.

They were cops. More precisely, detectives. Down, dirty, and very good at their jobs. Right now they were also a little drunk.

Fedorchuk's ancestors might've been cossacks—or the serfs they persecuted. He was big and sloppy and his suits never fit quite right. He was also never late for check-in and never sick, traits which endeared him to his superiors if not his colleagues. Not that he was especially dedicated or devoted to his profession. It was just that he had nothing else to do, and he knew it. So he went to work. He'd been a good street cop and he made an adequate detective. In the eyes of his superiors, his punctuality more than compensated for his lack of intuition.

His partner Alterez was quieter, which in comparison to Fedorchuk didn't mean much. Alterez was one of the boys, a classification he took pride in. For a former homeboy he'd accomplished a lot, striving to make himself indistinguishable from the Anglos he worked with. As a result, he'd acquired many of his paler colleagues' bad traits instead of the good ones. Not that there were many good ones to pick up at the station house. He and Fedorchuk were ponderous, unimaginative, foul-mouthed, and efficient. They suited one another.

Fedorchuk bent over his drink and sipped from the wide-mouthed glass without using his hands to steady it as he gazed up at the flickering TV. His brows drew together when he lifted his head.

"I remember where I was. You don't forget something

like that, right? I was pissing off my balcony at the neighbor's dog!''

Since all those seated at the bar near Fedorchuk were of a similar mindset and attitude toward life, they found this pious reminiscence uproariously funny. Alterez only smiled. He was used to his partner's witticisms. Instead of commenting or replying to the joke, he turned his attention to the brightly lit TV. It did not matter that Duncan Crais couldn't hear him. What mattered to Alterez was that he could hear himself.

"Get to the goddamn ball scores!"

"You tell 'em, partner." Fedorchuk's eyes narrowed as he devoted all his attention to his glass. Locating the rim with his lips alone was always a trying challenge. He prided himself on accepting challenges, particularly those which were self-imposed.

A glance upward revealed that Crais had metamorphosed into a middle-aged professor from Cal Tech. She looked uncomfortable in her starched blue suit, her movements suggesting that her natural habitat was a white lab smock. But all bowed down to and complied with the demands of the all-powerful television tube. She was willing to sacrifice for science. Fedorchuk found himself wondering what she looked like beneath the suit.

"From the time mankind first gazed up at the stars there had been speculation about a visit by people from 'out there.' How ironic that when the first contact was finally made, the two hundred and sixty thousand occupants aboard the starship were as surprised as we were about their arrival. They awakened from frozen hibernation, a kind of extended deep sleep, only to find that a malfunctioning autopilot had landed them on our world by mistake. They were many degrees off course and many hundreds of light-years from their intended destination."

She looked as though she might have more to say, but something offscreen caught her attention and she went silent. The man seated on Alterez's left made a rude noise. Crais reappeared, taking the scientist's place. He was relaxed, immaculately coiffured, secure in his position and fame.

"These 'Newcomers,' we soon learned, were genetically engineered people, created to perform hard labor under difficult environmental conditions. It would not be appropriate to call them slaves, but they had been given no choice in their future. Their destiny had been determined elsewhere, without their consent. Destiny, however, did not count on a malfunctioning autopilot. Instead of their intended planetfall, they found themselves stranded here on Earth, their vessel's peculiar and so far incomprehensible fuel system exhausted, with no way to return where they came from nor to contact those who had sent them on their way so long ago. . . ."

Beer glasses rattled noisily nearby. Annoyed, a couple of the patrons glanced in the direction of the busboy, as quickly forgot his clumsiness to return to their own conversations, or to the documentary running interminably on the overhead screen.

In the interval, Crais had once more been replaced, this time by a woman in her mid-forties. She was standing on the front porch of a house with the sun shining heavily behind her. A dog ran through the picture in the background, chased by a boy of eight. Fedorchuk wondered cynically if both boy and dog had been acquired from Central Casting, or if they actually belonged to the woman smiling at the camera. Probably a second assistant director was standing somewhere offscreen left, tempting the dog with a steak and the boy with a fiver.

The detective downed the rest of his drink and left the empty glass where the bartender would see it. The tender here knew him and his partner well. The glass would magically refill without him having to make a request.

"When the Newcomers were first let out of their ship," the woman was saying, "they were quarantined in a camp not ten miles from the town here." She smiled. An uncoached smile, Fedorchuk decided, feeling a little better about Duncan Crais and his crew. "You can imagine how the people around here felt about *that*. But once they were processed and studied by the scientists and finally released from the camp and we got a chance to know them, we saw what nice, quiet *people* they really are.''

Someone nearer the TV muttered something coarse. A couple of other patrons laughed. The man who'd spoken rose and fumbled with the channel buttons for a moment. A half-hearted cheer went up as another news program filled the screen. It wasn't the scores, but it was less boring.

Fedorchuk looked back down at his glass. Sure enough, when he wasn't looking it had acquired another inch of pale golden liquid and two fresh ice cubes. His lips frozen in a perpetual thin smile of servitude and understanding, the bartender nodded once in Fedorchuk's direction. The detective smiled thankfully in return.

The bartender ignored the hulking figure hard at work behind him. The busboy was like all the rest of the Newcomers: massive, humanoid, difficult to tell from a normal human being at first glance except for his size. Only when he turned did the telltale marking pattern on his bald skull and the absence of external ears become apparent. He could have crushed the bartender with a single false step, but instead the alien functioned smoothly around him, always giving ground when it was contested, always making way. He held two full racks of beer glasses without strain. Fedorchuk called out to him.

"Hey, Henry!" All the Newcomers had been assigned human names when it was found that their own varied from the difficult to the unpronounceable. They accepted their new names with the same equanimity as they had accepted their fate at being cast upon a world they had not been designed to live upon. The shipwrecked do not debate the declarations of the natives.

"How you doin' tonight?" Fedorchuk continued. "Workin' hard? Work like that can be a pain, y'know."

Expressionless but aware he was being addressed, the Newcomer named Henry turned slowly. His face was almost as human as Fedorchuk's, which was not saying much. Still, the similarities between Newcomer and human being were extraordinary, the differences slight. Slight, but disturbing. A Newcomer never looked quite right.

Fedorchuk wasn't through. He was enjoying himself. "You got your green card, buddy? You didn't leave home without it? I wouldn't want to have to take you in."

There were other cops at the bar. Some knew Fedorchuk, others did not. Most found their colleague's clever sally amusing. Henry simply stared expectantly back at Fedorchuk. There was no malice in his eyes, no pain in his expression. He blinked once. Then he turned to carry the heavy trays of dirty glasses back into the kitchen.

## II

The car was as ugly as the section of town it was patrolling. Low and squat, multiple layers of paint having long since merged into an Ur-green, it trundled along the streets of the alien part of Los Angeles unappreciated and little remarked upon. Sykes and Tuggle wouldn't have traded it for the newest, hottest freeway cruiser in the department. The slugmobile had character if not class. Since its occupants had no class either, they found it quite satisfactory.

Its guts were a dirty mélange of parts ancient and new. Only one mechanic at the station garage dared go near it. The others were either disdainful of the arcane collection of machinery, or afraid of it. Or afraid of what detectives Sykes and Tuggle might do to them if they screwed up the precious pile of ambulatory junk. The two bore an unreasonable affection for their vehicle, even for men working in L.A., where divorce actions were known to sometimes center on custody not of children, but of the family road machines.

The slugmobile hardly ever broke down. Its profile was dangerous, but the old steel sides would turn bullets that would rip right through the flanks of the new carbonfiber composite auto frames. It took good care of the two men who used it to cruise the dark back streets of the metropolis, and they in their turn looked after it.

The alien section of Los Angeles wasn't all that different

from the rest of the great urban sprawl. A little dirtier than most areas, grimmer than many, with only the occasional unexpected touch to remind a visitor that it was populated largely by refugees from another world. Sometimes you had to know just where to look in order to be able to tell where you were. Sykes and Tuggle had been on the street a long time and knew where to look.

Newcomers filled the oversized chairs of a grungy all-night diner. The chair backs and seats had been locally modified to accept their expansive frames. Another Newcomer emerged from a double doorway off on their right as the slugmobile slid down the street. Tuggle noted the inscription on the window next to the doors. The old laundromat had been converted into a night school for aliens.

They passed a city park, still green despite an obvious lack of regular maintenance. City workers weren't fond of the alien end of town. Weeds had supplanted much of the original grass and had also invaded the cracks in the sidewalk, advancing on the once sacrosanct pavement itself. Despite the lateness of the hour a group of alien families had gathered to enjoy each other's company. They were engaged in an alien game of uncertain purpose and incomprehensible strategy. Sykes stared and shook his head, trying to make some sense of it and failing utterly as Tuggle pointed the slugmobile up Washington.

"Jeez, they call that organized gang-bang a game?" Tuggle pursed his lips. On the billboard to their right, an exquisite female alien displayed yard-high white teeth while pressing a cold Pepsi to her lips. The billboard was the only piece of new construction in the immediate neighborhood.

Tuggle slowed as they approached the next intersection, the light against them. As soon as they slowed to a halt, a huge palm slammed against the window close by Sykes's head. He jerked back involuntarily, startled, then relaxed when he got a good look at the hand's owner.

The Newcomer was a derelict. Mumbling in his own sibilant language, he stood next to the car, weaving in place while fighting to stay erect. Filth and grime coated his face and worn clothing and his eyes were half-lidded and bloodshot. One dirty, broken-nailed fist clutched a quart carton of milk. It looked small as a pint in the massive palm.

Tuggle glanced speculatively in his partner's direction. Sykes returned a look of disgust, shook his head negatively, then rolled down the window on the alien's side.

"Can't you see this is a cop car, buddy? Look, we ain't in the mood tonight. So take a hike, okay?"

As soon as he finished he caught a full whiff of the derelict's breath. Wincing, he rolled up the window as Tuggle pulled away. In the enclosed atmosphere of the slugmobile the smell was slow to dissipate.

Tuggle's eyes took in the rearview. "He's standing in the middle of the street, waving his arms."

Sykes didn't bother to look back. The disgust was still clear on his face, his nose still wrinkled against the odor. "No traffic and it's late. He'll move in a minute or two and find himself an alley somewhere." Digging into his pocket, he found a plastic container of breath mints and popped a couple into his mouth. Tuggle refused the offer of one and the container vanished anew.

"Why's it have to be sour milk that these guys get wasted on? What the hell's wrong with Jack Daniels, or *Thunderbird*, for crissakes?"

Tuggle shrugged, his favorite gesture. He was a lot less flamboyant than his partner, and consciously so. "Beats me. Beats some of the eggheads, too, from what I've read about it. The Newcomers' physiology is full of curves, some of 'em physical, some of 'em chemical. You got to admit one thing: it's a cheap drunk."

"Yeah." Sykes stared out the window, studying lights and lonely streets. "Slagtown. Wonder what this part of L.A. used to be called before the Newcomers moved in?"

"Don't ask me. I ain't no history buff."

Tuggle turned the slugmobile up Broadway, now home to all-night liquor stores and cheap parlor entertainments. The theaters were nearly all closed down, there as yet being no films directed specifically at the Newcomer communities. Hollywood was still working that one out. But a couple of places played the usual, struggling to draw enough Newcomer patrons to stay in business. No comedies. Human

comedy was incomprehensible to all but the most sophisti-
cated aliens. The majority preferred action-adventure stories
and, oddly enough, love stories. Alien housewives were
regular watchers of the morning TV soaps.

Newcomer hookers paraded near the theaters and restau-
rants, plying their trade. Not all Newcomer habits were
incomprehensible. The women were elegant and impossibly
tall, Sykes mused. He spoke as he stared.

"Wonder if their plumbing's the same?"

"It is." Tuggle spoke in his usual monotone, without
taking his eyes off the road. Sykes eyed him curiously.

As he was preparing to ask the inevitable next question a
long, lowrider station wagon pulled up alongside the
slugmobile, grumbling through its chopped 427 Chevy engine. It peeled off fast at the next intersection, but for all his
bravado the driver was careful to remain well within the
posted speed limit. He was giving the cop car the vehicular
finger, but masking it with caution. Tuggle cruised on, past
alien eateries and specialty shops.

Slow night, Sykes thought. Just the usual Slagtown de-
pression hanging like steady rain over the storefronts and
dark apartment buildings. Even the bums and thugs moved
slowly, tiredly here. He made a quick search of the dash,
locating his cup of coffee amidst the rubble of two weeks'
worth of collected embalmed fast food by the steamed circle
it made against the windshield. Tuggle was chewing on his
lower lip as if trying to decide whether or not to say
something. Sykes knew his partner would get around to
whatever it was eventually. You didn't ride with a man for
nine years without getting to know him pretty well.

It wasn't what Sykes expected to hear, however, when Tuggle
finally spoke up. Nor was it a subject he wished to discuss.

"So, you gonna go, or you not gonna go?" his partner
asked him tersely.

Sykes considered a response as he watched Tuggle expertly
scoop up and begin noshing on a triangle of limp, lukewarm
pizza. It was a delicate balancing act: driving, eating, and
somehow simultaneously managing not to decorate his suit
with cheese drippings or tomato sauce. Sykes couldn't have

done it. No matter how hard he tried he always ended up wearing full evidence of his previous days' meals on his pants and shirt. Tuggle never said a word. He didn't have to. The looks he gave his partner's attire after such assaults were eloquent enough.

"How can I go?" he replied, trying to make it sound offhand and inevitable that he not go.

Tuggle wasn't having any of it. "How can you not go? Don't give me your excuses. Put on your wash-and-wear suit and your clip-on tie, have your landlady tie your shoes for you, and show up at the church. Simple. Even for somebody like you." He paused a moment, focusing his attention on the row of illuminated storefronts sliding past on their right. "Me and Carol are going."

That got Sykes's attention. "What?"

"Hey, look, you got no cause to say anything. We've known Kristin since she was conceived in that cabin up at Big Bear." He sat a little straighter behind the wheel and tried to lighten the mood. "Remember that night? You and Edie banged the wall so hard, me and Carol were picking plaster out of our hair for a week. I knew we should have insisted on taking the upstairs. But naw, we had to go and be generous, let you guys have the king bed. Some vacation that was. No sleep."

"Edie and me didn't sleep much ourselves, but then you already had that figured out." Sykes's newly won smile faded rapidly. "Goddamnit, Tug, I want to see Kristin get married too, okay? More than I want just about anything else. But I . . ."

Tuggle finished it for him. "But you're bummed out because your ex and her husband are paying for the whole thing."

Sykes started to argue, changed his mind. Tuggle knew when his partner was lying and would be too polite to point it out. That took any fun out of trying.

"Shit, if Kristin had to get married where I could afford it, we'd be holding the reception at Buddy Burgers. So what could I say? Kristin's marrying money. Can't say that I blame her. We sure as hell never had any of the stuff."

"Look at it as Kristin's money. She'd want you to be there, buddy."

"I want to be there as much as she wants me to be there, but try and see it my way, Tuggle. Father of the bride, the poor relation. Everybody on the other side giving me those damn pitying looks rich folks reserve for the rest of us who'll never own one of their colored credit cards. I got too much pride left for that, Tug. It's about all I do have left."

"Screw your pride. You should go."

"Yeah, I know, I know. What're you, my goddamn fairy godmother?"

"That's me. Wanna see my wand?"

"What's to . . . ," Sykes broke off abruptly. Only half his brain had been concentrating on the seemingly insurmountable problem of whether or not to attend the wedding of his only daughter.

The other half—the other half continued functioning on standard detective op. Something he saw triggered the automatic alarm inside his head. It also had the virtue of taking the rest of his brain off his pissed-off mood. He nodded out the window.

"Uh-oh. Check it out."

Tuggle turned responsively, squinting. "Check what out? All I see is dark."

"Up ahead. By the corner right, two o'clock."

Tuggle slowed the slugmobile, straining to see whatever it was that had aroused his partner's attention. Sykes's night vision was better than his. Rumor at the station had it that Sykes was some kind of nocturnal throwback, that he actually saw better at night than during the day.

Both aliens wore long coats, and it wasn't that cold outside. Nor were they slouching along like a couple of drunken perverts. Perverts didn't work in pairs. Other kinds of vermin did.

The coats were different. One was black vinyl, the other a heavy black or dark blue that didn't look water repellent. Raincoat, as Tuggle immediately dubbed him in his mind, flaunted a zip-up dark shirt tight at the neck and fancy shoes. The other alien was partially hidden by his companion's bulk.

The two entered a small minimart that occupied the corner of the block, Raincoat looking back to check the street before following his buddy inside.

"Does that look at all suspicious to you?" Sykes murmured thoughtfully.

Tuggle affected an air of mock innocence. "Now whatever would give you that idea?"

He found an empty slot between parked cars and eased the slugmobile into the gap. Sykes had his revolver out and was checking the chambers as his partner cut engine and lights.

Automatically finding the right controls on the radio, Tuggle flipped to the proper channel without taking his eyes off the street. "This is One Henry Seven. We've got a possible two-eleven in progress at Porter's minimart, corner of Court and Alvarado. Requesting backup."

Sykes was starting out the door. "Let's do it, partner."

His friend's hand came down on his shoulder. "Easy, cowboy. One of these days you're gonna get your head blown off pursuing justice a little too closely."

Sykes stopped half in, half out the door, grinned back at Tuggle. "I like to keep close enough to see her backside. That's what they told us at the Academy. 'Never lose sight of Justice.'"

Tuggle sighed, shook his head, and replaced the radio mike on its hook as the dispatcher sputtered acknowledgment back at them.

The old buildings looming over Alvarado had been built a long time ago, before the heyday of the two-car family arrived in Los Angeles. The detectives were grateful for that. It meant there were few garages, which meant little in the way of off-street parking, which meant plenty of cover as they dodged behind the lines of battered Toyotas and Buicks in their stealthy advance toward the brightly lit convenience store.

Two minutes later they were near enough to see the interior through the dirty plate glass and burglar bars. Porter's minimart was unimpressive, the shelves sloppily stocked, with none of the neatness familiar from Circle K's or 7-Elevens. The ceiling lights hung from naked chains, the harsh fluorescents illuminating dirt and dust.

They could also clearly see the aged alien proprietor. He was standing behind the counter conversing animatedly with one of the two aliens who'd just entered. He stopped talking when the taller Newcomer reached into his coat and withdrew a blunt, combat-grade pump-action shotgun and aimed it at his chest. Raincoat extracted a similar weapon from the depths of his black slicker and whirled to confront the deserted doorway. It was hard to make out the Newcomer expressions at a distance and through the glass, but Sykes thought Raincoat looked nervous. The one facing down the proprietor was relaxed and all business.

"Christ, you see what they're carrying?"

"Yeah." Tuggle's expression had gone grim. "Backup better get here quick. Don't do anything stupid. Or brave."

"Who, me? You got your vest?"

Tuggle winced as he was reminded of his bulletproof chest protector. "Of course. Nice and safe according to regulation, right next to the spare in the trunk."

"Yeah, that's comforting, ain't it? Mine too."

They were both tense because of the unexpected heavy firepower the two aliens had produced. Combat shotguns hardly seemed required for holding up mom-and-pop groceries. Maybe the thieves were insecure.

The larger alien was gesturing sharply with the powerful weapon. Though they couldn't hear anything out in the street, they could see the Newcomer's lips working rapidly, could see the terror that came into the old proprietor's eyes. He started filling a brown paper sack with cash from the register.

Tuggle nodded tensely. "Back of the room, rear right." Flicking his eyes past the pantomime being played out before them, Sykes saw that the proprietor's wife was standing frozen-faced near a back portal. Out front, Raincoat was hopping from foot to foot to relieve the tension. No human being would have moved in quite that fashion, could have managed quite so perfect a succession of cross-steps without preplanning. The emotions, if not the dance steps, were the same. It only served to remind the two detectives crouched across the street that none of the people inside the grocery were human.

The proprietor continued shoveling money into the bag. It was taking a long time because his hands were shaking and he kept dropping bills. This only made his tormentor angrier, which in turn made the old fellow more nervous still.

Raincoat wasn't the only participant in the nighttime drama who was getting antsy. Tuggle nodded at a car parked near the market.

"Watch the driver. I'm going for a better angle on the door."

Sykes glanced down the street, back at his partner. "Thought you wanted to wait for a backup?"

"They'll be here in a minute. Got to make a move now. The driver."

Sykes turned back to the street, leveling his pistol. "I got him. Don't get pinned going in."

His partner nodded curtly, then took off like a scared crab, running crosswise across the intersection. Sykes waited until his partner was under cover once more before returning his attention to the store.

The larger alien was grabbing up the sack of cash and shoving it into his coat pocket. Bills tumbled to the floor. The thief ignored them. Sykes frowned at that but had no time to work it out. The hair on his neck stiffened as it began. He felt like a man watching a slow-motion striptease, unable to react, unable to interact. It was insane. It made no sense.

Madness.

Without any warning of any kind, the robber whipped the shotgun up and fired. At close range the twelve-gauge shell opened up the old proprietor's chest like a demolition charge, slamming him backward into shelves crammed with cans and packaged goods. He never had a chance. And there was no reason for it, no reason at all.

As if to compound the craziness, as the oldster slid to the floor the thief leaned over the counter and pumped another round into the crumpled body.

"Aw, shit." Sykes was rising from his crouch.

Tuggle had almost made it across the street when the first shot was fired. He dropped instinctively, then raised his head for a clear look. As he did so a horn blared and both men looked in surprise down the street.

Sedan, late model. The horn howled a second time, a disembodied voice fleeing the pavement. Sykes barely had time to see that the human driver was starting his engine before all hell broke loose.

Reacting to the horn's shriek, the two aliens inside the market turned in time to spot Tuggle crouched out on the asphalt. They opened fire instantly, blasting through the plate glass. One shellburst struck pavement. Another hit a civilian car rolling through the intersection, perforating its radiator and bringing it to a halt nearby. The terrified alien driver had the good sense to stay inside and out of sight.

Tuggle rose and made a dash for the cover of a nearby lamppost. As he did so, the human driver of the getaway vehicle emerged to level a machine pistol in the direction of the fleeing detective. Sykes immediately turned his attention to this new threat, hoping the two aliens would elect to stay under cover inside the minimart. As the driver fired at him, Sykes was forced to duck down behind the car that was providing his own cover. The rapid-fire machine pistol raked the metal and safety glass above his head.

A moving van came trundling down the street, its driver unaware of the battle raging intermittently before him. The getaway driver grinned and came around in front of his car, a new clip punched into the belly of his pistol. What he failed to see was that as he advanced under cover of the slow-moving van, Sykes was already racing around its front. The driver of the van barely had time enough to look shocked as Sykes burst in front of him, leveled his revolver, and put the getaway driver on his back.

Now the aliens had no driver and it was Sykes who was using their vehicle for protection. There was a potential hostage present in the person of the proprietor's wife, but they chose to ignore her. Sykes stayed low, occasionally rising long enough to get off a couple of shots in the store's direction, ducking back down when an answering shotgun burst howled inside.

And where the hell, he wondered frantically, was their damn freaking backup?

With only the thin lamppost for cover, Tuggle was much worse off. Seeing this, the aliens were concentrating their fire in his direction and ignoring Sykes's wild shots.

Sykes leaned around the front of the sedan. "Tug, get outta there!"

Tuggle heard him and nodded, leaned left, and immediately drew back as twelve-gauge shot rattled off the post. "I can't! Do you mind?"

"I'll cover you! Get outta there!"

"Well, if you're gonna insist."

Sykes made a face in his partner's direction, then rose and rapid-fired an entire clip in the store's direction. It was enough to make both robbers temporarily dive for cover. Seizing the opportunity, Tuggle scrambled out from behind the lamppost and ran like hell for the nearest real cover, which happened to be the radiator-pierced car stalled nearby. Throwing himself onto the hood and rolling down the other side, he got his feet under him before slowly rising for a look through the glass.

His attention was distracted by the car's occupant. The elderly alien driver was still inside, lying flat on the front seat and breathing hard. He eyed Tuggle desperately.

"Can I get out now?"

"Come on, move it!"

He all but dragged the oldster out of the seat, watched as the Newcomer scrambled for safety around the nearest corner. His legs were moving fast enough to belie his real age.

"You okay?" Sykes's voice, concerned.

"Yeah! We having fun yet?"

Sykes didn't reply to that one. After checking his pistol, Tuggle rose and took careful aim at the store. The aliens were taking their time reloading, but it was hard to pick them out inside among the shelves and counters. His individual blasts in their direction drew heavy return fire. For some reason the shotguns' echoes lingered longer in the night air than they had earlier.

Glass shattered above his head as the car windows were blown out. That didn't bother him. What widened his eyes was a shuddering in the body of the vehicle he sat crouched behind. Metal ripped and smoked off to his right. That last shot had gone right through the whole car. Through the car. As he stared dumbfoundedly at the ragged hole, a second blast tore through the thick sheet metal barely inches from his shoulder.

Panicked, he scuttled toward the front of the car, blasts and exit holes following him in neat, orderly succession, until only the fender remained. Nowhere left to go except to the next car. Not too far away up the street. Ten feet. A lousy ten feet. No time left to think, either. He rose and ran.

Two steps from the second car the next blast hit him in the side, knocking him to his right, his arms flailing wildly at the air like those of a rag doll dropped from a speeding car. A second blast caught him in the chest as he was spun around by the first, but it didn't hurt him. He couldn't be hurt any further. The first shot had cut through his spine. He was dead before he struck the asphalt.

Sykes saw it happen and could only stare. Tuggle had been his partner for nine years. Tuggle had been his friend for nine years. And Tug was down hard in the street.

The big alien loosed one, two, three additional shots in the direction of the motionless detective. One blast caught the prone body and tumbled it over like a loose stone. Then he grabbed at his buddy and threw him toward the rear of the market. As he did so the shotgun fell from Raincoat's fingers. Neither paused to recover the dropped weapon as they searched wildly for the store's rear exit.

Sykes could have charged in then, might have had a good shot at them. Instead he was racing across the street. He slowed as he approached Bill Tuggle's body. There was no need to check for a pulse, no need to turn it over for closer inspection. The three powerful blasts had reduced the body of his partner to something unrecognizable.

One minute he'd been nearby, exchanging sour gags,

alive and warm and wise-cracking across the pavement. Now he was gone. It wasn't always necessary to check for the heartbeat of a gunshot victim. Sykes had been on the street a long time. He didn't check. Nobody had ever looked deader than Bill Tuggle looked right then.

"Aw shit, Tug, Jesus! Goddamnit!"

Sometimes all you can do is stare and curse. Not all cops pray in the conventional sense, but most do something similar. Sykes's lips didn't move, but anyone could see what he was feeling in his eyes. Words and images rushed through his dazed brain, all jumbled up together like one of Edie's stews, and his lousy mind wasn't equal to the task of sorting them out. He couldn't make sense of any of it.

Then his expression changed, his gaze came alive with something else. It spilled over into his entire being and took possession of him. By rights he ought to have stayed where he was. Sirens were wailing against the night. Their backup on its way, too late, too far away. By rights he had no business leaving the scene to pursue, one against two. Crazy, insane, madness. Why not sweep him up in it also? What did anything matter, with Tug a limp pile of meat in the middle of a Slagtown street?

He took off toward the store, eyes wild, rage giving wings to his feet.

The store was deserted, the proprietor's wife having fled. He nearly fell twice, slipping and sliding on broken glass, heedless of sharp-edged shelving and the possibility of catching a surprise shell. The rear door stood ajar. He plunged through just in time to catch a glimpse of the two tall aliens rounding the corner at the far end of the service alley. He felt as though he were flying along, his feet hardly touching the ground, the years seeming to fall away from his muscles as he built up speed in pursuit. He wasn't worried. Not yet. It was difficult for Newcomer fugitives to find places to hide. The department learned that early on. Size wasn't always an advantage to a mugger or purse-snatcher. They made nice, big, fat targets. The gun in his hand was light as a feather.

By the time he rounded the corner they'd vanished. The

street ahead was open and uncluttered, well-lit by bright overheads. The shops were closed, the storefronts mute and dim. Despite the absence of parked cars there were plenty of shadows and hiding places. He advanced more slowly now.

Cops who'd survived years on the street didn't have the sixth sense, but they had something else: caution developed through fear.

It was a small noise, insignificant. Anyone else would have paid it no heed. Sykes immediately turned toward it, toward the base of a high, overbearing billboard mutely advertising beer clenched in an alien fist. The tall alien had given himself a difficult angle for the shotgun. Without thinking, Sykes dove to his left.

What was brutally effective at close range was hard to aim with distance. The blast blew apart the top of the crate the detective flopped behind, but not the part he'd chosen to use as cover. Still intact, he scrambled on his belly, cursing the inventors of all shotguns, moving deeper into the pile of empty crates like some hyperkinetic centipede high on speed.

A new sound caused him to rise to his knees. It was a sharp click, loud and metallic in the quiet night: the sound of a hammer dropping on an empty chamber. His grin turned feral as he rose.

Dropping from the bottom of a fire escape and tossing the empty shotgun aside, the alien took off up the street. Sykes followed. He was closer now, a good deal closer. Close enough to see the Newcomer turn the next corner. He followed without slowing. The robber had sacrificed his lead for a failed ambush. Sykes wouldn't lose him now.

There was a pedestrian tunnel ahead, a black gaping hole punched through a concrete wall. No other way out, no other way in. He slowed, his nerves screaming with tension, his brain flashing that big red caution sign.

The concrete was cold and damp against his back as he started inside, his finger taut on the handgun's trigger. Then he realized it was the usual dry L.A. night and that the dampness came from the perspiration that was pouring down the back of his undershirt.

The murkiness inside the circular opening expanded to

engulf him as he edged slowly inward, trying to control his breathing so he could hear clearly. It was drier inside the tunnel than out. The only sound was the scuffing his shoes made on the ground.

Very dark but not completely so, shadows distinguishable but not shapes. That's when he heard the footsteps. Not subtle or cautious like his own, not trying to conceal their presence, but loud and pounding. The only problem was that in the darkness he couldn't tell which direction they were coming from because the sound bounced like mad off the concrete walls of the tunnel. He was surrounded by looming echoes.

He barely spun around in time to confront the massive shape as it lunged in his direction. It uttered something violent in a nonhuman tongue that was all sibilant hissing and glottal stops. Vinyl slapped at his face like the wings of a fish-catching bat.

Somehow he brought the pistol up in time to fire once, twice, three times. Raincoat stumbled backward, his knees collapsing an inch at a time like the legs of a folding ladder, until he finally lay on his back on the tunnel floor. Sykes found time to breathe, then advanced slowly.

With an inhuman bellow, the alien abruptly snapped erect and reached for the detective with both long, outstretched arms.

A startled Sykes jumped backward and fired twice more at the dim silhouette. This time when the raincoat-clad figure went down, he stayed down.

Damn aliens, Sykes thought. His heart was pounding hard enough to break ribs.

Only his street-sensitive hearing and his unwavering caution had saved him, had allowed him to react to those last, closing footsteps. Just as they made him turn now.

This noise was peculiar, an almost childish soft tinkling. Metal against metal, jangling like toys or cheap jewelry. Jewelry. He turned in a circle, the pistol extended before him, saw nothing, and only looked *up* at the last possible moment.

As one of the two aliens dropped down on him from directly above.

They both went down together, the alien grabbing with huge hands, Sykes rolling frantically and somehow managing to hang on to his gun. As he tried to bring it to bear, the alien swung the side of one palm and connected with the detective's wrist. Pain raced through his hand and the gun went skittering across the floor.

Sykes tried to run, found himself being lifted into the air as if he were a child. The alien threw him up the tunnel. More pain, racing through Sykes's back and arms as he hit the unyielding surface hard. A damn good thing, he thought crazily, that the Newcomer hadn't thought to throw him into the wall. That would likely be next.

Far off in the distance an angel was calling through the haze that filled Sykes's brain. A siren, mournful yet promising. Too far away.

The alien was coming for him now; confident, silent, unopposable. As he approached, Sykes heard the distinctive clinking sound which had almost warned him in time. It was dark and his eyes were full of dancing Christmas lights, but he still caught a quick glimpse of the source of the noise. It was jewelry, yes, but not cheap. An exotic silver bracelet of obviously alien design dangled from the Newcomer's right wrist. As the links slapped against one another they produced the musical metallic tones that had tickled his hearing.

The Newcomer loomed over the fallen detective, his head scraping the tunnel ceiling, one fist raised to deliver a final blow. At the same time, the formerly faint echo of the siren grew much louder, as if it had turned a nearby corner. Lights, flashing and glorious, illuminated the front entrance to the concrete tunnel.

The alien turned to glare in their direction, the red and blue glow coming from outside throwing him into sudden sharp relief. Then he turned, and without another glance in the direction of the fallen detective, jumped over the prone, helpless body and sprinted off down the tunnel.

Sykes listened to the fading footsteps as he fought to get back on his feet. He was still stunned, his vision still unfocused. He fought to rise. Damned if the bluecoats would find him moaning on the floor.

Then an alien face was gazing close into his own.

Without hesitating or thinking, he brought his right fist up and around with all his might. He couldn't have been that bad off because his punch landed square in the center of that alien visage. Caught by surprise, the staring Newcomer tumbled to the ground.

Don't let him get up, Sykes found himself thinking frantically. Don't give him a chance to get up. He rose and tottered forward, trying to position his right foot for a crippling kick.

Only to find himself grabbed from behind and held tight as he tried to attack. He half turned in the restraining arms, relaxed only when he saw that beneath its blue cap this new face was wholly human. The golden badge riding the crest of the cap gleamed in the bad light like an Aztec relic.

"Whoa, whoa, hold it! Take it easy!" the cap's owner was telling him. Sound advice, Sykes mused. Useful advice. Not to mention welcome. Suddenly he was conscious of how much running he'd done, of how exhausted he really was. Some of the tension drained out of him.

The uniform was still talking, but not to him. Instead, he was gazing with concern at the alien still on the ground.

"You okay?"

Easier for the eyes to focus when you stood still, Sykes told himself as he tried to make sense of what he was seeing. The aliens were tough because they were big, but they were not invulnerable. The proof of that was the one he'd just decked, lying sprawled on his ass ten feet away. As Sykes looked on, the Newcomer sat up and recovered his cap. A blue-badged cap, just like the one Sykes's restrainer was wearing.

At that point the detective realized he'd just flattened a fellow cop. A Newcomer cop.

"I am all right." His enunciation was very precise, with none of the accent that afflicted so much Newcomer English. Whoever he was, he'd spent a lot of time with voice tapes. The result was accentless, yes, but somewhat stilted.

He didn't look all right. A trickle of purplish blood was trailing from his left nostril. The human cop studied his colleague for a moment, then decided his medical needs weren't serious.

"I'd better call in." He stepped around Sykes and headed up the tunnel.

The alien watched him leave, then rose and came toward Sykes. The detective tensed. He'd popped the Newcomer pretty hard. But retaliation wasn't what the cop had on his otherworldly mind. He ignored Sykes as he moved past him to kneel beside the dead alien. Fingers groped Raincoat's upper arm, hunting for a pulse. Sykes mumbled a desultory query.

"Nothing." The Newcomer's tone was emotionless. "He's quite dead." Rising, he turned to see Sykes cradling the bruised fist he'd struck out with. The detective took a step, stumbled. Instantly a massive arm went around his upper body to support him. Concern entered the alien's voice.

"Your hand will require attention."

Sykes jerked himself free, stumbling a second time but angrily refusing additional assistance. "Get the hell away from me! I don't need your goddamn help!"

Obediently the alien released his grip. Sykes nearly lost his balance, had to steady himself against the tunnel wall. He was a picture of impotent rage and frustration. One alien dead was good. One still on the loose was infuriating. His reactions to the Newcomer cop standing stolidly nearby and gazing back at him with that slightly inquisitive expression they always wore when trying to comprehend the vagaries of human nature provoked feelings inside Sykes that lay somewhere in between.

# III

The lights hanging from the ceiling of the minimart were supplemented by the harsh glare of the coroner's floods. Had to make sure every inch of every wound was properly illuminated for the cameras. Don't miss any important details or you'll have the boys from Forensics all over you before you can say "severe trauma to the skull." Movietime. Sykes had seen enough contemporary coroner work to last him a lifetime. It was enough to make you curse the invention of the camcorder. Stills were easier to look at. But stills were never as thorough. Or as graphic.

They'd brought what was left of Bill Tuggle into the market for the usual preliminary study, which considering the force of the blasts his body had absorbed had taken plenty of time. Now they were loading the body bag into the back of the meat wagon. Sykes stood and watched. There wasn't anything else to do and he was already wondering if he'd be able to stand going to Tug's funeral. Right now he was still numb enough to watch.

Hopefully, he was going to be very busy very soon.

The store and the street outside were crowded, packed with Los Angeles Metropolitan Police Department black-and-whites, Forensics vehicles, and cops trying to keep back a crowd of alien rubberneckers who'd gathered to stare. Two of the cops working the crowd were Newcomers, like the one Sykes had floored. A few humans stood out in the mass of onlookers. Everybody loves a catastrophe, the detective mused dully.

They were closing the doors on the wagon now. Not even a lumpy outline left to stare at. Nine years. No ring, no flowers, but plenty of beer and gags and good work and pleasant memories. A lot shared. Just the memories left now. Oh yes, and something else. Some unfinished business he had to attend to. He shuffled into the overlit store.

It was fuller than it had been in a long time, but not with customers. The team on the scene was all over the place; checking for prints, digging shotgun and police special shells out of the walls and groceries, taking photographs of every foot of the interior. A laserscan unit was hard at work in front of the blood-splattered counter, searching for microscopic samples of blood and dried perspiration. The scanner operator wore a cumbersome outfit and harness while his partner's eyes stayed glued to the remote readout screen. Several uniformed cops milled around, chatting and trying not to look bored.

Sykes moved aimlessly through the mob like a stranger at a party, talking to no one. Those he knew had also known Tuggle. They knew what had taken place here, and knew enough not to speak to him.

His attention was caught by the proprietor's wife. The tall old woman was standing near the body of her husband, her stance peculiarly rigid. A thin, keening sound came from between her lips, an eerie yet somehow comforting alien dirge. You had to be close to even hear it. No screaming or wailing, no flailing of arms in agony here. Just that simple, hardly varying wail. Sykes wondered what it meant, then shrugged and moved off. It wasn't the first time he'd been unwilling witness to a tragedy like this, but it was the first time involving Newcomers. Their reactions were not so very different.

A uniformed female cop was alternately trying to pull and urge the woman away from the body. Ballistics was finishing up and the coroner's people needed to get at it. Sykes hoped the copy was persuasive. She didn't have a chance in hell of budging the Newcomer woman physically.

Thinking about Ballistics made him think of Minkler. Sure enough, there he was, over by the shattered chips-and-dips section, tagging the pump combat shotgun Raincoat had dropped when his partner had yanked him toward the back alley. The ugly uniform mooching around next to him was Natuzzi. Neither of them noticed his presence until he moved close and offered his unsolicited opinion.

"Looks like a standard combat pump-action."

Minkler was recording on the little memopute he always carried with him in his breast pocket. "It is."

Sykes studied the weapon thoughtfully. "I don't see any modifications."

"None to see."

The detective nodded toward the street. "So what punched holes clear through the old Chevy out there? You saw the holes?"

"We saw 'em." Natuzzi wasn't half as mean as he looked. He knew better than Minkler what Sykes was going through, knew the effort of will required for the detective to stand there asking calm questions.

"Wasn't woodpeckers," Natuzzi added.

Minkler made a face. "A gun doesn't hurt you, Sykes. The gun's standard. It's the shells that ain't."

"I'm real tired, Minkler. Don't make me ask every question."

The ballistics man bent and extracted an evidence baggie from his work box. He fumbled around inside, pulled out four unfired twelve-gauge rounds, and held them out for Sykes's inspection.

"BRI sabot slugs. These puppies are nasty. Two plastic sabots fall away in flight leaving a fifty-caliber slug going two thousand feet per second. Tug might as well've been hiding behind a rosebush."

Sykes studied the shells. "Strictly military issue, right?"

Minkler nodded in confirmation. "Strictly military, yeah. Wanna buy some? I can give you three contacts on the East Side alone."

That was typical, Sykes knew. "Pretty heavy artillery to haul around for knocking over a minimart."

A new voice joined the conversation. It sounded vaguely familiar, a little too precise to be normal.

"An identical round was used in the shooting of a Newcomer named Hubley, two days ago."

A surprised Sykes turned to see that the voice belonged to the alien cop whose nose he'd mashed. He wasn't particularly pleased to see him again, but wishing wouldn't make him go away. He had as much right as Sykes to be where he was. Maybe more. And he had some information.

The detective's response was automatically belligerent. "Yeah, so what? That still doesn't explain why the extra firepower here."

The alien considered briefly. "Perhaps because even the larger-caliber handguns aren't always effective against my people."

"That's no bullshit." Natuzzi made everything he said into a grunt. "I seen one take five hits once and keep on coming. Even a Magnum'll sometimes only slow 'em down."

Sykes wasn't listening to the other policeman. He didn't want to get friendly with this Newcomer cop, but he wanted information badly.

"You're saying that the slimeballs who did this wanted to make sure the old geezer behind the counter was gonna be dead? I don't care what anybody says. A handgun would've been enough to do in an old fart like that." He said nothing about the alien robber firing a second shell into the proprietor after he'd fallen to the floor. Let Forensics earn their pay.

"It is possible," the Newcomer admitted.

Once Sykes's brain got revved it was impossible to turn him off, no matter how bizarre his thoughts became. "So maybe what you're suggesting is that there's some connection to this other homicide you just mentioned?"

"So both killers had some BRI's," Natuzzi observed. "Coincidence. Stuff like that's on the street all the time."

"So maybe baby," Sykes growled nonsensically. He wanted the alien's opinion, not Natuzzi's.

Before the Newcomer could respond, the female cop who'd been wrestling with the widow stepped up. "Hey, gimme a hand with this woman, willya, Samuel? We've got to get her down to Division for her statement and she won't budge, and I sure as hell can't make her.''

The Newcomer cop nodded at Sykes. ''Excuse me.''

Sykes was reluctant to let him go. ''So, you think there's a connection, or what? Hey!''

But the alien Samuel was already walking over to the proprietor's wife and speaking in smooth alien sing-song. Sykes was left to draw his own conclusions from his own thoughts.

There wasn't much upstairs to work with, and the memory of Bill Tuggle lying dead in the street kept getting in the way.

It wasn't much brighter inside his apartment building than on the street outside. He parked the slugmobile, made sure the alarm was set, and hauled himself to the front door. The double lock yielded to his magnetic key. He stood there, thinking. Tommy's down the street was still open. He could spend the rest of the night there and feel better about everything. Tomorrow would still be waiting for him, however, and he was on duty. Vengeance is mine, sayeth the hangover. With a sigh, he gave the door a resigned shove inward.

Anyone seeing the interior of his ''home'' would have instantly divined that it was the maid's decade off. Not that Sykes was a slob. Just indifferent. Also, he had no taste, which was one reason why he and Tuggle had gotten along so well. Tug had enough taste for three cops. The room was decorated in Sears Primitive: functional and nothing more.

His hand reached out to automatically slap the rewind/playback switch on the answering machine. It whirred as he advanced on the kitchen, he and the machine the only signs of life in the apartment. One time he'd put a funny greeting tape on the machine, a gag gift from a fellow officer. Only trouble was that his mother had called once when he'd been out and had been forced to suffer through the tape's bouncy barrage of four-letter words. All copspeech, unsuitable for mentally stable civilians. Now the machine requested its messages in a noncontroversial monotone.

The fridge didn't stink because he remembered to keep open boxes of baking soda on all the shelves. You always got something out of a marriage, he mused. He'd taught Edie how to load and fire a .38 and she'd taught him about baking soda. Fair enough.

Unfortunately, there were only so many recipes that called for baking soda, and there wasn't much else occupying the stained glass shelving. Leftover takeout pizza carton. Leftover takeout Chinese in little cardboard boxes with wire handles. Leftover takeout burger wrappers. Perfectly normal. His life was a succession of leftover memories.

One of them jostled his brain even as the empty fridge was jostling his gut. The answering machine had finished its rewinding and now spoke in his daughter's voice. As he listened, he removed an ancient carton of milk and set it on the counter. The beer was in the back and the cow juice had been in the way.

His daughter talked steadily, her voice full of youth and life and love. He listened as he tried to track down a semi-clean glass.

"Hi, Daddy, it's me. I'm over at Danny's parents' house. We're all talking about Sunday, natch. There's so many things to do, so many arrangements to make, it's unreal. I don't think I'll do this more than once."

She laughed then and the sound of it made his fingers clench unconsciously against the beer can.

"I thought maybe you'd be home by now. I guess not, but talking to the machine's better than not talking at all, right? Besides, you can play it back as often as you want. You're never home anyway, you work such crazy hours." She laughed again. "You know me. I can't ever remember things. So I have to get them out when I'm in the mood. I just keep going on and on, always something new, like you've always told me.

"Anyway, it's really nothing. Not important. I just wanted to call and say hi, and tell you that I love you. I love you, Daddy."

He made himself relax his fingers. Where were those damn glasses?

She'd been giggling to herself. Now she stopped. "Uh-oh, I shouldn't a done that. Knowing you, you'll probably pull this tape out of your machine now and save it, in that same drawer where you keep every card I ever gave you. And all my old baby teeth! Gross! Anyway, Daddy, don't save this tape. Use it again because that's what they're for and I bet they're expensive. I'll buy you more tapes if you want. But I do love you, and I'll talk to you again before Sunday."

The glasses were hiding behind a big empty pot. The pot was clean because he'd never used it. Like he never used a lot of the things in the apartment, because they were part of his "share" from the divorce and he couldn't bring himself to use them. The last time they'd been touched, *she'd* touched them.

Kristin wasn't through. "Oh, Tug and Carol came by and met Danny last week." That made him stiffen despite his resolve. Tough guy you are, he thought. Sure. "Danny thought Tug was the greatest, but then, who doesn't? Anyway, love you, talk to you soon. I gotta go. Something about picking flowers. Bye."

Behind him the machine finished with a crackle-pop. Sykes took the glass and the bottle of vodka—the Russkies still made the best vodka in the world, even if they didn't drink near as much of it as they used to—and shambled back into the living room. On the way to the couch he switched off the humming answering machine.

Halfway past the bedroom he stopped, staring off into the distance. Then he turned and thumbed the eject switch on the machine. He studied the tiny cassette for a moment, then pulled it out and tossed it into an open drawer full of similar tapes. Cards and opened envelopes provided a clean bed for the tape collection.

He didn't bother to put a clean tape back in the empty machine.

The squad room the next morning was the usual *olla podrida* of busy cops coming on duty, night personnel bumping exhaustedly off walls and each other like lost steel balls in an arcade game, bored hookers waiting to be bailed out by their pimps, druggies and drunks settling down for their morning naps, and clerical personnel doing their best to ignore everything except the precious papers they carried protectively in both hands or beneath their arms. Nobody paid the slightest attention to Sykes, which suited him just fine.

He'd managed four hours' sleep, which under the circumstances was reason for half a dozen Hail Marys. His brain was up and alert while the rest of him was still going through the motions. Though awake, he looked like the heavyweight contender's latest sparring partner. The pint-sized Styrofoam cup whose contents he was stirring mechanically steamed like a ghost snake.

Check-in was perfunctory and automatic. Ignoring the duty board and his own desk, he moved straight for Fedorchuk's. Its owner was bent over some paperwork, his brow furrowed. Fedorchuk always said it was the heat in the station house, but Sykes knew the man was paranoid about his reports. Fedorchuk could contract cancer of the colon from a mistyped heading.

It was a lousy beginning to an undoubtedly lousy day-to-be, and Sykes wasn't in the mood for small talk. So he didn't waste any time.

"So what've you got on Tuggle's killers?"

Fedorchuk responded with a pained expression. "Jesus, Sykes, it's been less than ten hours. Me and Alterez are on it, okay?" Alterez turned from the file cabinet whose contents he was ruffling and smiled thinly. "I promise you, we'll keep you updated."

Sykes gulped coffee. It burned his throat and warmed his belly. "Which says to me that you don't have squat."

"Ten hours." The grumbling Fedorchuk squinted over at his inquisitor. "You ever try to make a case in Slagtown? The list of Newcomer informants is about as long as the list of Mexican War heroes. Nobody talks to nobody down there, and they sure as hell don't talk to us. Half of them don't speak English and the other half only when it suits them. They're real nice and polite when you run into one somewhere else in town, but down in the Slag sometimes they ain't so nice."

"I've been there. You got a short memory."

"The hell I do. What I'm saying is that you were just doing routine patrol. You haven't had to do any legwork. When you want information it's different from hauling in drunks or passin' out tickets. This is gonna take some time."

"Yeah, I know it's gonna take time. Like until the Ice Capades opens in Hell, with you two in it."

Alterez looked back from his filing cabinet and glared across the room. "Up yours."

As he usually did, Sykes had the perfect comeback. He wasn't given the opportunity to deliver it because the Captain's door banged open on the other side of the room and Warner emerged. He studied the squad room intently, like a trainer inspecting his lions and tigers, before his deep voice boomed out. It sounded clearly above the morning chatter and the hum of computer terminals.

"Nobody wander off! I got an announcement. Get your asses back here where you can hear."

That was Captain Warner, Sykes ruminated. Quiet and thoughtful. At least you never had to ask anybody else what he meant. The detective sipped at his cooling coffee and chose a spot near the back wall where he could see clearly, hear clearly, and get the hell out of the room fast without being noticed if he so desired.

A pair of younger detectives on their way out stopped at the declaration and turned to pay attention. Probably afraid Warner had already spotted them. If he had, the Captain wouldn't say a thing. He'd just ignore possible deserters while making his announcement. But two weeks, or a month later, the duo who'd tried to flee would find themselves pulling patrol duty in the worst part of town on graveyard shift, without ever being able to figure out why they'd been so unfairly singled out.

A crowd assembled in response to Warner's klaxon. The Captain was holding up a single sheet of typeout fresh from the maw of some overworked printer. Nobody offered him the microphone that rested, powered up and ready for use, beneath the big display screen. Warner didn't need one.

"I'll make this short." Somehow he managed to read and scan the room simultaneously, missing nothing on paper or on the floor. "This is a directive from Chief Evaner, who is acting on orders from the Mayor, who is under mandate from the Federal Bureau of Newcomer Relations. As of nine o'clock this morning, one Newcomer uniformed officer has been summarily promoted to the rank of Detective, Third Grade."

Moans of anguish rose from the crowd. A few others let loose with more descriptive and less polite commentary. Warner didn't wait for the disaffected to finish.

"And we've got him, people." This provoked further groans of dismay from the assembled men and women. "Volunteers for duty with the new detective should see me in my office. It's a guy, by the way." Somebody near the back of the squad room offered an exceptionally obscene comment. Warner's gaze sought him out and the offender was instantly silenced. "If no volunteers are forthcoming," he finished, "I'll choose one myself. That is all."

Ignoring the discontented rumble that was mounting behind him, he turned and disappeared into his office. After a few moments of animated, angry discussion, reality returned to the squad room. There were assignments to be carried out, reports to be collated, leads to be pursued. The crowd splintered into smaller clusters, the clusters themselves then fragmenting as officers and civilian employees alike returned to their work, their temporary outrage at Warner's announcement subsumed in the crush of morning duty.

Sykes hadn't moved. He leaned against the wall while gazing thoughtfully toward the Captain's office. The walls were double-thick bulletproof glass, nice and clean so the office's occupant could keep a steel eye on his people outside. It also allowed the detective to see inside.

He straightened away from the wall. Warner wasn't alone. A thin, balding man in a severe suit was speaking to him. But that wasn't what had caught Sykes's attention.

Standing off to one side and dominating the office by his

sheer bulk was a Newcomer in a gray suit. His shirt looked freshly pressed and his skin was immaculate. The russet patterns on his bald, rising skull were more distinctive and memorable than most.

It was the same alien officer he'd decked in the tunnel.

A few diehards remained in the middle of the room, continuing to argue as Sykes gazed thoughtfully at the Captain's office. Fedorchuk and Alterez were among those hanging on, venting their frustration and anger at anyone within earshot.

"Unbelievable bullshit," Fedorchuk observed sagely, shaking his head in fresh outrage.

Alterez would've spat if they'd been outside. "How long has this Slag been on the force, anyway? A year, max—right? Couldn't be any longer than that, even including time at the Academy. Less than a year and he makes detective. You know how long I had to slave in a uniform to make grade, man?"

"Yeah, I know. We all know." Fedorchuk's gaze swept over the small group of malcontents. "I dunno about the rest of you, but I sure as hell ain't gonna sit still for this. I'm calling the Union, pronto, and I don't give a shit what the Feds say. We don't have to take this!"

A couple of the others ventured verbal support for this proposed course of action, one quoting the number for the Union office from memory. Another nodded and headed for a free phone. Meanwhile Fedorchuk found himself frowning as he spotted Sykes strolling unconcernedly toward the Captain's office.

"You see that?"

Alterez turned and saw, was puzzled but not upset. "I thought he clocked in on time."

"He did. Where the hell's he going?"

Sykes never hesitated. He knocked on the door, face expressionless, waited a polite moment, and then popped the door and stuck his face inside. Warner looked at him in mild surprise.

"Yeah, Sykes?"

"Captain, I'd like to volunteer for duty with the new detective."

It wasn't often anyone caught Warner badly off guard. He tried to hide his reaction but wasn't quite fast enough. He hadn't really expected to get a volunteer, was certain he'd be forced to assign some unfortunate low-ranker with little seniority to the task, and didn't know quite what to say now that his little problem had been so quickly and painlessly removed from his problem file. He never would have expected Sykes. Especially after what had happened to Detective William Tuggle.

However, as his problem file was always the thickest one on his desk, he wasn't about to hesitate over the offer.

"That's very thoughtful of you, Sykes. Very." He stared as the detective entered and shut the door behind him. Sykes's expression was blank, unreadable. Warner stared at him a second longer, then shrugged mentally and turned to face the massive alien.

"Detective Sergeant Sykes, this is Detective Francisco."

All the aliens had names like that. They'd been assigned them arbitrarily upon arrival and processing through camp. Not one had raised objection either to the procedure or to any of the names.

The Newcomer peered solemnly over at the detective and didn't bat an eye. "We have met."

Warner's naturally suspicious nature instantly clicked into high gear. He put a questioning eye on Sykes, who ignored him. Something smelled, and it wasn't the men's toilet up the hall. Even so, Sykes *had* volunteered, which took a load off Warner's shoulders. But if they already knew each other . . .

His thoughts were interrupted by the action of his other guest. The slim gentleman had moved to shake first the Newcomer's hand, then Sykes's. He was smiling cheerfully as he greeted them.

"Victor Goldrup, Mayor's Office, special liaison for Newcomer Affairs. Congratulations, gentlemen. This is a historic moment in Human-Newcomer relations and a historic day for the Los Angeles Police Department. I am proud to be a small part of it. You're both going to find yourselves in the history books."

It had taken Warner those couple of moments of introduction to make the connection he'd been seeking. His initial suspicions were well grounded. It was just that everything had happened a tad too fast for him to put it together. Now he glared hard at the uncharacteristically altruistic Sykes.

"You are to have nothing to do with the investigation into Bill Tuggle's death. You know that. Leave that for Fedorchuk. It's his baby, his and Alterez's. I won't have my people butting into each other's business, no matter how noble their motives."

If he expected an argument he was disappointed. Sykes merely nodded agreeably. "Departmental policy."

"That's right, and don't forget it." By way of afterthought, Warner glanced over at the alien. "You understand too?"

"Yes, sir." The Newcomer didn't nod. They could, when they wanted to. The lack of a nod bothered the Captain but he couldn't say so. That was also departmental policy. The situation was delicate enough, having a Newcomer uniform on the premises. Going and making one into a detective had potentially explosive ramifications among the rank and file. No point in making things worse. So if he didn't want to nod, fine.

"Good."

Before he could say anything else, Sykes stepped forward, trying not to appear overly anxious. It helped that he was dead tired from emotional fatigue and lack of sleep.

"If it's all right, Cap, considering the uniqueness of our situation and all, there's another case I'd like to take. Sort of start out with something I'm a little familiar with, you know?"

Warner didn't look up at him, but his tone was still wary. "What case?"

"A homicide. Newcomer named Hubley."

Warner pretended to study the papers carpeting his desk. Goldrup was ignoring everyone, off in some bureaucratic heaven of his own. Probably contemplating the potential

PR. So no one noticed the look Francisco threw Sykes. The aliens weren't always so inscrutable. It was plain that the Newcomer knew his volunteer partner was up to something. But he didn't comment, and Sykes took pains to avoid his stare.

"Granger and Pitts are already on it," Warner said brusquely.

Sykes pressed his argument. "Granger and Pitts have one hell of a caseload. They're also doing the Wilcox murder, and they've been stuck on the Silver Lake rape for six months now. They might be able to come up with a lead on that, if they didn't have sixteen other things to do. Now you're gonna dump this one on 'em."

"Granger and Pitts are my best investigative team."

Sykes let that one pass. "They're only human, Cap." The humor slipped past his listeners. "They need a break or they won't find piss on anything. I would've thought what with Francisco here being the first Newcomer plainclothes, and Hubley's body being found over in the Newcomer community, it would only make sense for the two of us to take the Hubley case."

"Don't tell me what to think," Warner told him sharply even as he found himself mulling over the detective's words.

The thrust of the conversation had drawn Goldrup out of his daze. "He's got a good point, Captain Warner. That's the sort of thing we should be doing with this early-advancement program. Much better than sending them out on something routine like patrol and search. If we're going to get any airtime out of this we're going to have to go for something kind of exciting, if you catch my drift."

Yeah, I catch it, Warner thought sourly. Right in the ass, where I usually catch dorks like you. The Captain bore it with the air of the long-suffering martyr compelled to endure yet another fiendish torment. There was nothing he could say and what the hell difference did it make anyway? Other than the fact that the victim was a Newcomer, the Hubley case was your standard Homicide One, Unsolved. So Sykes was interested in it, so what? Everybody knew how weird Sykes was. Around the station, Bill Tuggle had been regarded as a saint for putting up with the guy for nine years. Sykes would be in a nuthouse somewhere, or the gutter, if not for one unarguable fact: he was a good detective.

Obviously his volunteering to work with the Newcomer had something to do with Tuggle's death at Newcomer hands. Just as obviously, he wanted the Hubley case because it also involved a Newcomer. Was that anything to worry about? So long as he kept his nose clean and left Tuggle's murder to Fedorchuk and Alterez, his other motives need not concern Warner.

I've spent far too much time worrying about it already, he thought abruptly. I've got a precinct to run.

He sighed deeply, and recognized it for the acquiescence it was. He tried not to smile.

# IV

The door that blocked off the bottom of the ground floor stairwell was solid steel, intended not only to keep out aggravated street types and unwelcome media mavens but bullets and fair-sized explosives. It banged noisily against its hinges as Sykes slammed it wide. Francisco followed close behind. Even allowing for the fact they were from different worlds, they made an odd couple. Sykes had slept in and looked it, while the Newcomer in his neatly pressed suit more closely resembled a canvasser for the Jehovah's Witnesses.

They'd spent the rest of the day talking, going over official procedures, doing what was expected of new partners. Because of his recent advancement, Francisco had plenty of additional paperwork to deal with. He handled it adroitly. That surprised Sykes as he watched his new partner at work. Maybe this guy Francisco was real smart. That wasn't necessarily a good thing.

Black-and-whites were pulling out on the evening watch as the two detectives made their way across the parking lot. Sykes was doing all the talking. He'd been lecturing Francisco most of the afternoon, ever since the Newcomer had tidied up the last of his official forms.

"... And we work my hours. I'll do the driving, *you* do the paperwork. You gotta learn it, so you might as well do it. I saw you back there." He nodded in the direction of the station house. "You handled yourself okay. But filling out personnel chits isn't the same thing as making out an arrest sheet or trying to describe an arsonist's state of mind at the time of arrest."

"I have done my homework." Francisco spoke quietly, smoothly. A moment later he added, in a tone only slightly different from the one he'd employed all day, "Sergeant, I'd like to thank you for what you're doing."

"What's that?" It made no sense to Sykes until he realized what the alien was referring to. "Look, get one thing straight in your pointy head. We're not pals, we're not married, and we ain't gonna take long moonlit walks together. So don't thank me. We're just partners. All we do is work together. The rest of the time we're on opposite sides of the moon, got it?" The alien listened intently and without comment.

"One more thing. Don't call me 'sergeant.' Call me Sykes. Or Matt, if you have to. No, Sykes would be better."

"I understand the significance of being on a first-name basis. I would not presume. By the way, mine is Samuel."

Sykes nodded absently and they continued on until his expression contorted and he called a halt again.

"Wait a minute. Let's make sure I've got this straight. Your name is Francisco. Samuel Francisco?"

The Newcomer nodded.

"Wasn't that a mission padre or something? Some guy who built shit for the Indians and taught them how to make adobe, stuff like that?"

Again the alien nodded.

Sykes shook his head doubtfully. "You look about as much like a Spanish friar as a chilied chicken." The Newcomer didn't react to this sally, not that Sykes had expected him to. Tug, now . . .

Forget about that.

"This won't do. Francisco's bad enough, and people are gonna start whistling the same old tune at you. I'm damned if I'm gonna run around calling you 'Samuel.' That's not gonna carry the right weight if we have to use the radio." He shook his head, grinning to himself.

"I've heard some good ones for you guys. Humphrey

Bogart, Harley-Davidson. Could'a been worse in your case. I guess the people at Immigration got a little punchy after awhile, coming up with names for a quarter of a million of you. Samuel Francisco might cut it for a mortuary worker, but not for a cop. Understand?''

"It sounds too much like a familiar California city."

Sykes nodded vigorously. "Besides the padre business. So you're not a total jerk. Good. The Francisco can stay, but the Samuel's gotta go."

"My true name is SS'tangya T'ssorentsa'."

"Gesundheit. I'd call you ST, but that's too close to another bad joke. How does 'George' strike you?"

"Strike me?" The Newcomer was puzzled. If only they had external ears instead of those damn holes, Sykes thought. Then they wouldn't look half so bizarre.

"How does it sound to you? Any objections?"

"Why should I object," the alien replied blandly, "when the name Samuel Francisco was not one of my choosing either?"

"Fine. Glad you understand." Sykes completely missed the implied bitterness, which was just as well. "George it is, then. Nobody can object to that. It still sounds a little silly, but not half as silly as the other. Anyway, what's it matter to you if we think it's funny, right? Whatta you care?"

"That is quite correct." The alien's face was devoid of expression, which was fortunate in the light of what he said next. "It is like your own name. Sykes."

The detective frowned slightly as he scanned the parking lot. "What's wrong with Sykes?" There was the slugmobile, right where he'd left it. He turned to his left.

"Nothing—as far as you are concerned. I'm sure it doesn't bother you at all that it sounds like 'ss'ai k'ss', two words in my language which mean respectively 'excrement' and 'cranium.' "

Sykes paused on the driver's side after unlocking the internals. He wore a perplexed look, so the Newcomer took the liberty of elaborating.

"Shit—head."

He climbed in, squeezing his bulk through the too-small passenger door on the other side, leaving Sykes standing there alone. The last vestiges of the smirk the detective had been wearing all afternoon were falling rapidly from his face.

There was plenty of traffic, most of it law-abiding. Sykes ignored the violators. He wasn't interested in maintaining the speed limit or ticketing Valley housewives whose taillights had burnt out. He wasn't even interested in pausing to verbally flay the pair of teenagers they'd caught vandalizing a vacant house. He had only one thing on his mind, though it took him awhile to get around to discussing it.

At least the alien had good command of the language—for a Newcomer. Too many of them bordered on the non-verbal, at least in English. But then, he reminded himself, George wouldn't have made detective even with the aid of the special Federal program if he hadn't been reasonably fluent.

Sykes eyed his partner. George was more than slightly cramped by the passenger's seat. Detroit hadn't started building wheels to Newcomer dimensions. Not yet.

"Let's talk Hubley," he said without preamble.

"What do you want to know?"

"Anything and everything." Sykes nodded toward the glove compartment. "You got the file?" The Newcomer nodded. "Then read it. Talk to me, George. Skip the procedural stuff."

Francisco opened the file and scanned the contents. "His body was discovered three days ago, in an alley off Central, near downtown."

Sykes kept his eyes on the road ahead. "With two BRI sabot slugs in the chest."

"*Through* the chest," Francisco gently corrected him. "Rupturing both the primary and secondary hearts."

The slugmobile skidded abruptly rightward, avoiding a Jaguar sedan that had slowed for a left-hand turn. Sykes yelled irritably out the window. "Nice signal, dickwad!"

The unexpected outburst, not to mention the peculiar commentary, threw Francisco off stride. The aberration appeared to be temporary, he decided, since his new partner was once more sitting silently behind the wheel and concentrating on his driving. Humans were prone to such inexplicable and unpredictable outbursts, but they were still startling to observe. Very little about human behavior was predictable. At times the entire race seemed hell-bent for a collective nervous breakdown. He wondered if a response was required, assumed from Sykes's continued silence that one was not. He hefted the file and continued reading.

"He was employed at the Northwest Petroleum Refinery in Torrance and was manager of the methane facility there." Francisco flipped the page and read on. "He was also a principal partner in a real estate venture to develop low-cost housing for Newcomers."

Sykes made a face. "Terrific. A real pillar of the community. Which tells us squat." He rounded the next corner, ignoring the red light and chewing on his lower lip as he thought hard and fast. "Was Hubley missing anything when they found him? Had he been ripped off?"

Francisco checked a form in the back of the file. "There was no wallet. Hubley wasn't wealthy, but he had a good job and other investments. It is reasonable to assume he would have been carrying a modest amount of cash as well as appropriate credit cards. However, when found he was still wearing a watch and two rings."

"What about them?"

"The watch was a Seiko. Nothing fancy, worth perhaps twenty bucks on the street. The rings were both gold, however, one set with some small but good-quality diamonds."

Sykes was smiling to himself now. "Sound familiar? Anybody who'd kill a guy for his wallet wouldn't leave stuff like that behind even if he had to slice the fingers to get at the rings. The guys at the minimart last night made a half-assed grab at the money in the till, but I don't think that's what they were there for. I think we got us a couple'a executions on our hands, George. How's that strike you?"

Francisco closed the folder quietly as he tried and failed to find a more comfortable position on the narrow bench seat. "The murder which occurred at the minimart is not our case. The Captain stated quite specifically that . . ."

An obviously pissed Sykes interrupted. "Look, you want to fit in here, right? You want to learn how to get along, be like all the other detectives? How you can blend in with the group and go with the flow—at least as much as you'll ever be able to?"

"Yes."

Sykes relaxed a little then as he turned back to his driving. "Well, there's a thing about partners, about being somebody's partner. You won't find it in the manuals they gave you to read at the Academy, and you won't find it posted on the duty board at the station. You *do* for each other. And that means that other people's rules don't mean shit. It's the rules you set up between the two of you, that's all that counts. It's got to be that way because your partner is the guy who's guarding your ass on stakeout or take-down, not somebody talking rules back by the duty board. If the two of you don't have a private understanding, then you got nothing. You haven't got a partner, you've got deadweight.

"You've got to be with somebody you can count on no matter what the 'rules' say, count on every second, because one second might mean your life. You've got to be able to read each other without talking. You've got to know what your buddy's thinking so you can react without thinking. Understand?"

Francisco nodded slowly.

"Okay. See, there's nothing real complicated about it, so don't make this out to be bigger than it is. My friend and partner was murdered last night and I'm after the shitbag that did it. As my partner I'm asking you to respect me and help me find him."

The Newcomer pondered the human's words thoughtfully. Sykes tried not to watch his shifting alien expressions. Not that you could tell much of the time what one of them was really thinking anyway. Francisco would be quite within his rights to take everything Sykes had just told him straight to Warner. That would result in new partnerships for both him and Francisco, as well as Sykes's being assigned to track down some guy for nonpayment of back child support off somewhere safe like the North Valley. He'd taken a calculated risk laying it on the line with the Newcomer. Whether it paid off or not was up to Francisco.

The Newcomer finally responded, though not as Sykes had hoped.

"And as *my* partner, I must ask you to respect *me* and my desire not to break with procedure. I realize the death of your friend has put you under a great deal of stress. Please keep in mind that as the first Newcomer to achieve the rank of detective in a human police department, much less in one as visible and important as that of the city of Los Angeles, I will be subject to constant scrutiny both by the civil authorities and by my own people. This unending attention will be difficult for me to deal with, as I am by nature more of a private than a public person. I am having troubles enough dealing with external forces without having to worry about violating procedure. The results if I should do something wrong will be much worse for me than for you."

Sykes gave him an exasperated stare, abruptly slammed on the brakes, and threw the transmission into park. Francisco banged into the dash, recovered, and quickly took note of the fact that they had halted square in the middle of traffic. Horns began blaring behind them. Drivers leaned from their windows to bombard the slugmobile with inventive invective. Sykes ignored it all.

"What is wrong?" Francisco muttered.

Sykes was very calm as he turned to face the much bigger Newcomer. "Nothing's wrong. I just want to get something straight. I just want to make sure that we're operating on the same wavelength here. You agree that there's a good chance these two shootings are somehow related, right?"

The yelling outside was much louder now. Francisco was obviously unsettled by all the chaos they were causing. His natural, not to mention his professional, instincts told him to get the car out of the way. But Sykes was behind the wheel, not him, and Sykes continued to sit and stare expectantly. His foot went nowhere near the accelerator, his hand nowhere near the shift lever.

In spite of the confusion and the ringing in his head where he'd struck the dash, Francisco managed to concentrate on the detective's words.

"Well—yes. Quite possibly they are, given the similar

MO involved and the lack of an apparent interest in serious larceny.''

"*Possibly*. Good. Well, would you be willing to consider the theory, George, that possibly examining the evidence from one case could shed some small ray of light on the other? Does that sound unreasonable to you? Does that not violate accepted procedure?''

"Yes—no, it is not unreasonable. Although I . . .''

"Great.'' The detective settled himself back behind the steering wheel and put a ready hand on the gear shift. "I'm sure glad that's settled, aren't you? Isn't it great that partners can talk things out and solve problems between themselves this way? That's what it's all about, George.'' He put the car in drive and roared away from the line of furious drivers stacked up behind them.

"I think we're really starting to click now, George. See how easy it is when you just talk to one another? Why, there's no problem too complex for a couple of partners to solve. And everybody goes on and on about how difficult it is for two guys from different social backgrounds to get along with one another. They don't have the slightest idea what they're talking about, do they?''

Unsure what to think, Francisco sat quietly. It took ten minutes before he realized they were headed in the wrong direction.

"I thought we were supposed to be going downtown to check out the murder site?''

"What for? You've seen the pictures. Forensics has been all over the place. There's nothing for us to find there. If you want to know more, check your book.''

"Then where are we going?''

"County morgue.''

Francisco eased back in his seat, reassured. "Ah. To run a check on Hubley.''

"To run a check, yeah. But not on Hubley. At least, not at first.''

The Newcomer's defenses instantly went back on full alert. "You are contemplating another violation of procedure, aren't you?''

"Who, me?" Sykes looked offended. "I'm just following up on the obvious lines of investigation in our case, like I told you. Relax, enjoy the ride."

Francisco tried, but found he could do neither. Sykes whistled merrily as they cruised through the traffic on the Hollywood Freeway. The whistling did nothing to improve his new partner's mood of unease.

The morgue didn't bother Sykes. He'd paid the massive, old, small-windowed structure too many late-night visits, seen too much of its guts as well as those of its transitory inhabitants. Only the echoes occasionally bothered him. Buildings like the county morgue always seemed full of echoes. Your footsteps always had company. Most of the time that didn't matter, but if you were strolling the hallways late at night you had a tendency to hear extra echoes. There was never anything behind you when you looked, but that didn't keep the toughest cops from sneaking the occasional peek just to make sure.

It was obvious from the start that the visit wasn't troubling to his new partner, and why should it be? Ninety-eight percent of the building's occupants held no more interest for him than would a standard text on mammalian physiology. He might be curious, but he wouldn't be queasy.

Winter was Deputy Medical Examiner, and he owed Sykes a couple of favors. Not that the request the detective put to him was out of the ordinary. It was the timing that made things slightly awkward. But Winter proved obliging enough. As he led the two nocturnal visitors down the corridor he read from the file case he was carrying.

"What's with all the interest in this stuff? I didn't know you were on this one too, Sykes."

"Relates to another murder, like I said. Associational," Sykes informed him casually.

"Yeah, well, you know I've already been all over this material with Fedorchuk and Alterez this morning. Why can't you just talk to them?"

"Because Fedorchuk's a blob and Alterez can't talk worth shit. What's it to you? Come on, Winter. You got nothin' better to do, cushy county night job like this one. You oughta thank us for coming by on a slow day. Keep you from getting bored. You can't keep reading those bondage mags all day long.''

The Deputy Examiner eyed him sharply. ''Who says I read that stuff?''

Sykes grinned. ''I'm a detective, remember? I get paid to find things out. Hey, don't look like that. I could care less. But some of the bluenoses on the promotion board might find that kind of easy reading a little funny for a guy in your position.''

''Some of those old farts would find anything 'funny,' '' Winter replied morosely. ''You threatening me, Sykes?''

''With something as petty as that? Gimme some credit, Jack. If I wanted to threaten you, I'd mention the time that stripper who'd OD'd on crack was brought in for autopsy and you . . .''

''Jesus, keep your goddamn voice down!'' Winter was looking around nervously as they pushed through a double swinging door.

The room they entered was filled with metal tables, gurneys, instruments, sterilizers. Some of the platforms were occupied with sheeted lumps. Others gleamed naked beneath the fluorescents like chrome on a new Italian car. Winter continued talking as he led his visitors through the maze of tables.

''Anyway, according to the sheet, the guy you nailed outside on the night of the holdup . . .''

''The human.''

''Yeah, the getaway driver.'' Winter checked his file quickly. ''He was one Martin Helder. White male, twenty-seven. Let's see . . .'' The Examiner flipped a page. ''Wrap sheet shows one armed robbery conviction, a couple for sale of a controlled substance. He also beat a number of raps back East.''

''Whereabouts?''

''Jersey City, Passaic. That was a couple years back. Then he decided to pick up and move to sunny Southern Cal and carry on his preoccupation with bad habits in our backyard. Forfeited a grand and a half bail. Small-timer. Oh yeah, and he was wired on coke when you stopped his clock. If you're looking for somebody with credentials, our man Helder ain't your boy.''

"Where's the other one?"

"Over here."

Winter paused by a table supporting a covered body. The concealed mass was by far the largest in the room. He unceremoniously yanked the sheet aside to reveal the pale, hairless body of a Newcomer. Sykes recognized the corpse instantly: Raincoat. His sheer bulk was impressive. But not as impressive, he reminded himself, as the one in the overcoat who'd gotten away.

Francisco studied the cadaver with professional detachment. "Have you identified this one?"

Winter shrugged. "So far he's a John Doe. Or a Sam Slag, if you prefer." Francisco smiled politely, his expression noncommittal. Winter read on. "No ID on him, and—well, you know. No fingerprints. So it could be tough. Your buddies went through the mug book this morning but couldn't make a facial match."

Successful adaptation, Sykes mused. Hardly here long enough to learn the language and already the Newcomers had their very own mug book.

"I'll bet they looked real hard," he sniffed sourly. "But that doesn't mean a damn thing. Fedorchuk couldn't find his ass with both hands in his back pockets."

While he and Winter chatted amiably, Francisco studied the alien body. That suited Sykes fine. The Newcomer detective wouldn't inhibit the discussion with the Deputy Examiner.

Winter finally broke off the small talk long enough to indicate the alien corpse. "You took this guy out too, didn't you?"

"Yeah."

"Lucky for you, you got him in both of his—well, what we loosely refer to as 'hearts.'" Winter shook his head in amazement. "They look a lot less like us on the inside, you know. Basically humanoid, though sometimes I wish I could specialize. It's fascinating stuff. I try to keep up, what with L.A. being home to most of them. Some of the stuff that's out in the literature would blow your mind, Sykes. They have a kind of group shyness about their internal workings, so it's tough to find things out, but we're learning. The double heart setup isn't the half of it, and they aren't really hearts as we understand them. They move the blood, all right, but they're not the same size or shape, and instead of chambering they've got the damndest most complicated ventricular setup you ever . . ."

Sykes was bored by the first sentence. "You think I was lucky? Lucky my ass. I had to empty my damn gun into him. I thought he was down for the count after my first shot and started to check him out. If I hadn't watched my step it'd be me you'd be lecturing George about."

"That's the way these people are." Winter was studying the body, still obviously intrigued by what he didn't know. "They're so damn big and dense that if you don't hit both pumps or the brain you just piss them off. Maybe one of these days we'll have a Newcomer on the staff to help us with explanations, but right now we don't know what half the goop inside them is even *for*."

"Me, I don't want to know. Mind if I see that?" Sykes reached hopefully for the report.

The Examiner hesitated, his gaze taking in the unlocked door. They were still alone in the morgue. "Okay, but just here. No copies."

Sykes smiled thinly. "Yeah, right. Just here."

Francisco was making a detailed examination of the body, starting with the feet and working his way up. As he reached the right hand he absently turned it over to check the palm—and frowned. Something on the skin made him lean closer. He studied the dead flesh the way a counterfeiter would examine a batch of freshly printed fifty-dollar bills.

Letting the hand fall back, he reached up and carefully peeled back the dead alien's upper lip. What he saw made him frown anew, but neither the busily reading Sykes nor the indifferent Winter glanced in his direction. Finally he removed his fingers from the breathless mouth and straightened.

Three lab assistants had entered a few moments earlier and were busy at their respective tasks. One bulked much larger than his companions. A glance showed that Sykes was going to be occupied for a while yet. Making his way across the floor between tables empty and full, he introduced himself to the alien lab assistant. They began conversing softly in their own tongue. The other pair of lab workers ignored them.

Eventually Sykes returned the folder. "Thanks, Winter. Do you a favor sometime."

"You know what they say. Silence is golden."

"Not where I work it ain't. You got anything else?"

"You've seen it all. Oh, wait." Winter fumbled with the folder's back pocket. "Since you're so interested, here's an extra head shot if you want one." He passed an $8 \times 10$ Polaroid of the dead Newcomer's face to the grateful detective.

"Sure you won't miss this?"

"No problem with photos. It's the synopses and analyses the boss gets touchy about passing around." He nodded in the direction of the corpse. "We're just about to start cutting in. You're welcome to stick around and watch if you want. I guarantee you'll learn a lot. Every time we open one of these guys up there's a new surprise."

"Yeah, I'll bet." Sykes had what he'd come for. Sliding the photo into his own folder he scanned the morgue in search of his partner, found him deep in conversation with the Newcomer lab worker.

"Take it easy, Sykes." Winter offered a final smile.

"Easy as I can." But he wasn't paying attention to the Deputy Examiner anymore.

His first impulse was to go gather up his Newcomer, and get moving, but he hesitated. If he strained his hearing he could make out snatches and bits of alien conversation. The lab assistant appeared by turns to be animated, sullen, and unsettled as he responded to Francisco's questioning. Then he was nodding as if agreeing with something the detective had said—or like someone who'd just agreed to do something for someone else.

Unable to stand it any longer, Sykes walked over and stared straight into his partner's face.

"What's this, what's going on?" At his intrusion the lab worker melted silently back among the work benches.

Francisco replied as blandly as usual. "Going on? Why, nothing."

Sykes's brows crinkled. "Nothing?"

The Newcomer's gaze rose to the table across the room that held Raincoat. "We have examined the two bodies and obtained what information we could. Shouldn't we now examine their personal effects? They could be revealing." He headed for the door.

Sykes glared at the retreating back for a long moment, then followed, his thoughts churning.

Ortiz was pretty enough. Sykes had no serious interest in her, though. She was too young for him, and busy working her way through college. Smart women made him uneasy. Not that he felt intellectually inadequate in their presence, whether he was or not, but Edie had done the college bit. Anything associated with his ex-wife's likes and dislikes made him uneasy.

She glanced up from her homework and recognized him. "Sykes, isn't it?" He nodded. "Been a while. You not working homicide much these days?"

"Naw. Just got back from six months in the Bahamas. What do you think?" He smiled to indicate his sarcasm wasn't serious.

She rose and went behind the property counter. "What do you need?"

"A tall blonde, a Tesstarossa, six figures in the bank, and a new face."

She grinned playfully. "No got. What else?"

He sighed elaborately. "Effects of two stiffs named Hubley and John Doe. The latter's an alien, gunshot, brought in in a black vinyl raincoat. I doubt you've got more than one of those."

She shook her head. "Only the one is right. Wait here."

A few minutes later she was back with the requested materials. Young, yeah, but efficient. College, he thought, and dismissed the thought irritably. Everybody had different abilities, and his weren't measurable by quarter-end tests and weekly quizzes.

The pair of regulation-issue storage packets she unceremoniously dumped on the counter were both filled. Sykes went through the effects of the dead alien while Francisco studied Hubley's. Ortiz watched for a while, then returned to her homework. She'd seen it all a hundred times before.

Francisco paused with a small foil packet, held it up to the light before confessing his confusion to his partner. "What is this?"

Sykes looked over. "A rubber." When Francisco failed to react he added, "You know. A condom. Coney Island whitefish?" The Newcomer detective still looked dubious. "Men—human males, put them on their, uh, penises to protect against having babies."

It was clear that his new buddy was having a tough time with something that was clear as crystal to Sykes. He glanced back at Ortiz.

"You need this?" he asked her, indicating the packet.

She looked up from her books. "Nope. Anything you guys don't use gets shoved back in storage."

Sykes nodded, turned to Francisco with his hand outstretched. The alien obediently passed over the foil packet. Ripping it open, Sykes unrolled the contents and dangled the condom before the Newcomer's curious gaze.

"Get the picture now? Or should we stop by a bookstore on the way out and buy you a manual?"

Francisco frowned at the pale membrane. "And that *fits*?"

It wasn't exactly the response Sykes expected. "Well, yeah. It's rubber. It stretches."

"And still it fits?"

The detective stared hard at his partner for a long moment, but Francisco's expression was utterly serious. Finally he tossed the condom and empty packet back on the counter and continued probing the dead Newcomer's effects. Francisco returned to his examination of Hubley's pile. The subject of birth control was not mentioned again.

Sykes started in on Raincoat's clothes. The heavy workboots the alien had been wearing came last and he handled them gingerly. They were still coated on the sides and sole with some thick, viscous black material. He took a tentative sniff of the stuff and was gratified it wasn't what it might have been. Sticky, but not tar or asphalt. Either of those would have dried to rock hardness by now from their time in storage.

The stuff was still malleable enough to come off on your fingers, though, as Sykes quickly discovered. Looking disgusted, he hunted for something to wipe his hand. Francisco looked over.

"Problems?"

"There's some kind of goo all over these boots." He held out his sticky fingers for examination. "What is this stuff?"

Francisco studied his partner's outstretched hand. "If I am not mistaken, it is a resin."

Sykes stopped hunting for a loose rag or towel and looked up in surprise. "Oh. A resin. Well sure, I mean, that's obvious, isn't it?"

Francisco wasn't finished. "Newcomers working with methane at oil refineries must paint it on their boots to protect against sparks that could set off an explosion."

The detective's jaw fell slightly. "How the hell do you know that?"

As it turned out, there was a perfectly good reason. Francisco was knowledgeable, if no genius.

"A large number of my people were hired by refineries in the Los Angeles-Long Beach area because the methane fumes that are produced as a byproduct of certain refining processes are not harmful to us. Our lungs can tolerate a number of different gases which humans would find harmful and sometimes even lethal. This fact is widely known." Sykes bridled only slightly at the implied criticism. "My spouse's brother is one such worker."

"I see. And you saw the stuff on his boots one day and asked him what it was." Francisco nodded.

"We frequently exchange information. It is the only way we can learn about the world in which we find ourselves."

Sykes's thoughts were racing. "So the Slag they're cutting into upstairs worked at a refinery. Just like Hubley worked at a refinery.'' He glanced significantly up at his partner. "That suggest anything to you, George?''

"I am not unaware of the line of thought you are following, Matt.''

Sykes was nodding to himself, obviously pleased. "I'd say that 'possible' connection between the two cases just got a hell of a lot more possible. Okay, next step." He was silent for a moment, gazing at the far wall. Then he blinked and turned back to the silently waiting Francisco. "I gotta go talk to the wife of the Slag storeowner who got blown away last night.''

"I believe I should be the one to interview the widow.''

"Yeah, sure, you can be there too. Probably need you, if her English ain't too good. Might even be a question or two you'd think to ask that wouldn't occur to me.''

"You do not understand. I am saying that I think I should interview her alone. By myself, yes?''

"Yes—I mean, no! Why the hell . . . ?''

He stopped himself. Francisco wasn't smiling knowingly, but he might as well have been. Sykes was among the first to recognize that his bedside manner at such times could be less than sympathetic to the victim of a recent tragedy. Interviewees tended to shrink from him when they ought to be spilling information. Relatives of homicide victims were the worst. It made no difference that the subject of their visit was going to be Newcomer. Where those kinds of emotions were concerned there was no difference between species.

Sykes had his pride, but he wasn't dumb. He wanted information, not ego boosting. "Great, fine," he muttered. "*You* talk to the wife.''

Francisco looked pleased, but had the courtesy not to comment.

# V

The last time they'd seen the minimart it had been aflame with police lights and noise and activity. Now it was silent, the shattered windows boarded over with three-quarter-inch plywood. After several rings the door was opened with obvious reluctance by an elderly Newcomer woman taller than Sykes. He stood behind Francisco, letting his partner do all the talking in the softly hissing Newcomer language.

My day to play chauffeur, he mused as he strolled through the empty store. The shelves were empty now, the stock having been sold or given away. A For Rent sign was already stapled to one of the plywood panels out front. Empty and deserted, the minimart didn't look like much.

There were a few isolated goods left on the back shelves. Some he recognized, others he didn't. American manufacturers were still trying to adapt, some with far more success than others, to an entirely new group of consumers unexpectedly dumped in their midst. In their place alien entrepreneurs had stepped in, repackaging old goods to appeal to their own kind, creating new products out of what was available. The Newcomers often acted silly and slow, and deserved many of the jokes told about them, but they weren't all shambling stupes. They had their share of brains, even if it seemed much of the time that they weren't evenly distributed.

Take Francisco, now. Like all his people he was almost

59

too quiet, too precise in his speech for Sykes's liking. The detective smiled to himself. If they had to be together as long as six months, Sykes would have ol' George spewing every cuss word known to the L.A. Police Department, which because of the city's polyglot population included most swear words known to modern man. Given some time he might be able to make the Newcomer into something resembling a real detective.

The less time they spent together the better, of course. Molding George wasn't his job. His task right now, his only task, the only thing that interested him at all and made him get up in the morning was the burning need to track down Bill Tuggle's other murderer. For that he needed Francisco, in spite of all the frustrations that came with working with a Newcomer. For that he could endure any number of snide remarks from Fedorchuk and Alterez and the rest of the bozos at the station.

For that he could handle anything the world chose to throw at him.

The proprietor's widow was speaking calmly to Francisco. There were few gestures. As Sykes looked on, the alien detective extracted a picture from his pocket and showed it to the woman. She studied it intently, nodding and talking fast. Sykes could hear it all clearly without being able to understand a word of it.

"Turn in here."

"I saw the sign, damnit." Sykes had to hit the brakes hard because he actually hadn't seen the sign, but he was damned if he was going to let Francisco know that.

Steam and scrubbed smoke rose from the enormous complex of pipes and conduits and buildings that comprised the refinery. There was just enough of a breeze blowing in off the South Bay to keep the air over the hellish installation clear. You could feel the presence of exotic chemicals in the atmosphere as you drove through the lot, or so Sykes imagined. Men and a few women scurried busily through the maze, ants tending to their hill. Everyone wore a hard hat.

They located the Visitor's Office and Sykes received the

sort of welcome commonly reserved for inquiring police: reserved and correct. The Methane Section manager who was summoned from his regular duties to escort them was a little more friendly. His name was O'Neal. Unlike the majority of the workers they'd encountered, he wore a tie and shirtsleeves.

Companies were strange in their habits, Sykes mused. A guy working this place needed a tie about as much as a longshoreman did. It was more a badge of rank than anything else, a long straight chevron that differentiated O'Neal from the peons who slaved over the pipes and wheels and gauges.

He was amiable enough, though, as he led them deeper into the complex. More important, he was talkative. Sykes soaked up everything he was saying. Never knew when you might find some gold shining among the shit. Around them dozens of workers went about their assigned tasks, none of which Sykes could make sense of. A few O'Neal acknowledged, others he ignored. The work crew appeared about evenly divided between humans and Newcomers.

The Section Manager had to shout to make himself understood above the clank and roar of the machinery around them.

"Mr. Hubley was an all right guy, and a damn good manager. The men liked him. Even the Newcomers liked him. Hell, I got his job, but I'd give it back in a minute if it would do him any good. I'm really gonna have to scramble to fill his shoes. I wasn't expecting to be in this position for a couple of years, at least. Now I'm gonna have to work tough to keep it."

"Maybe what you say is largely true," Sykes told him, watching his steps as they advanced up a catwalk, "but one of his men didn't like him so much."

O'Neal frowned, stopped when Sykes handed him the Polaroid of the alien who'd recently taken up residence in the County Morgue. They were approaching a massive sealed door leading to the Methane Section. As O'Neal examined and his two guests waited patiently for him to comment, the door groaned open. A trio of workers emerged, chatting softly among themselves. They were all Newcomers.

The Section Manager tapped the photograph. "You think this is the guy who did it?"

Sykes wore his air of professional nonchalance. "We think he coulda been involved, yeah. You know him?"

O'Neal examined the picture one last time. "I'd like to help you fellows out, but to be honest it's hard to say. I might, and I might not."

"That's what I like about this job," Sykes muttered. "You keep finding one indisputable piece of evidence after another."

"Hey, I'm sorry. I hate to admit it," and he glanced furtively in Francisco's direction, "but they all still kinda look alike to me."

"Try to learn to recognize the cranial coloration patterns," Francisco told him. "They are quite distinctive. We often recognize others that way ourselves. It is no good for long-term police work, however, because they tend to change with age."

"Who else can I ask around here?" Sykes inquired impatiently.

O'Neal still held the photo, trying to make a connection for them. "I'm not sure that—wait. You know who it looks like?" He nodded to himself. "Yeah. Anderson. Uh, James Anderson. He isn't in today. If I'm remembering the shift roster right he was scheduled to take the afternoon off."

Sykes grunted. "I think you're gonna find he's taken the rest of his life off." Ignoring O'Neal's reaction, the detective nodded toward the heavy door. "That where Anderson worked?"

"Yes, it is." O'Neal turned as two more Newcomer workers emerged from inside. "Thirty-five percent methane in there. I don't know how these fellas do it. They breathe oxy-nitro just like you and me, but that stuff doesn't start to faze them until the concentration hits fifty percent."

Francisco spoke again. "Our lungs can carry out a kind of selective filtration which yours cannot. Greater capacity has something to do with it, as I understand the difference, and there are significant differences in the structure of the alveoli.''

"Uh, yeah," said O'Neal. Sykes simply gave his partner a look before turning one final time to the Section Manager.

"If you see a Newcomer who *does* look like the guy in the photo, give us a call." He handed O'Neal one of his cards. "If neither one of us is there, leave a message. We'll get back to you fast. We'll get back a lot faster if this Anderson character shows, though I'd bet my pension you'll never see him within a mile of this plant again. Never know, though. Even Newcomers can do dumb things. Right, George?"

"That's right, Matt."

"Ain't he a card?" Sykes left O'Neal gaping as he and Francisco departed.

The Section Manager continued to follow them with his eyes until they reached the gate. As soon as the slugmobile had pulled out into traffic he retraced his steps, heading for the section control room. The one monitor on duty ignored him as he went to the rear wall phone and dialed rapidly.

It was dusk by the time Sykes pulled up in front of the modest three-bedroom home located on the outskirts of Slagtown. From an architectural standpoint it wasn't much to look at: composition roof, stucco walls, lawn and bushes, two-car garage at the end of a narrow concrete driveway, and a solitary but sturdy maple dropping leaves out front. One thing even Sykes noticed right away was how clean the place was. Not a weed poking its rough-maned head through the perfect lawn, not a candy wrapper or bit of tin foil on the sidewalk, not a mark on the house. The windows looked new but were probably only well maintained.

An attractive and conservatively dressed alien woman was watering the lawn with a garden hose. In her huge but still feminine hands it looked like a flex-straw. A six-year-old alien boy rode a specially modified bicycle along the sidewalk.

Everyone had expected alien children to have even more trouble integrating into human society than the adults, but the opposite turned out to be the case, especially once they advanced past puberty. Sykes had heard that the girls still had a difficult time, but even the scrawniest alien boys were welcomed with open arms to local high school football teams by their coaches and fellow players. The Newcomer boys ran a minimum of fifty pounds above the average for children their age, and they never demanded to play quarterback. If they ever developed real quickness they'd revolutionize pro sports.

Sykes studied the bucolic scene and rolled his eyes. "Geez. Welcome back, Ozzie and Harriet."

He leaned on the horn. Francisco looked up from where he'd been waiting for his son, then while Sykes waited he went to kiss his wife goodbye. Lastly a kiss for the boy, atop the naked skull. Oh well, Sykes mused. Every race to its peculiarities. At least they kissed.

As he looked on, the derisive expression he'd worn when he'd parked by the curb began to soften. It was too corny to be fake, too genuine to be ignored. Sure they were aliens, out of place and time and society, but the innocence of it cut across interspecies lines. Even interstellar ones.

He turned forward as Francisco opened the door on the passenger side and climbed in. Only one thing mattered anymore, he reminded himself, and that was finding Tug's killer.

Which probably meant finding this Slag named Anderson.

The Biltmore was still the grand dame of downtown L.A. hotels. Completely renovated in the eighties, it clung to its glory like a wealthy dowager in her prime. Cars pulled out in front of the main entrance and slickly dressed men and women emerged. Not all were human. Not every Newcomer still lived in Slagtown. Some had come a long ways in a short time.

There was muzak in the air and the cheesy aroma of canapés on trays. Waiters moved obsequiously through the crowd, dispensing Perrier and champagne and soaking up a month's worth of gossip which the more astute among them would peddle a little at a time and for high fees to the city's more prominent columnists. Not all the waiters were human, either. Newcomer integration had reached every level of society, though it remained concentrated near the bottom.

At the moment the hall men's room held but a single occupant. His custom tuxedo had been tailored to fit his massive frame. He checked the stalls, then the doorway, before removing the small, thick plastic object from his inside suit pocket. It resembled a flattened toothpaste tube with a tab dispenser near the top. As he lifted it to his lips a faint but distinctive clinking sound echoed through the bathroom. It was made by the links of the exotic silvery bracelet he wore around his left wrist.

Placing the dispenser to his lips, he extended his tongue and thumbed the stud near the tip. Like the dispenser itself, the tab control was designed to accommodate an alien-sized thumb.

The tube released a small dab of bright blue gel. He pulled it in with his tongue, inhaling wetly through thick lips, and let it rest near the back of his mouth for a long moment as he savored the sting. It dissolved slowly in his saliva. When it was nearly gone, he swallowed.

Almost immediately, his pupils dilated and his eyes widened. As the rush overcame him he sucked air.

And whirled as the door to the men's room banged open. He calmed himself as he saw that the intruder was only a balding, middle-aged human whose sole interest was the nearest urinal. The man was half drunk and didn't so much as glance in the gel-sucker's direction.

The name of the owner of the seemingly innocuous dispenser of blue gel was Kipling. He hurriedly pocketed his little dispenser and strode toward the exit, taking care to keep his face turned away from the peeing human. His caution was excessive. The man was having enough trouble focusing on his business. He didn't notice Kipling depart.

If you squeezed your eyes shut until they hurt, the lights of L.A.'s army of autos changed from blinding blobs to heart-breakingly beautiful streaks of color. Sykes never did it intentionally, but sometimes he got so tired he experienced the same hallucinatory effect from sheer exhaustion.

They'd been driving awhile in silence, each sunk in his own thoughts. The radio crackled and complained, dense with high-caloric crime. Just an average L.A. night, no more than the usual number of muggings, purse snatchings, domestic disputes and DWI's. No murders yet. No rape. No arson. One major burglary, safely out of their vicinity.

When Francisco eventually spoke up he did so without looking at his partner. "Mrs. Porter is not taking her husband's death well."

Sykes tried to sound sympathetic and discovered he could not. He'd had to take statements from too many widows. The underside of Los Angeles had kicked most of the sympathy out of him years ago. Not that he wanted to be that way, but it was a matter of self-defense for a lot of cops.

"Pity. Did you learn anything from her?"

"A week ago two men came to see her husband. After they left he was very frightened. She identified one of the men from a photo I showed her. It was Hubley."

"Aw-right." Sykes sat a little straighter behind the wheel. "What about the other guy?"

"She didn't know him. But she said her son might."

A little of Sykes's elation seeped away. He'd been hoping for a positive ID on the surviving killer. Still, taking a make on Hubley was important. The visit hadn't been wasted.

"What about the son? Did you talk to him?"

"He has not been home since that day. But she told me where we might find him."

Sykes nodded. Patience, he told himself. Two pieces to fit in one side of the puzzle, two more on the other. Borders first, then fill it in.

The main ballroom of the Biltmore was a sea of black, white, and all shades of gray. Tuxedoes and evening gowns were the rule, though since this was Los Angeles "formal" could include any color in the rainbow and often did, depending on its wearer's profession. The Hollywood male contingent boasted more ribbons and rhinestones than the gaudiest of the female guests.

Circulating through this select gathering a very few Newcomer faces were visible, not including the servers, security personnel, kitchen help, and others who happened to be working as opposed to attending the gala. Kipling was one of the select. He managed to thread his way unobtrusively through the crowd toward his goal. None of the celebrants paid him the slightest attention. He was simply another guest. The sight of a Newcomer in a tux was no longer a novelty.

The crowd's attention was on the Mayor, who was holding forth from his position at the speaker's table. Nobody minded the fact that instead of directing his words at them he was speaking to the half dozen television cameras lined up on the table's right. He would have been doing exactly the same had he been pontificating at the opening of a new bowling alley. No matter what their social status, Los Angeles audiences always shared one thing in common: media sophistication.

"Our guest speaker tonight has done so much in his community and for his community in such a short period of time," Hizzoner was declaring. "And I must add that as the founder of the first Newcomer owned and operated business to be incorporated in the state of California, he certainly has come a long ways in the last few years. Granted, though, not as far as he came in the years *before* reaching Los Angeles."

It was a good line, and the audience was spared the necessity of laughing politely. They liked the current Mayor. He was a lot more easygoing than his predecessor, who'd been unlucky enough to preside over some botched earthquake relief. The city preferred a laid-back style for its elected officials. The Mayor was a relief, an antidote, a feel-good alternative to the 7.3 that had smashed the San Gabriel Valley a year ago. Nobody paid much attention to his real politics, though behind the smiling, wisecracking veneer he seemed serious enough about his office.

As his rambling discourse held the attention of both the audience and the TV cameras, Kipling slid into an empty seat at the front table, then leaned over to whisper into the head of the individual seated to his immediate right. The tall figure listened without once changing his expression or taking his eyes off the Mayor. Occasionally he would respond with the slightest of nods.

When he'd said all he had to say, Kipling straightened and joined everyone else in listening to the Mayor. Leastwise, he looked intently in his direction. Kipling actually had no interest in politics of any stripe, human or Newcomer.

The Mayor was winding down. A few of the reporters were starting to look bored and the last joke had drawn only a few chuckles instead of the hoped-for big laugh. Like any good politico-performer the Mayor knew when to quit a winner. So he ditched the rest of his speech and turned to his left as he marshaled his concluding words.

"As Mayor of this great city, the greatest in the country, it gives me great pleasure to introduce someone who has so readily made our city his home, someone who has added greatly to its stature while adding simultaneously to his own. Who has literally built something vital and important out of nothing, and who has done so under the most trying and stressful circumstances imaginable. Someone who has made all of us who live here his friends." He gestured magnanimously with his right hand, and the TV cameras genuflected approvingly.

"Ladies and gentlemen—William Harcourt."

Everyone seated at the tables and standing on the ballroom floor applauded vigorously as the TV lights and ballroom spotlight swung away from the Mayor to the newly designated doyen of media attention. Having been forewarned, the camera people knew where to aim their autofocusing equipment. The lenses came to rest on the outsized figure Kipling had been whispering to moments earlier. Kipling tried to stay out of the lights.

Harcourt dwarfed the humans seated at the front table with him. For that matter, so did his strikingly beautiful alien female companion. Everyone recognized him, including those invitees who were attending as guests of guests. Harcourt had appeared on TV and in the papers more than most Newcomers. He was handsome, even suave-looking, despite his lack of hair. His manner was charming and his cool blue eyes could weaken the knees of females of both races. Men stood a little straighter when that gaze focused on them. He was much more than admired. He was well liked.

William Harcourt was the epitome of the successful Newcomer, someone who had moved beyond integration to acceptance. His success was real and of his own making. As his warm smile swept over the audience the Newcomers waiting tables and passing hors d'oeuvres felt a shared sense of pride in the achievements of one of their own.

Harcourt winked down at his date as he stepped behind her to approach the podium. Once there, he further brought the audience into the palm of his outsized hand by making a production out of trying to raise the microphone high enough to reach his lips. As the laughter subsided he shielded his eyes from the spotlights, studying the crowd. When they had quieted, he reached into a breast pocket and extracted his carefully prepared notes.

"Thank you all for that very warm reception." He paused to scan rapidly through the notes, then looked back out at the crowd of expectant VIPs. "I'm particularly grateful because I actually had the gall to write that in my notes." He changed his tone to that of a man reading from a news monitor as he "read."

" 'Thank you all for that very warm reception.' Imagine how embarrassed I would've been if it hadn't been such a warm reception."

Fresh laughter from the crowd as they realized that here was an alien you could warm up to, an individual of charm and candor, who was not above self-parody or having a joke at his own expense.

"I don't have a great deal to say tonight." Harcourt turned to the Mayor and his entourage. "You have His Honor and three council members here tonight. I'm sure if I fail in my poor jests that we won't lack for entertainment." More chuckles bubbling up out of the crowd, just the right amount.

"As for myself, I stand before you a simple businessman. What you call a capitalist. I'm still not sure of certain English terms. Your politics are also still strange to me. But then, you appear to find them rather peculiar yourself. Still, one doesn't need to know all the words to be a success in this country, does one? Perhaps even one of my background may dream someday of reaching for high office."

A few encouraging cheers rose from the back of the crowd. Harcourt was silently delighted to see that they came from young humans, not Newcomers. It was a measure of how far he'd come that he could generate that kind of enthusiasm among members of the host race. It made him feel very good inside. Confident.

They had a hell of a time finding a place to park. Sykes finally decided the hell with it and squinched into a red fire zone. Francisco politely pointed out that it was illegal for them to park there except in emergency situations.

"This is an emergency," Sykes groused as he headed for a side entrance, hands jammed deep in his pockets. "I'm ten minutes overdue for a trip to the can."

"But I think we should . . ."

"Shut up, George, and just follow me, okay?"

Francisco nodded once, reluctantly, as they entered the hotel.

The official function was over and the long line of limos out front had traffic backed all the way up to Fourth Street. Sykes and Francisco forged on through the cavernous hotel, homing in on the buzz of departing guests. As it was they were almost too late, but Sykes spotted the man he was after as he was exiting the main entrance.

"Move it," he snapped at his partner. Francisco did not have to lengthen his stride to keep pace.

Harcourt didn't look at the approaching detectives. He was too busy smiling and chatting and shaking hands with his human equals. But Kipling recognized Sykes right away. His instincts told him to get away, and fast. But if he left in a hurry that would make him stand out when all he wanted to do was blend into the crowd. Humans rarely recognized individuals of his kind at first sight. He made the hard decision to remain at Harcourt's side. He needed to know how the policeman would react to his presence, and he badly wanted to hear what he had to say. So he held his ground and kept his face turned toward the street.

Sykes saw him, but only momentarily. His gaze and thoughts were on Harcourt as he mentally readied his questions. A slight sense of unease came over him and he couldn't isolate a cause. He shook it off as he came around in front of the alien.

"William Harcourt?"

The entrepreneur turned, still smiling broadly. "Yes?"

Sykes flashéd his badge, returned it to his breast pocket. "I'm Detective Sergeant Sykes and this is my partner Detective Francisco. Los Angeles Police Department."

"Pleased to meet you, Sergeant." Harcourt nodded condescendingly. His gaze was on the silently staring Francisco. "Detective. I wasn't aware any Newcomers had achieved the rank of Detective yet."

"I am the first," Francisco informed him.

"Congratulations. This must be the evening for declaration of achievement." He added something brief in his own language. Francisco said nothing, instead responded with a peculiar jerking movement of his head.

Ignorant of whom he was addressing, Harcourt then gestured unknowingly to his companion. "This is my administrative assistant, Rudyard Kipling." Kipling flinched at being pointed out.

Sykes gazed curiously in his direction. "Rudyard Kipling? No shit?" Kipling held his ground tensely, staring at the street, and let out a long slow breath when Sykes turned innocently back to Harcourt. "Listen, we need a minute of your time."

Harcourt's smile faded slightly. From inside the idling limo his date beckoned impatiently. He gestured to her, then turned back to Sykes.

"Always glad of an opportunity to be of assistance to the police. The Mayor and I often discuss law enforcement matters. What can I do for you two gentlemen?"

Francisco took a step forward. "We'd like to ask you about a business associate of yours. Warren Hubley."

Sykes was watching Harcourt closely, but the businessman didn't miss a beat. "Ah, yes. I heard about poor Warren. It was in all the papers, but I knew about it earlier than that. Since I work hard to keep tabs on my many interests, something like that would immediately come to my attention. Tragic."

"You were partners with him on some Slag—uh, Newcomer real estate venture."

Harcourt nodded easily. If he was trying to hide something he was doing a good job of it.

"That's right. He and I, along with seven or eight others." The smile vanished altogether as Harcourt checked his expensive watch. The custom band encircling his wrist was fashioned of gold bars. "Gentlemen, I will be happy to assist you in your investigation in any way I can. Unfortunately, that must wait as I am already overdue at another function. If you will call my office for an appointment I am sure I can spare you a few minutes some day late this week. Kipling?"

The assistant passed a business card to Francisco, who accepted it without looking at Kipling's face. A loud voice cut through the crowd noise and they all turned to see the Mayor and his wife approaching.

"William?"

"Mr. Mayor." Harcourt's smile had regained its previous brilliance.

"William, I was wondering if you wouldn't rather ride with Luisa and me. Two limos trying to make it across town in all this traffic, we're bound to be later than we already are. You know how the Santa Monica can get this time of night."

"I certainly do. What an excellent idea." He turned to gesture at Sykes, taking the sergeant by surprise. "Ray, I wonder if you know two of your fine police officers. Detectives Francisco and Sykes."

The Mayor shook Sykes's hand first, then lost his in Francisco's huge mitt. "A pleasure," he said professionally without really seeing either of them. "William, we really should be going. Can't keep the constituents waiting."

"That's something I'm learning fast, Ray. I've learned a lot watching you."

Sykes had a whole raft of queries to put to the Newcomer entrepreneur, but the presence of the impatient Mayor took the wind out of his sails. He was impressed despite himself, not the least by the fact that the Mayor and Harcourt called each other by their first names. Confronted by Harcourt's courtesy and the Mayor's impatience, he quietly gave up.

Harcourt's concern didn't make him feel any better.

"Don't look so distraught, Sergeant. Your world's an impatient place, you know. Please feel free to call my office Monday for an appointment. I promise I will answer all your questions." He turned and extended his hand to help his date out of their limo.

As he started off, something made him pause and he turned to gaze back at Francisco.

"Congratulations again on your promotion, detective. Remember, you're out there setting an example for all of us. When you accept a high-profile position you are also taking on a great deal of responsibility. With so much bad press it is vital for those of us in a position to counteract it to be aware that we are every day working under a microscope. I'll be keeping an eye on you and following your progress with great interest."

Francisco met the entrepreneur's stare unflinchingly. Sykes ignored them both. He was left frustrated and angry as the Mayor and Harcourt strolled off practically arm in arm.

"Let's get out of here." He spun on his heel and began pushing his way back through the rapidly thinning crowd.

"I thought he was most cooperative," Francisco commented gingerly.

"Just shut up, George."

Francisco eyed him uncertainly but acquiesced. Asking questions wasn't the best way to learn human behavior.

Kipling touched Harcourt's arm lightly. Turning from his date, Harcourt noted the expression on his assistant's face and allowed himself to fall slightly behind the other members of the Mayor's party. His date didn't miss him. She was conversing merrily with the Mayor's wife, thrilled and awed to find herself in such exalted human company. Harcourt was not so easily impressed.

"Something bothering you, my friend?" He spoke softly in English. That would draw less attention than speaking their own language. It was considered impolite to speak the Voice of Origins while in human company. English conversation would be ignored by those around them. He continued to smile and nod at faces in the crowd, never failing even as he listened to Kipling to acknowledge someone he recognized or who recognized him. Every contact was a potentially useful one. Amazing how you could make a human your friend simply by judicious use of the expression they called the smile.

It was an indication of his considerable self-control that his own smile did not vanish completely at Kipling's next words.

"That cop, the one who was just talking to you? The human?"

"What about him?"

"He was the one who killed Anderson and the driver."

Harcourt nearly stopped in his tracks. Nearly, but not quite. "This is becoming a serious breach of security. We have to put a stop to it immediately. There's too much going on, everything is going far too well to risk something like this now. I don't have the time to deal with it. Everything is at a very delicate stage of development."

"I know." Kipling smiled, but it wasn't anything like Harcourt's expression. Where the entrepreneur's was warm and reassuring, his assistant's was feral. "Don't worry. He didn't recognize me."

"I'm not worried about some 'ss'askli human cop. It is his new partner who concerns me."

Kipling nodded thoughtfully and turned to search the crowd. But the persistent human detective and his tall partner were already gone.

* * *

Maffet had retired years ago, but like some career cops he couldn't keep away from police business. There was always a job for lifers like him, and the younger cops viewed him with sympathy. As for themselves, they couldn't understand a mindset like Maffet's when all they wanted was to do their time with as little trouble as possible and retire early. Not Maffet and his kind. They loved the rapid-fire banter of the station house. Maffet wasn't an enthusiast. He was an addict.

The old man had a special fondness for guns. So they'd put him to work down on the firing line. The range was empty now, quiet, only half the lights on. Footsteps echoed through the subterranean chamber as the old man led his visitors through the grill that served as a gate. The clang of it shutting behind them boomed in the enclosed space.

Stepping behind the counter, he unlocked the cage that held the range supplies and removed a bag of reloads and a handful of silhouette targets which he passed to Francisco. The Newcomer detective glanced questioningly at his partner.

Sykes gestured rangeward. "Go on ahead. I'll be right in." Francisco nodded, turned to leave. As soon as he was out of sight, Sykes whispered to the old man. "Okay, what did you dig up for me?"

Maffet's eyes gleamed. He glanced a last time in the direction of the entrance, more for effect than need. Others would be arriving soon to make use of the range, but they still had the facility all to themselves.

"I could catch hell for this if anybody finds out I did it for you."

"Nobody's gonna find anything out, you paranoid old fart. You think Francisco's gonna tell?"

Maffet leaned over the counter and looked toward the range, where the Newcomer detective was loading his own weapon. "How the hell can you be so sure of him? He's a Slag."

Sykes's expression twisted. "Hey, sure he's a Slag—but he's an okay Slag. Got me? As far as you're concerned he's a detective."

Maffet looked up sharply at Sykes. "Don't tell me you actually *like* him?"

"I don't have to tell you nothin'. You're a civilian now, remember? So what did you find for me?"

"Okay, okay. Don't get your ass in an uproar." Maffet's sour look vanished when he unlocked a drawer beneath the counter and pulled it out. The bag he withdrew didn't contain groceries.

Maffet reached into the bag and pulled out the biggest handgun Sykes had ever seen. Plenty of custom jobs in the shops came equipped with longer barrels, but that had nothing to do with power. The bore on Maffet's baby was immense, capacious enough to hold a shotgun shell. Nor was bore size the gun's only unique characteristic. The whole weapon; hammer, cylinder, trigger guard, scope, everything down to the screws, was fashioned of solid stainless steel.

There was reverence in Maffet's eyes as he handed it over. Sykes accepted it gingerly, studying it as he flipped it from one side to the other, finally hefting it in one hand to aim it experimentally. It was heavy, yes, but not unwieldy.

Maffet looked like a proud parent at Christmas. "You said you wanted the biggest thing I could find. Well, there she is. Cost about a grand."

"You'll get your money, pops. What is it?"

"Casull .454 Magnum. You're talking twice the impact energy of .44 Magnum hot loads. Place called Freedom Arms makes these puppies somewhere up in Wyoming. See, it even has a scope."

Sykes looked back curiously. "What the hell would anybody want a scope on a handgun for?"

Maffet was having a good time. "Hunting." He nodded toward the huge handgun. "Deer. Maybe bear."

"Bear, yeah." Though he wasn't smiling, Sykes gave every indication of being satisfied with the old man's choice. He flipped the cylinder open to examine the weapon's interior. "Only holds five cartridges."

"Yeah. The shells are too big to fit six in a cylinder. Hell, Matthew, you don't need but one."

Sykes fought to hold the pistol at arm's length, taking casual aim in the direction of the range. "Heavy, but not impossible. I won't ask about recoil."

"You won't have to." Maffet grinned. "Find out for yourself." The sound of the grill being opened made him look toward the entrance. "Better get started. This time of night the place can fill up fast once the guys start coming in."

Sykes nodded. Picking up the gun and a couple of boxes of very expensive shells, he went looking for his partner.

Francisco stood near the far end of the range, looking bizarre in his ear protectors. Unlike most articles of human attire which were cut too small for the average Newcomer, the ear shields were too large. They didn't fit tightly enough over the flat aural openings in the side of Francisco's head and he was readjusting them constantly. Duct tape would probably work better, Sykes mused.

The alien was taking careful aim with his regulation .38. His finger barely fit in front of the trigger. Up the range, recent arrivals were beginning to load and fire.

"Let's see what you got," Sykes asked him. When Francisco didn't respond, Sykes rapped him on the arm.

The alien lifted his ear muffs, looked querulous. "Sorry, Matt."

"I said, let's see what you got, Cochise. Gimme six in a row, rapid fire."

"Please bear in mind that I am still not comfortable with the firearms they issue." This confession made, the detective replaced his ear protectors. Sykes slipped into his own and looked intently at the paper target downrange, which only made his partner more nervous.

Francisco let fly methodically, all six shells. Every one struck the target, but that was the best you could say for his aim. The bullet holes were spread all over the paper in a highly dispersed, sloppy grouping.

Sykes lowered his ear shields and proceeded to demonstrate the tact and diplomacy for which he was famed throughout the precinct.

"How long you been shooting? That's pitiful. Didn't they

teach you anything at the Academy? Cripes, the last thing they do is show rookies what a gun is for. What are you gonna do if somebody draws down on you? Wave your scores on the written exam at 'em?'' As he spoke he was sliding thumb-sized cartridges into the cylinder of the Casull. The pop and bang of handguns being fired filled the range and he had to shout to make himself heard above the din.

Francisco listened, taking it all silently. Only when Sykes had finished did he speak up unexpectedly. ''Why did you do it?''

''Why'd I do what?''

''Agree to work with me. You don't like me. You don't like any of us. You have nothing but contempt for my kind. That has been plain to see these past few days. Your attitude is obvious in the way you address me, in the way you refer to other Newcomers, in the way you look at us. You make no secret of it, so do not try to deny it. I am not surprised. Your attitude is the one that still prevails among most humans.

''And yet you make yourself an outcast among your fellow detectives by volunteering to become my partner. I wish you would explain this to me, Matthew Sykes, because I wish to learn as much as possible about human behavior.''

Sykes turned sharply. ''All right. I'll tell you why I'm working with you. Because my partner is dead! Because one of you bastards killed him before disappearing down a rathole in Slagtown, where he's home safe and dry 'cause in Slagtown nobody sees nothing, nobody says nothing, and a cop like me's about as welcome as a visit from the Federal Forced Resettlement Bureau.''

Turning away from Francisco, he angrily wrenched a Kelvar-IV bulletproof vest from a nearby wall hanger and slapped it over the hanging target silhouette in front of him. As the Newcomer looked on impassively, Sykes flicked the wall switch and ran the vest-covered target down its transport wire, all the way to the end of the range. The stink of cordite filled the subterranean shooting gallery and it was loud even with muffs on.

Sykes was still talking as he waited for the target to reach the end of its line. "But there's something the son-of-a-bitch didn't figure on. He didn't figure on *you*, George. That's why I closed my eyes and stuck up my hand when they asked for a volunteer to babysit you. That's why I've kept my ears shut and taken all the crap at the station while I've been working with you. Don't think I did this because I'm some kind of saint, or because I'm overflowing with the milk of human kindness, or because I felt bad for you. I did it because I need you. You're the only one who can help me find Tug's murderer." The target had stopped swinging.

"You're going to get me through that wall of silence, George. You're going to make them talk to me. You're going to help me find that Slag son-of-a-bitch. Comprendo?"

"Procedure. We spoke about . . ."

"We spoke about a lot of shit, George," Sykes said, interrupting him. "We also spoke about what it means to be partners. Remember?"

"I remember, Matt, but . . ."

"And if Fedorchuk and the boys in the bullpen don't like it, screw them," he continued, "and if the Captain doesn't like it, screw him, and if the computer doesn't like it, unscrew it, and if all the Slags down in Slagtown don't like it, why hell, screw them too!"

Francisco was about to reply but his following words were drowned out by a thunderous, echoing roar as Sykes raised the Casull in both hands and let rip. It sounded as if someone had set off a small bomb in the range. The target nearly flipped a 360, swinging wildly on its stressed clips as the shell slammed clean through the paper and the state-of-the-art bulletproof vest.

That's how he learned about the recoil. It slammed him a step backward and brought his arm up sharply. Fighting down the pain, he grimly resumed his position and fired a second time. Another gaping hole appeared in the vest. Fragments of cardboard drifted like snow to the floor of the range, illustrating graphically how the target was being shredded by the impact.

As Sykes kept firing it grew quieter and quieter uprange. The other shooters were leaning out and looking downrange curiously, trying to locate the source of the awesome explosions.

Sykes set the pistol down, saw that his hand was bleeding. It would take awhile to get used to the Casull. He felt only satisfaction as he studied the still swaying, devastated target.

# VI

Few humans ventured beyond the outskirts of Slagtown at all save for government workers, and even the police preferred to avoid this end of the alien ghetto. Only the X-Bar seemed at home, a brightly hued carrion feeder set down among dark storefronts and boarded-up apartment buildings.

The menial laborers lounging in front of the bar looked like rejects from the Raiders' offensive line, big and battered. They glared with undisguised antagonism at the two detectives as they emerged from the slugmobile. Sykes took in the sullen expressions and threatening gazes phlegmatically.

"Okay," he told his partner. "I do this all the time, so just stay back and watch me. Watch and learn, watch and learn."

"Whatever you say, Matt." Francisco obediently followed Sykes into the bar.

Sykes expected bad lighting. That much was evident from outside. But he wasn't prepared for the near total absence of illumination. A few indigo-colored ultraviolet lamps made the place resemble the nightmare end of an old fun house. Shirt and socks glowed eerie blue. Sykes knew the ultraviolet wasn't for effect. The Newcomers could see farther into that region of the spectrum than any human.

His eyes adjusted slowly to the dimness. Gradually he picked out the long straightaway of the bar and the massive humanoid shapes hunched over the plastic wood counter.

The floor was spotted with chairs and tables, islands adrift in an ocean of ultraviolet.

"I can't see dick in here." Francisco didn't comment.

Booths lined the far wall. They were mostly empty. He tried to take a headcount, thought maybe twenty inhabitants shuffled silently through the purple haze. All of them had been chattering animatedly in their own language when the detectives had entered, making the place sound like the snake house at the zoo. As the presence of the intruders was noted, the conversation died.

He sauntered toward the bar, to all outward appearances utterly unconcerned about his safety and ignorant of the hostility that was rising like steam all around him. His walk was casual, unhurried. He might've just dropped in for a drink and a chat, like the rest of them. Except that he wasn't thirsty, and he wasn't like the rest of them.

Easy enough to grab their undivided attention. He addressed the general silence. "Which one of you Slags is Porter?"

A voice rose from an unseen source near the far end of the bar. "Who wants to know?" The English was crude, the alien accent heavy.

Sykes squinted into the darkness, without result. He needed to be an owl in this place. Instead he felt like a mole, blind and groping his way. He mumbled softly to his partner.

"I can't make 'em out. Who said that?"

Francisco replied in a low whisper as he gestured with his right hand. "At the end of the bar."

Nodding, Sykes headed in that direction. "My name's Sykes. Detective Sergeant Sykes. I'm with the L.A...."

An alien voice interrupted, rich with disbelief. *"Ss'ai k'ss?"*

The individual roared with laughter. It spread like a wave through the bar as the information was passed from table to booth. Too late, Sykes remembered what his name translated into in the alien tongue. His face was burning, but it was probably too dark even for the damn Slags to note the change. Most likely none of them would recognize the significance of heightened skin color among a human anyway.

He was having plenty of trouble focusing on the distant

speaker, so it wasn't surprising he missed the size-16 work boot that emerged from one of the booths to trip him. He stumbled but didn't go down, spinning to confront the offender. But the booth was suddenly filled only with lavender-tinged shadows. Laughter taunted him, accompanied by soft alien admonitions.

A new voice reached him, leavened with amusement. "Careful, ss'loka'. You might hurt yourself."

More laughter, but this time Sykes spotted the speaker. He stared hard, then calmed himself as he resumed his march to the end of the bar. True to his word, Francisco kept his mouth shut, trailing silently behind.

The Newcomer Sykes found himself confronting was as big as any he'd seen. He wore greasy, stained coveralls. Beneath the hapless overdose of cologne he stank to high heaven. If possible, his boots were larger than the one which had just tripped the detective.

But Sykes abruptly found himself much more interested in the smaller Newcomer seated on the last stool. He was dressed and coiffured in postpunk style. Unlike his oversized neighbor, he was making obvious efforts to render himself inconspicuous. Sykes smiled tightly to himself. The Newcomers made lousy poker players. Their emotions always showed in their posture and expressions.

Sykes kept staring without speaking. Sure enough, the Newcomer couldn't keep himself from turning to catch a glimpse of the two cops staring back at him. His expression underwent a drastic shift when he spotted Francisco, but the alien detective was looking elsewhere at the time and missed it.

Sykes's attention kept shifting between the two Newcomers. Just because the punk wore a guilty air didn't mean he was the one they were looking for. Frankly, the big guy seated next to him appeared a much more likely candidate for serious antisocial behavior.

"You Porter?" Sykes said to the broad back.

The Newcomer ignored him, sipping at his mug. It was half full of sour milk. Sykes didn't waste time, grabbed the guy by the shoulder and spun him round. Given the alien's bulk it wasn't an easy move, but he managed it. Practice compensated somewhat for his lesser mass.

The Newcomer flicked the detective's fingers from his shoulder. He slid off the stool and stood up. Kept standing up, locking eyes with Sykes. Meanwhile the punker who'd been seated nearby was edging off his seat.

Francisco grabbed him before he'd made it to the end of the bar, speaking for the first time since they'd entered. "No, Matthew. I believe this is the one you want." As he spun the younger alien around, the detective got his first good look at him. It confirmed his initial suspicions.

Sykes favored the big alien with a final warning look, then gratefully stepped past the giant to rejoin his partner. He turned his frustration on the punk.

"Your name wouldn't happen to be Porter, would it?"

"Uh, Matt, if I may . . ."

Sykes snapped at his colleague. "Back off, George."

"But I . . ."

"I'll handle it. Just do as you're told." Francisco reluctantly let go of the punk's shirt and stepped back.

The youth wasn't nearly as big as the millworker Sykes had just confronted, but he was still plenty impressive. Sykes made a show of his frustration.

"Geez, are these questions too tough for you? I know some of you guys are slow, but it's not like the music's drowning me out, right?" He sighed melodramatically. "Let's try it one more time." He framed the words with his lips. *"Is . . . your . . . name . . . Porter?"*

The punker replied in a monotone. "Ss'kya'ta."

Sykes made a face, glanced at Francisco. "What's that?"

"Screw you," his partner informed him without batting an eye.

"Screw me? That can't be right," he said amiably.

Having warmed to his subject, Porter became positively voluble. "Ss'kya'ta ss'loka. Sss'troyka ss'lato 'na'!"

Sykes's voice dropped dangerously. "What's all that mean?"

Francisco sounded nonplussed. "You don't want to know."

"Tell me."

"Matt, really, I'd rather not bother with . . ."

"Tell me, damnit."

The detective swallowed, said rapidly and without pause, "Your mother mates out of season."

Sykes relaxed, smiling appreciatively. "That's very colorful. However, it doesn't mean zip to a human. We mate all the time, see?"

"I know. That's precisely the point."

"He can make all the points he wants about my love life. But see, now I've got a problem. I don't seem to be getting much cooperation from you, Porter. So I guess we're gonna have to take this little session down to my office, ya know? Everybody down there mates out of season, in case you're interested, and when they haven't mated for a while they get mean and nasty and impolite. Does that translate into anything worthwhile, George?"

"It makes a point."

"I'm glad something does."

He could tell Porter was getting ready to run. Sykes wasn't utterly ignorant of Newcomer characteristics. He dug in his pocket for a plastic tube. Not the Casull, but a flashlight with a high-intensity krypton bulb. As Porter tensed to break, he flipped on the light. The Newcomer let out a cry and turned away in obvious distress. So did every alien within range of the white light. Even Francisco, half expecting Sykes to do something, was taken by surprise and had to flinch.

Being able to see better in the dark, Sykes reflected grimly, also came with disadvantages.

By the time Porter knew what had hit him, Sykes had the alien pinned up against the bar and was working with his cuffs. But it was hard to manipulate flashlight and handcuffs simultaneously. As the light waved around, Porter got a hand free and grabbed the end of the tube. Massive fingers convulsed and the plastic splintered, smashing down into the fragile bulb. Blood trickled from the punker's hand, but the light was out.

Sykes cursed himself for not bringing a regulation aluminum flash, but he'd decided the Casull was enough extra weight to lug around. Now it might cost him. Darkness regained the room and Sykes's sense of satisfaction vanished with the light.

Porter hurled him onto a table, shrugging him off easily. Sykes hit hard, winced, and scrambled back onto his feet. Francisco was moving.

"Matt, you don't have to do this."

The detective was shrugging off the pain in his sacrum. "Stay back! I'm okay. I told you I'd handle this." Looking doubtful, Francisco retreated.

Taking a deep breath, Sykes charged Porter, brandishing the broken flashlight like a club. The punker took a shot to the face which drew blood but didn't put him down. He worked at parrying the detective's punches. Sykes was faster, the alien far stronger. The longer the fight lasted, the more Porter's confidence grew.

It didn't do any good to land blows on your opponent if they had no effect, Sykes realized tiredly. Aware he was doing nothing except getting good and winded, he made another rush, feinting high with the light, then bringing his knee up sharply into the alien's groin. Porter doubled, and almost as quickly straightened. He was smiling. That was not the expression Sykes expected him to be wearing.

"Don't they teach you anything about us in cop school, little ss'loka'?"

Porter grabbed Sykes by the front of his shirt and lifted him off the ground preparatory to delivering a final crushing blow. Another arm flashed through the darkness to block the punch. Porter looked over in surprise.

Francisco was glaring at him. "Enough."

The punker stared back. "Ss'tangya T'ssorentsa. You're a cop." He didn't try to conceal the contempt in his voice. "It fits you."

Francisco replied in the alien tongue. Porter eyed him for a long moment, then slumped slightly as he let loose of Sykes and shambled toward the rear of the bar. Sykes pulled himself together, straightening his clothing and his composure. The laughter in the bar had died down. The show was over, and normal conversation echoed from tables and booths. The patrons now chose to ignore the detectives, which was fine with the shaken Sykes.

"You know the guy?"

Francisco nodded. "From quarantine, from when we first arrived on your world. You may recall that we were grouped randomly, with no attempt at preserving family groups or friends." He nodded in Porter's direction. "He and I were housed together."

Sykes frowned. "How could a straight-arrow like you ever pick a roommate like him?"

"In the camps we were lodged four to a room. You must remember that the processing was overseen by the military. It was all done very arbitrarily and in considerable haste. We were simply told which room to go to after we had been issued bedding, identification cards, and toiletry articles— and new names."

He passed Sykes, moving toward the bar's back exit. Sykes looked after him, then followed, careful to watch where he put his feet.

The alley looked like any big-city alley. The Newcomers had not had time to build housing to their liking, and they left human structures pretty much alone, adapting to them without extensive modification. They hadn't had much choice. It was easier to rent than to build, especially in a city as expensive as Los Angeles. A few attempts to build specifically to Newcomer needs had been made by entrepreneurs like William Harcourt, but their projects were isolated and few.

To make it worse, wealthy humans drawn to anything new and different outbid those few aliens with money enough to buy a house for the slightly alien structures Harcourt and his partners built.

Porter was leaning against the far wall of the alley, hands jammed in his pockets and looking sullen. His accent was thick and liberally laced with a weird mixture of human and alien street slang. It hadn't taken the younger Newcomers long to learn that there was more than one kind of English.

Francisco confronted him, keeping out of easy reach. "You don't know what your father and these two men who came to visit him that day were arguing about?"

"I told you." Porter spoke without looking at the big detective. "I was in the back of the store. I just heard muffled voices. I had the box on and I couldn't hear any words. Just talking sounds, like."

Francisco sounded doubtful. "You didn't try to listen in, maybe learn something useful? A deep-holed 'ss'yuti' like yourself?"

"I told you, I didn't hear nothin'!" Porter responded defensively. "I didn't give a damn about the old man and his friends. He had a lot of visitors. I always figured it was just business, so I stayed out of it. That kind of ss'loka crap never interested me."

"Didn't it?" said Sykes. "Why do I have this tight feeling inside that you're not telling us the truth?" When Porter didn't comment he tried a different tack. "One of the two men was named Hubley, right?"

"What if it was?"

Sykes ignored the challenge. "What about the other one? Did you see him?" Sykes leaned in close so that the punker couldn't avoid his eyes. "You're not being helpful enough, Porter. It would please me if you were a little more helpful."

The younger man shifted uneasily against the wall. "Okay, what of it? Yeah, I seen him around. Highroller dude named Strader. Joshua Strader. Runs a club on the West Side. 'Encounters,' I think it's called."

Sykes was nodding to himself. "Yeah, I heard of it." He spat in the direction of the X-Bar's exit. "Caesar's Palace compared to this rathole."

"That's all I know." Porter was shifting nervously from one foot to the other, like a cat that's been too long in a box on its way to the vet. "You want to know anything more, you ask somebody else."

He turned and waited expectantly. After a long look, Francisco moved aside to let him pass. As the punker mooched through the doorway leading back into the bar, the Newcomer detective had a final word for him.

"I am sorry about your father."

Porter threw him a last, inconclusive look. Then he was gone, swallowed back up by the alien hissing and ultraviolets. Sykes and Francisco headed up the alley toward the main street.

Francisco paused once they'd reached the slugmobile. "If I may make a suggestion, Matt?"

Sykes looked across at him, the door open and his hand on the handle. "Like what?"

"We have different weak spots than you do. If you intend in the future to try extracting information from one of us by the use of physical force, you should know exactly how to go about it." He raised his right arm and pointed. "There are sensitive nerve centers here, beneath each arm. A blow to this spot will produce the effect I think you were looking for."

"Yeah, sure." Sykes didn't look at his partner as he climbed into the car. "I knew that all the time. I just never got the opening, that's all."

Francisco's face was expressionless as he slid in alongside his partner. "Of course . . ."

Sykes studied the menu mounted above the serving counter. It was late and the burger stand wasn't crowded. The menu was in both English and the alien language. To the detective the Newcomer hieroglyphs looked like the scribbles Kristin used to bring home from kindergarten.

Teenage humans and aliens mixed freely behind the counter, working together to produce both varieties of fast food. Sykes envied them their easy camaraderie. It just proved what everyone knew all along: if you put any group of kids together and kept 'em away from the adults, they'd get along fine. It took experienced grown-ups to really screw things up.

They'd been waiting less than five minutes when the pretty brunette brought them their food. She didn't so much as glance at Francisco. Sykes noted that all the cashiers were human. Given time, that too would change.

"Six forty-two," she demanded boredly. Her attention was split three ways: among her two customers, the night manager working the grill, and the tall gangly boy her own age presently shaking oil from the latest batch of fries.

He shelled out bills and change, waited while Francisco methodically counted out his share. They argued briefly over a quarter, with the result that their server gained an unexpected tip.

"Missing a chocolate shake," Sykes told her.

Her eyes flicked over their tray and she nodded without commenting, headed for the shake machine. While he was waiting, Sykes found his attention drawn once more to the brightly lit overhead menu.

"I don't think I could ever learn to read that shit. Looks like a bunch of worms screwing." He glanced curiously at his partner. "How long did it take you to learn English?"

Francisco gazed down at him. "You find my English acceptable?"

Sykes shrugged. "Got a ways to go, but it ain't bad."

"Thank you. It took me three months." At the look that came over his partner's face he added, "Certain things we learn quickly. We may sometimes appear to be stupid, but we are not, Matt. It is simply that our talents are concentrated in certain areas. Some things that you do easily and well I do not think we will ever be able to manage. Other tasks we find hard but can do. A few things we are very good at because we were designed to adapt to them. It is our strength, what we were bred for. To adapt to difficult environments. To survive. Learning a native language is an essential survival skill. Your own early explorers of your planet knew this as well."

The girl returned to put Sykes's shake on the tray.

"That's a large?" Sykes eyed the Styrofoam container dubiously.

She nodded. "New cups. Complain to the management."

"Where? In Chicago?" He picked up the shake and put it in the bag atop his burger and fries. The detectives headed for the door, digging food out of their sacks as they talked.

"My neighbor's kid has a Newcomer girl in his class. She's six years old. The basketball coach at the high school down the street's already trying to get her family to commit."

"Our physical size has been of benefit to us, which is fortunate." Francisco held the door for his partner. "We arrived with nothing but our bodies. Many of us have been forced to make a living on strength and size alone." They were out in the parking lot now. "Considering that much of the reaction to our arrival has been less than friendly, can you imagine what our situation would be like if instead of being bigger and stronger than the average human, we were smaller and weaker?"

Sykes's brow furrowed as he considered this new thought. Then he brightened. "Actually, it might've been easier on you. Big as you run, there are always some folks who are going to view you as a threat."

"Such people, I think, would also tend to view humans bigger than themselves as threatening. Are you saying that had we been smaller we could have relied more on the goodness of human nature to ease our acceptance into your society?"

Sykes hesitated outside the slugmobile, pondering that one carefully. Finally he declared around a mouthful of greasy fries, "Don't go asking a cop about the goodness of human nature, George." He slipped in behind the wheel and started unwrapping the rest of his food.

Except that it wasn't his food. His expression contorted as he fought to mute his reaction. "Oh, God. I think I got yours here." He held up two neatly sliced strips of raw meat. Patches of animal fur clung to the unskinned exterior.

He wasn't alone in his disgust. Francisco could barely stand to hold on to the dripping cheeseburger he'd just unfoiled. They quickly swapped handfuls.

Sykes bit gratefully into his burger, savoring the taste of grease and fried beef and processed cheese. It helped settle his stomach. But he couldn't restrain his curiosity.

Porter had been wrong. They did teach you a little about Newcomers in cop school. They just never taught you enough.

He nodded at the unwrapped meat in his partner's hands. "Which kind is that? Raw what?"

Holding one of the two strips like a piece of jerky, Francisco bit off a few inches. He replied while chewing slowly, clearly delighting in the taste of the dreadful stuff.

"This is mole. We are extremely fortunate in that our

digestive systems are similar enough for us to ingest local foods."

"Geez, don't call that garbage 'food.' Have some respect."

"Furthermore," Francisco went on, "we find much of what you call vermin extremely palatable. This works to your benefit as well as to ours, since our culinary preferences coincide neatly with your dislikes. There is a new restaurant on the West Side, I am told, which specializes in serving heaping platters of..."

"George! Just eat your crap, will you, and keep your mouth shut when you're not chewing?"

Francisco hesitated, then obediently took another bite out of his meat strip. The second one rested on his lap, atop yellow wrapping paper. The foil it had been served in was identical to the square which had held Sykes's cheeseburger except that the script on it was all alien. The burger chain's instantly recognizable logo was also unchanged.

"It is good," he said around his mouthful, a bit defensively.

"I'll bet." Sykes couldn't keep from staring in fascination as his partner masticated. Thank God the Newcomers naturally chewed with their mouths shut. "I got a kitchen question."

"I will try to answer."

"Would it really put you out if they tossed that on the grill for a minute or two?"

"It is not only a question of taste, Matt. If the food has been cooked, our bodies cannot assimilate the nutrients."

"Kind of like with rice and vitamins, huh?"

"I believe it is something like that. I have made a minor study of our different food habits. Serving is a hobby of my mate's. Did you know that in Southern America, in the regions crossed by the Andes Mountains, guinea pig has been a staple food of the local humans for thousands of years?"

Sykes's stomach did a complete flip-flop. His daughter had kept guinea pigs as pets for several years. They were fat and furry. The thought of eating one cooked, much less raw...

Francisco rambled on, oblivious to the look on his partner's face. "The word for them down there is *cui*, pronounced 'koo-ee' in English. I have seen pictures. Sometimes they are served in stews, sometimes simply gutted and split and unfortunately boiled with sauces. Often the hair remains on. I imagine that even after being dreadfully seared by flame the hair is still nice and crunchy on the way down.''

"George, I've got a large-caliber handgun in my shoulder holster, and if you don't shut up I may have to use it.''

Francisco responded with a wide smile, not quite sure if his partner was merely engaging in the usual human hyperbole or if his suggestion was serious. Sykes blanched at the smile.

"Oh, that's real attractive. You got fur in your teeth, George. Come on, man, do something with yourself, will you? We can't go out like that. We're gonna be talking to people— Geez.''

The Newcomer made an effort to pick the fur out of his teeth. It caught under his fingernails and he scraped the accumulated fuzzy lumps off on his serving paper. Sykes watched a moment longer. Then, his appetite gone, he shoved the remainder of his supper back into his sack and tossed it into the back seat.

He gazed quietly out past the parking lot, trying to watch the pedestrians and cars, taking his thoughts slow while praying for his partner to finish as rapidly as possible. Unfortunately, Francisco decided to linger over his second mole strip.

Better to talk about anything than sit listening to those munching noises, Sykes finally decided. Clinging to the wheel and his stomach, he asked, "So what was that other word for human everybody was using? 'Slow ka? That's what that jerk kid Porter was calling me.''

"Ss'loka'.'' Francisco corrected him gently. "It means literally 'small but intelligent creature.' ''

Sykes looked over at his partner, uncertain whether he approved of the definition. Francisco must have noticed something in his expression, because he added reassuringly, "It loses much in the translation.''

"I see.'' Sykes mulled this over, found himself getting nowhere. Linguistic subtleties weren't his forte. "And what was that one about my mother? That was a good one. Even if it didn't mean zip to me."

"Ss'troyka ss'lato 'na'."

"I'm damned if I can figure out how you make sounds like that with just your mouth."

"You must learn to move your tongue properly against your upper palate."

"Say what?"

Francisco demonstrated. The result was a pure hissing sound. "Press your tongue against the roof of your mouth where the accents fall. The trick is to make the '' sound by inhaling, not when breathing out. Your linguists have learned how to do this."

"Yeah, but two years' high school Spanish is as far as I ever got."

"With a little practice I think you could do it, Matt. Try. I will help."

Sykes took a deep breath. "Say it one more time."

"Ss'troyka ss'lato 'na'."

"Yeah, that's it. Again. Slowly."

Francisco complied, stretching out the peculiar consonantal combinations and exaggerating the hissing sound where appropriate. Sykes tried, failed miserably, then tried again. He kept trying. Each time he sounded a little better.

"I can almost understand you," his partner said encouragingly. "Let us try one word at a time now. Then we will put it all together."

Sykes nodded determinedly. "Right. And don't be afraid to correct me, okay? I use this on some Slag, I want to make sure he gets my point."

They worked on it steadily, until Sykes had achieved near fluency with the phrase. It was only three words and a lot of hissing, but he felt oddly elated when his partner pronounced him perfect.

# VII

The difference between the Encounters Club and the X-Bar was the difference between the Plaza Hotel and the Bates Motel, between the disintegrating depths of Slagtown and the upscale West Side, between night and day. Well, between evening and day, anyhow. It couldn't compare to the all-human clubs up on Sunset, but compared to the best downtown Slagtown had to offer it was damn impressive.

The place was full of young professionals, mostly human but with the occasional Newcomer individual or couple. They tended to cluster in the corners and against the walls, where the darker lighting helped them to blend in with the human clientele. Sykes wondered if they found the dance floor lighting painfully bright and suffered it for the sake of being able to mix freely with human company. If he got the chance he'd have to ask George.

One thing to be said for steady drinking, he mused. When you were falling-down drunk you didn't care what planet your drinking buddy hailed from.

Music blared from several sources as their hostess led them through the maze of tables. They walked past the dance floor, traveling from the realm of technopunk to Newtone. She found them a small table not far from the stage, then moved slinkily away. Sykes watched her legs through the slits on the sides of her skirt, finally forced himself to concentrate on the stage.

The music changed abruptly and a new dancer appeared on the runway. The beat was familiar but the dancer was not. She was well over six feet tall, not unusual for a Newcomer female, and appropriately proportioned. Her high naked skull was covered with a silvery wig, her makeup an exotic combination of human and alien tastes. With the full wig you didn't even notice the absence of external ears.

Not that anyone was likely to be looking for her ears anyway, Sykes decided.

As she danced to the pounding rhythm, the silvery nylon wig bounced wildly. Sykes observed the entire performance in total silence, fascinated by some of her inhuman movements as well as her more familiar attributes. Francisco merely sat stolidly and looked on with what could best be described as nonjudgmental politeness.

Sykes had expected to be bored, turned off. The strength of his reaction and interest surprised and startled him, so much so that he was actually disappointed when the music died and the dancer fled the stage. She was instantly replaced by another performer, human and pretty, who seemed somehow very small.

Francisco was resting a big hand on his shoulder. "Let's go."

Sykes shook himself. "What?"

"If we do not hurry we may miss her."

"Yeah, right." He rose and followed his partner to the left of the stage.

The guard there tried to stop them, shrugged indifferently when Sykes flashed his badge.

They found her as she was making her way back to the dressing rooms. She studied them with interest, her gaze lingering curiously on the towering form of Francisco.

"Aren't you boys in the wrong place? Next show's in an hour. I don't do private performances."

"You are Cassandra?" Francisco inquired formally. This time Sykes said nothing about his partner keeping silent.

She stared back at him. "That's right. Not much point in denying it, not with my face plastered all over the front of the building."

"We are with the Los Angeles Police Department."

She responded with a strange whistling noise. "Gee, I never would've guessed. You both hide it so well."

Francisco took her sarcasm in stride. It was nothing compared to dealing with Sykes. "This is Detective Sykes, and I am . . ."

A look of astonishment crossed her exquisite face before she burst out laughing. "Ss'ai k'ss? Perfect."

It was Sykes's turn to ignore her comment. "We're looking for your boss, Strader. Not much point in denying who he is, either."

Her eyes flicked rapidly from the human detective back to his Newcomer partner. Then she shrugged and turned, assuming correctly they would follow.

The backstage corridor was narrow and unpainted. Cassandra spoke as she led them up the narrow passageway. "Of course he's my boss, but if you're looking to talk to him you're out of luck. He's not here. Why ask me about him, anyway? He just signs my checks. He doesn't keep me posted on his personal itinerary."

Francisco spoke up. "The young woman at the front said you might know where he is."

"Did she? Well, she was wrong. That's Mandy. She's wrong a lot of the time, even more so than your usual human female. Now if the two of you will excuse me, I have to change for the next show."

"No problem," Sykes said casually. "Shouldn't take very long if your new costume's as small as the last one."

She smiled sardonically, pushed through a door. Sykes followed too closely for her to shut and lock it. Francisco was right behind him.

It wasn't much of a dressing room and it was anything but private. There were half a dozen stalls, each with light-lined mirror and stool. Cassandra grabbed a handful of clothes from a rack and went into one of the empty stalls.

"Look," Sykes told her as he tried to see around the curtain, "we're not here doing an interview for the school paper. This is a homicide investigation. You're not under suspicion, you're not involved, so why not be nice and cooperate? You've got nothing at risk."

"If I'm not under suspicion," she replied from behind the curtain, "then I've got nothing at risk by telling you shit."

"On the other hand," Sykes said less politely, "if you don't stop jerkin' us around on your boss's whereabouts, I'm ready to start playin' hardball. Just because you're not under suspicion now doesn't mean that can't change in the future. In fact, I feel myself gettin' a little suspicious right now."

Francisco stood quietly by the door. Sykes motioned silently for him to have a look around while Cassandra was occupied changing clothes. The gesture was wasted on the detective, who responded with a look of anxious bafflement. Sykes grimaced, found himself peering at the stall. The curtain didn't close tightly.

"Oooh. Hardball," she whispered huskily. A flimsy halter flipped over the curtain rod like a glitter-coated bird settling on its perch. "That sounds interesting. Are you going to strike me? You'd be surprised how similar many of our less-publicized tastes are. You could tie me up and do whatever you want with me. I've got my own ropes. Or you could use your handcuffs. Real police handcuffs. That would be exciting. I think they would fit my wrists. Wouldn't it be fun finding out what fits and what doesn't?"

Sykes replied while still miming frantically at his partner. "Does that cost extra or do you throw the ropes in free?"

"You've got me all wrong. I'm a dancer and that's all. I don't charge money for something I myself find pleasurable. What a peculiar concept! But you humans are full of many such alien notions."

That made Sykes think. He'd never considered himself alien, but realized that was how the Newcomer must view all humanity. *They* were the normal ones. The innumerable little ss'loka's were the ones who were strange and abnormal.

Francisco finally got the idea. He replied much too loudly, in the stagey, uncertain voice of a bad actor. "I am going out to the car. I will meet you there."

Sykes winced as he watched his partner exit into the corridor, but now wasn't the time for a lecture on believability. Besides which, Cassandra was just emerging from her stall, having completed her change. She wore a long, stylish low-cut dress that revealed plenty of her spectacular figure. From the neck down it was impossible to tell her from a human—on the outside, anyway. Sykes raised his gaze with an effort, knowing she had to be aware of the effect she was having on him.

She confirmed his thoughts, cooing, "Why, Detective Sykes, is this part of normal police procedure?"

"Can it. We're just here for information."

She sighed and let loose with an elaborate shrug, all sliding movement, that sent his blood pressure up fifteen points. "Look, I'm sorry, but I don't know where Mr. Strader is. He comes and he goes. I just do my routines and pick up my check each week and go home. I'm not interested in what he does when he's not around to watch. If he has a special lady he confides in, it's someone other than me."

Sykes's eyes kept trying to fall from her face and he had to fight to keep them level with hers. It was a development he hadn't anticipated and it was making him acutely uncomfortable. He wished now he hadn't sent Francisco out searching. It was warmer in the room than when they'd entered.

"The girl out front mentioned Strader's assistant, somebody named Watson. Maybe he'd know."

She tensed unexpectedly. You couldn't miss the reaction, and Sykes didn't. He was instantly on alert.

"Mandy loves to babble, doesn't she? The trouble is, she never has anything to say. That would be Todd. Todd doesn't know where Mr. Strader is, either."

"Now how would you know that?"

"Because Mr. Strader is a very private person." She'd moved closer, now reached for him with a long arm. Her fingers worked the lapel of his coat. "I know what. Why don't you hang around for a while and let me entertain you? There are a lot of things I'd like to learn about men and I'm sure you could think of one or two questions to ask me, if you can stop being so professional for a couple of minutes.

Can you do that, Detective Sykes? Ten minutes? Five? If you can forget who you are for five minutes, I guarantee I can make you forget everything else.''

He should have stepped back, should have pushed her hand away, but there was too much body too close, too much heat in the cramped dressing room, and maybe he was just a tad too curious. Her eyes gleamed.

She grabbed the other lapel with her free hand. Now he would have had a hard time retreating if he'd wanted to. He didn't want to.

''Now tell me the truth,'' she purred. He said nothing, losing himself in those faraway eyes. ''Have you ever made it with one of us?''

Sykes swallowed hard. ''Not unless I got real drunk and nobody told me about it afterward.''

She threw back her head and laughed. ''That answers my question, because if you had, nobody would've had to remind you. You would've remembered.'' She was staring at him hungrily. ''A virgin. I find that *very* arousing. Do you know what one of us is capable of when we're really aroused?''

He tried to take a step backward, discovered he could not. Or maybe he didn't try all that hard.

Francisco could move very quietly despite his bulk. It was a useful talent he'd discovered early in his police training and one which he cultivated assiduously. It was not a particular Newcomer trait. Plenty of his people were awkward and clumsy in their movements.

He'd made it up to the second floor without being seen. Now he walked softly up the corridor, taking in everything, keeping an eye on the shadows behind him. Music filtered up through the floor from the stage somewhere below, occasionally interrupted by enthusiastic shouts or hoots of delight. He ignored it, listening for voices and footsteps. There were none. To all outward appearances this floor was deserted.

He put massive fingers around a door knob and twisted, found it locked. Letting it slip quietly back to its original position, he continued down the hall and tried the next one. This time the door opened to his touch. He eased it open a few inches and peered into the darkened room beyond. Entering, he was careful to close the door quietly behind him.

A human would immediately have bumped into the furniture. Francisco had no such problem in the dim light, finding his way without trouble around chairs and a filing cabinet. He was in an office. A desk sat off to the right, near a shaded side window. The blotter atop the plastic was buried beneath papers and small notebooks. The detective started riffling through the pile, careful to place each paper and booklet back exactly where he'd found it.

It was all very commonplace: letters of application from prospective employees, resumes from dancers looking for work, customer complaint forms, order sheets, business forms. He finished and started to leave when he spotted something sticking out from beneath a pile of computer paper. It was inconspicuous, but something about the shape piqued his curiosity.

Picking it up, he saw that it was a small plastic container, a thumb-operated dispenser of some kind. After examining it intently, he popped the top and studied the interior. It contained a trace of some dark, viscous substance. There was barely enough left to stain his finger.

Bringing it cautiously to his nose, he inhaled deeply. The sample was so tiny it was impossible to tell for sure what it might have been. But coupled with the type of container it had come from, it aroused his suspicions about what it *could* be.

He stood silently in the darkened office where no one could see the concern and worry on his face. Or the fear.

Cassandra was as close to Sykes as she could get without being inside his shirt. One hand pressed against the small of his back. She was using the other to guide his imprisoned fingers over her facial ridges, shuddering with delight as contact was made with sensitive nerve points. Though it was comfortably cool in the dressing room, Sykes found himself starting to perspire.

"There're a lot of things I haven't done," he heard himself mumbling feebly, "but this ain't high on my list. Don't take it personally. At heart I'm just a conservative kind of guy."

"I don't believe you," she whispered softly. "I think you're just a little scared right now, about what you might find once the lights go out. A little scared, and a lot curious. Aren't police made detectives because they're the curious type? Maybe you're more curious than you want to admit to yourself. I can understand that. But doesn't that turn you on a little, all that curiosity and wonder swishing around inside you together? I know it does me." Her lips were close to his ear now. "Just relax and let it happen. Think of it as broadening your horizons."

He struggled in her grasp. "I like my horizons narrow, thanks. Easier to keep track of where you're going that way."

She kept pressing herself into him. "Your voice is saying no, but your body is saying yes."

Finally he managed to give her a serious push and disengage himself. "My voice, body, and everything else is saying I'll be back in two hours looking for Strader, and he damn well better be here."

He fumbled with his wallet until he located a business card and shoved it toward her. She took it indifferently, obviously disappointed.

"You're making a big mistake," she told him.

"Yeah, that's the story of my life. One big mistake after another." He left the dressing room with as much decorum as possible.

Once safely outside he paused to take a long, deep breath, closing his eyes and standing motionless for half a minute. Then he blinked and headed up the hallway.

Behind him, Cassandra's disappointed look gave way to one of concern. She studied the card Sykes had passed her before turning and hurrying to the wall phone. It doubled as

an intercom, and that was the half of the device she
activated.

Francisco was looking through a cabinet when he heard
the intercom buzz in the room next to the office he was
searching. The walls were thin, the building having been
repeatedly and inefficiently subdivided during the previous
twenty years of its existence. Walking over to the wall, he
pressed his head to the wood and found he could hear the
conversation on the other side clearly. Meanwhile he blessed
the inventor of speakerphones, who enabled him to overhear
both ends of the conversation.

A male voice answering: "Yes?"

Then a woman replying, her voice distorted by the
speakerphone but still unmistakably that of the exotic
dancer they'd just been interviewing. "Todd, it's me."
Francisco thought she sounded worried. "The police were
just here, looking for Strader. And asking about *you*."

Amazing, Francisco mused, how rapidly connections could
be made with the aid of one little overheard conversation,
just a couple of sentences. He drew his gun as he edged
along the wall toward the door that led to the adjoining
office. The floorboards were warped with age and squeaked
despite his caution. He kept moving.

The connecting door was unlocked. He found himself
torn between the need to move fast and the need to move
quietly. The door opened silently to his touch and he peered
through the gap.

The next office was much more elaborately decorated
than the one he'd been searching. Obviously this was the
owner or manager's inner sanctum. The speakerphone sat on
the desk, next to a small flexlamp. A cigarette smoked in an
ostentatious crystal ashtray. But the chair behind the desk
was unoccupied. Either the room's occupant had already
fled, or he'd gone through still another connecting door on
the far side of the room from the one Francisco was peering
through. A bathroom, perhaps. The detective opened the
door wider and stepped into the room.

The chair that hit him did not break. It was solid, heavy,

and connected with his shoulder and the side of his head. Francisco went down hard, the gun slipping from his grasp to go skittering across the carpet.

He was down, but not out. Dazed, he rolled instinctively away from the blow, as he'd been taught to do at the Academy, trying to put space between himself and his assailant. Warm weight landed on his side and a fist struck him hard in the face. He turned, trying to fight while shielding his eyes, his vision blurring. He might lose, but he'd damn well get a good look at his attacker.

Whoever had ambushed him was strong but not particularly skilled at fighting. If he could hang on to consciousness until he recovered a little, he might get in a strike to a vulnerable area. At the same time he became aware that his assailant was no longer trying to hit him as much as he was attempting to disengage so he could reach the .38 which lay on the carpet a few yards away. Francisco absorbed one punch and kick after another while clinging determinedly to his opponent.

Sykes was prowling the second-floor corridor in search of his partner when he heard the sounds of fighting from behind the closed door on his left. When he tried the knob and found it locked he didn't waste time requesting admittance. There wasn't much room in the hall to get up speed, but he managed. The lock gave on the third try and the door flew inward. He had the Casull out and aimed before he came to a complete stop.

"FREEZE! NOW!"

The individual atop Francisco complied, his frightened gaze taking in Sykes and the big handgun simultaneously. He was battered and breathing hard, but still in control. Now he rose slowly, hands in the air, keeping his eyes on the muzzle of the small cannon Sykes held firmly in his grasp. Francisco caught his breath and staggered to his feet.

Something hot and heavy hit Sykes from behind, knocking him sideways. Perfume and flesh: Cassandra. Sykes fought to recover his balance.

Seizing the opportunity, Watson gave the off-balance and

still dazed Francisco a shove that sent the detective careening into the desk, sending papers flying. He sprinted through the open door and turned up the hallway.

There was a window at the far end. Wrenching it open, he clambered out onto the fire escape outside. Sykes tried to keep an eye on him while he wrestled with Cassandra. She wasn't trying to seduce him now, but while she was nearly as strong as he was, she knew little about fighting, and nothing about fighting human males. She kept jabbing him under his right arm, looking frustrated and surprised when he didn't react.

A disheveled Francisco appeared in the doorway, ready to give chase but ignorant of the path their quarry had taken. Sykes yelled at him while trying to knock Cassandra's legs out from under her.

"Fire escape! End of the hall!" She hit him in the stomach and he winced as he tried to pin her arms.

Francisco nodded tersely as he took off up the corridor. The window at the far end was small, but he managed to squeeze through the opening, found himself on a steel platform outside.

Meanwhile Sykes managed to get one handcuff on Cassandra's wrist, the other around a pipe sticking out of the wall. She was screeching and cursing in her own language as he collected the Casull and rushed off in his partner's wake. He left her with a few parting words.

"Sorry, sweetheart, but you're wasting your breath. It all sounds like a broken boiler to me." He grinned mirthlessly. "What are you so upset about anyway? I thought the idea of being handcuffed was supposed to turn you on?"

She added something undoubtedly vile and insulting, sounding like a cross between a stiffed hooker and a berserk python.

Francisco was moving like a runaway eighteen-wheeler as he pounded down the fire escape. He saw Watson reach the lower level, shinny down the bottom ladder, and take off fast toward the parking lot. Muttering under his breath, the detective ignored the ladder and vaulted over the final railing. He hit the ground hard and the shock went all the way up into his hips. But everything still worked. Shutting out the pain, he took off in pursuit.

Watson looked back, saw the huge detective closing in on him. He zigzagged desperately through the parked cars. Francisco followed silently, occasionally cutting across rows as he tried to make up ground between them. Once, he vaulted a Corvette's hood, but Watson turned a different direction and he actually lost ground.

Sykes came rattling down the fire escape, far behind but moving fast. He duplicated his partner's fifteen-foot jump to the pavement, bending his knees to cushion the impact. He still would have lost track of both aliens if not for the fact that Francisco's high, bald skull stood out like a forlorn basketball above the roofs of ranked cars.

He couldn't match his partner's stride, and he was older, but he'd always had fast feet and stamina. Dodging through the vehicles required more agility than pure speed.

Watson reached his Alfa Romeo and fumbled with the lock. Flinging the door open, he threw himself inside and fought to insert the key in the ignition. The engine finally rumbled to life.

Francisco heard the engine catch and skidded to a stop ten feet behind the car, aiming his pistol carefully. In his massive hands the gun looked like a toy.

The backup lights winked on on the Alfa and the car started to move. Francisco stood like a rock, the gun leveled, and hesitated. Because the shooting of a fugitive by a Newcomer cop would make headlines. Because there might be another, better way to do this. Because he was running on education but not experience.

While he hesitated, Watson floored the accelerator, tires screeching as the sportscar wailed in reverse. Francisco threw himself to one side as the car sped over the spot where he'd been standing. Relieved, the assistant manager of the Encounters Club jammed the five-speed into first and looked for the nearest exit.

What he saw instead was Sykes, standing right in front of him. Again he thromped the gas. The detective jumped, but not to the side, as his partner had done. Instead, he threw himself spread-eagled onto the hood of the car, blocking the driver's view.

Trying to see around the grim-faced detective, Watson lost control of himself as well as the car and plowed into a couple of parked sedans before picking up much speed. Sykes slid halfway off the hood, scrambled to his feet and around to the driver's side of the stalled car.

He was delighted to find that the panicky manager had forgotten to lock the door. Watson's head had struck the steering wheel and he wasn't going anywhere in a hurry. A big, gnarled fist reached through the open window and grabbed a handful of expensive suit, yanked hard.

The manager stumbled out of the Alfa reluctantly, started to gather himself when he saw that his captor was only a mere human. He drew back a huge fist to flatten the detective. As he did so, Sykes swung both arms around in a couple of wide arcs, his fists parallel to the pavement. Both landed squarely on the nerve centers beneath Watson's arms.

The manager let out a dull "oomph" and clutched at his armpits as he fell to his knees. Sykes stood over him, both fists still clenched, panting hard and ready to strike again. It wouldn't be necessary. Right now Watson had no interest in fighting, or trying to run, or much of anything else except working through the pain that had paralyzed his body.

"I'll be damned." Sykes sucked in cool night air. "It worked." Noticing motion out of the corner of his eye, he looked up sharply, relaxed when he saw it was only Francisco. "How'd you like that, huh? Whammo! Both barrels. Dropped him like a sack of cement."

Francisco studied the immobilized Watson for a moment, then spotted something lying on the ground next to the Alfa. Walking over, he bent to recover the manager's wallet, flipped it open to examine the contents. Sykes looked on, keeping a wary eye on the kneeling Newcomer.

"Who is he, anyway?"

Francisco spoke absently while flipping through the wallet. "Todd Watson. The assistant manager of the club."

The individual Sykes had downed was still crouched over clutching his armpits, trying to draw enough wind to speak. "I don't believe this. Who the hell are you guys? What do you want with me? Look at my suit. Look what you made me do to my car! Do you have any idea what bodywork costs on those Italian jobs? I'm gonna sue your whole damn department."

"Fine. The LAPD's got a whole herd of lawyers sittin' around looking bored ever since they settled the Handley accidental murder suit. One of 'em will be glad to accommodate you." Sykes shook his head in disgust. "Your girlfriend put up a better fight than you did, pal."

Watson grimaced up at him. "What makes you think she's my girlfriend?"

"Gimme a break, Todd. You don't bowl over a cop holding a gun unless you're trying to protect somebody who's more than a casual acquaintance. I'd take real good care of her if I were you. That's some woman, even if she is bald as a bat under those wigs she wears."

"This small talk is most enjoyable," Francisco commented evenly, "but we have business to discuss." He tossed the wallet to Watson. "We are looking for your employer, Joshua Strader."

Watson tried to stand, found he couldn't quite make it yet, and hunkered over to wait it out. "He's out of town," he muttered glumly.

"Why should we believe you?"

"Because it's true, and there are ways you can check up on it. Besides, what else would I be doing working out of his office?"

Sykes made a rude noise. "Trying to get the feel of the boss's chair?"

Watson glared up at him. "It's easier to take phone calls and run the operation from there. That's all. What do you care?"

"I don't."

"Why did you run?" Francisco asked him calmly.

"Because you two were chasing me."

Sykes shook his head sadly. "We were chasing you because you ran, you dumb son-of-a-bitch. Isn't that obvious?"

"Look, I don't know about you, ss'loka', but when somebody comes sneaking up on me I react defensively, especially if he's carrying a gun. And if he and his buddy start chasing me, I run."

"When will Strader return?" Francisco refused to let the injured Watson change the subject.

The assistant manager shrugged. This time he managed to rise, breathing deeply as he straightened. Slowly he let his hands fall from beneath his arms.

"Who knows? He's the boss. He doesn't have to check in with me."

"I find it difficult to believe," the Newcomer detective went on, "that your employer would go off and leave the operation of his enterprise to his assistant without so much as hinting where he might be located in the event of an emergency."

"Strader's like that. Every now and then he just takes off without telling anyone where he's going. I think it's a weird way to run a ship myself, but what can I do about it?" He smiled wanly, seeking sympathy.

He wouldn't get it from the likes of Sykes. Sighing wearily, the detective adopted his best lecturing tone. "Watson, this here's my partner's first coupla days on the job after making Detective grade, and he wants to make a good impression. So he's being real polite to you, sort of handling you with kid gloves like, you understand?

"Me, though, the way I feel, this could be my last day, know what I mean? I could show up to clock out tonight and find an early retirement notice waiting in my box. Or I might just decide to chuck the whole rat race and take early re voluntarily, catch the red-eye for Miami or the Bahamas or someplace."

The Newcomer manager frowned at him. "I don't follow you."

"What I'm sayin', Slag," Sykes told him as he took a belligerent step forward, "is that if I don't start getting some real cooperation out of you right now, I'm ready to rain on you like a cow pissin' on a flat rock.''

Watson swallowed, glanced in Francisco's direction. To his credit, Francisco's expression did not change. This added to the alien manager's increasing discomfort. Who knew what an edgy human might do when pressed, especially a half-mad policeman?

"Look," he said placatingly, glancing around as if someone might overhear him in the middle of the parking lot, "Mr. Strader hasn't been around for a couple of days. I'm telling you the truth. He didn't tell me where he was going or when he'd be back. I know that doesn't make much sense, but that's how it is. I swear it."

Sykes locked eyes with the Newcomer for a long moment before turning to his partner. "What do you think?"

Francisco's tone had not changed at all. "I believe very strongly that he is most probably lying."

Sykes nodded agreement. "Through his ass." He turned back to Watson. "Next time you see Strader, tell him to call me. Unless you want us to keep coming down on you like a bad case of herpes. Or whatever it is that you guys get."

Walking over to the bigger alien, he shoved a business card into Watson's breast pocket, flicked a little dirt off the expensive material, and smiled up at him before turning away. Francisco followed.

Watson followed their departure with his eyes, then staggered over to his battered Alfa and slumped against the dented hood.

As they made their way back to the waiting slugmobile Sykes suddenly felt very tired. He ran over the events of the previous hour in his mind: the interview with Cassandra, his rejection of her advances, prowling the club, trying to bail George out only to let himself get knocked silly by an alien broad, and then the race down the fire escape and through the parking lot. His legs were throbbing from his calves up to his ass, his throat was raw, and the end result of the evening's stress and strain was little more than zero.

Francisco noted his partner's mood but didn't have sense enough to keep quiet. "Matthew, I feel that I must point out that you do not look at all well. Would it be impolite of me to inquire how you are feeling?''

"Not at all, George. I feel like old shit." He favored his partner with a lopsided smile. "Satisfied?"

"I wish it were otherwise."

"Thanks for the sympathy. I wish I was ten years younger. How you doin'?"

"I am doing well, thank you, though I am frustrated we could not learn more. I still think he was lying."

"So we agree on a coupla things. Watson was lying and I look like shit. And we got nothing for our trouble. Cripes." He ran a hand through his sweat-soaked hair.

"What does procedure suggest we do about it?"

Sykes looked sharply at him. "Procedure?" Suddenly he found himself grinning. "Official procedure—or Sykes procedure?"

Francisco considered the choice thoughtfully. "Following official procedure has not produced much in the way of results this evening, has it?"

"No, George, it ain't."

"Then I would think it would be in order to try any alternative."

Sykes looked pleased. "That's real good, George. Real good. You're learning."

"I am a fast study, Matthew. So they told me at the Academy." He opened the door on the passenger side and slid in.

"One more thing, George." Sykes flopped down behind the wheel. His lower back was killing him again, but he didn't have time to visit the chiropractor.

Francisco eyed him expectantly. "What's that, Matt?"

"From now on you handle the women, you mind?"

He put the slugmobile in gear and pulled out of the lot, not bothering to check his mirrors to see if anyone was interested in staking a claim to the same piece of pavement.

Watson heard them leave but paid no attention. He was far more interested in the damage to his Alfa. The right front side was crushed in, and the door on the passenger side had buckled in response. Damn! Broken glass every-where, both headlights gone, the windshield popped, and he'd probably have to order a whole new paint job to make any of it match. And no telling what was busted beneath the hood. Sss'malki' cops!

The sound of footsteps reached him, but he didn't bother to turn. He could care less what anyone might think if they saw him bent over his ruined car. Which was too bad, because if he'd shown more interest he might have been able to avoid the butt of the shotgun before it slammed into the back of his skull.

The assistant manager crumpled like used foil. Five figures surrounded the unconscious form, gazing down at it like handlers in a meat-packing plant. Four of them were human.

The other was Kipling.

The human in charge was named Quint. Without having to wait for orders, he gestured to his companions. "Okay, scrape him up."

One of the men grunted as he hefted a heavy alien leg. "You want us to be careful with him or not?" He took his directions from Quint, but he put the query to the Newcomer.

The alien was holding the sawed-off shotgun loosely by its stock, handling it as easily as a human would a handgun. He studied the limp body of the club's assistant manager.

"Take it easy with him—for now."

# ───VIII───

California beaches are occupied around the clock except during the winter, and even in cold rainy weather an occasional beachcomber or necking couple will claim a section for their own. The farther from the city one travels, the less chance there is of running into any of these hardy sand-lovers.

Zuma Beach lay on the fringes of the great metropolis, north of Malibu and a good drive from the San Fernando Valley. This morning the waves were rolling in from the Central Pacific unobserved by any save the crabs and gulls.

There was no one to see the big black limo as it oozed down the narrow access road that led to the lip of the beach itself. It was the northernmost end of Zuma, the part of the beach least likely to be visited on a good day, much less this early in the morning when the moon still usurped the sun's position as dispenser of light and the fog hung cold and damp over the driftwood.

The limo cruised past a lookout car occupied by two aliens who could have been kin to the types Sykes and Francisco had encountered in the X-Bar, except that this pair was alert and well-dressed. Acknowledging their presence, the driver took the limo right down to the sand's edge, parking alongside a nondescript late-model van.

Cutting the engine, he emerged and opened the rear door on his side, allowing William Harcourt easy egress. Polite as always, Harcourt thanked his driver and walked over to the waiting van. In order to get 'round to the rear he had to walk through some sand. Interested in everything new, he studied the granulated surface with fresh delight.

Kipling, Quint, and the rest of the little gang were waiting for him behind the van. Watson was there also, chained to the van's back bumper facing the rumbling sea. Quint held a bloodied tire iron in his right hand. Anyone wishing to know the origin of the dark stains could have easily divined them for themselves by taking a look at Watson's battered face. Quint prided himself on his work. The assistant manager was bloodied but still conscious.

Harcourt ignored the unhappy victim of Quint's attentions as he addressed his tormentor. "Any progress?"

The human rolled a shoulder, gesturing with the iron. "My arm's getting tired and so far we got zip. He's either real stubborn, real tough, or real dumb." He stared down at the sullen, frightened Watson. "Me, I'd guess the latter, but maybe you know more than I do, sir."

Harcourt smiled pleasantly. "I would consider that a rhetorical question, Mr. Quint." He turned to his assistant, raised an eyebrow.

"He is ss'verdlatya ss'alo to Strader," Kipling informed his boss.

Quint's expression contorted. "What's that mean?"

"Duty-bonded," Harcourt informed the man. Not that he owed Quint any explanations, but an ill-informed employee was an inefficient one. "His allegiance to Strader is above pain or life. It is not something you would be likely to understand, though friends of mine who have made a study of human history have found societies where such a concept would not only be understood but would have been valued. Your present-day society is not among them, however."

"You tellin' me this guy would die before he'd screw his boss and work for us? Nobody's that dumb."

"It is not a question of intelligence, Quint. It is something you can't comprehend." Kipling glared at the human. Quint stared right back at him but chose not to make an issue of it.

Harcourt went over to Watson and knelt beside him,

careful to keep the knee of his designer slacks clear of the sand. He examined the bruised face sympathetically.

"I am sorry for this, Mr. Watson. I would much prefer to have it another way. It distresses me when I'm compelled to resort to such methods. Clumsiness offends my sense of aesthetics, and this way is clumsy. You must believe me when I tell you that I find this kind of business distasteful."

Watson managed to lift his head high enough to glare at Harcourt out of his one open eye. The other one had swollen shut. "Yeah, you look like you're real upset."

Harcourt pursed his lips. "You doubt me. Well, given the present circumstances I suppose I cannot blame you for that. I understand you have for some time now been rejecting my offers. Your sense of duty to Mr. Strader is noble, but no longer an issue, I'm afraid."

"I don't follow you."

"Then I will explain so that you will understand, and in such a fashion that you cannot doubt." He looked at Kipling and nodded once.

Two of the humans climbed into the van and pushed something out the back. The large, bulky mass landed heavily on the sand. It was Strader, shot twice through the front of his silk suit at close range. Watson's eyes widened in fear.

"There. You understand now, don't you?" Harcourt was smiling; that famous, ingratiating smile that charmed human and Newcomer alike. It was wasted on the terrified Watson. "So you see why you no longer need feel bound in any fashion to Mr. Strader, since Mr. Strader no longer has need of your allegiance." His voice was all oil and sympathy.

"I will not make this offer another time. I want you to work for me, to manage the Encounters Club as Strader's successor and to handle a little side business for me during the day. It is a natural enough change. None will question it. I could of course put one of my own people in Strader's place and ease you out, but your experience in running an establishment that caters to both humans and Newcomers is unique. I know of no other such establishment of such caliber, which is why I require it to be part of my expansion plans.

"My interest will become clear to you at such a time as I feel you can be trusted with my confidence. Right now you need only know that you will be given a free hand in the Club's operations. I am not in the least interested in the details of its day-to-day functioning. I am not even particularly interested in whether or not it makes money, though that would be nice. I need it for something else.

"I am afraid this is not an either/or situation, Mr. Watson. I cannot allow you to work for someone else in a similar capacity since your talents applied elsewhere could conceivably jeopardize the success of my own operations. If you agree to work for me you will come to know a wealth and comfort our people never dared imagine."

Watson was still frightened, but managed a halfway defiant glare as he replied to Harcourt's offer.

*"SS'kya'ta!"*

Kipling bristled and stepped forward, but Harcourt waved him off. The big Newcomer halted reluctantly.

The alien entrepreneur studied Watson for a long moment, perhaps admiring his resolve, perhaps reconsidering the offer. It didn't take long for him to reach a decision. It never did.

"There are still some of us who have things to unlearn. It is a pity to perish for such an outmoded value." Straightening, he turned to the expectant thugs. "Mr. Quint, I believe it is time for our friend's swimming lesson."

It took a few seconds for the words to settle in Watson's brain, for him to understand what was going to happen to him. When he did he went crazy, screaming and bucking wildly against his chains. Harcourt watched him silently. The smile was still on his face, but it was different now, a smile few people ever saw. There was no humor in it, and those who saw it never forgot it. Kipling had seen that smile, and Quint, and one or two others, and despite their hardness it made them shudder inside.

"It is important to learn new skills," Harcourt was saying. "Essential to your growth as a person. That's one of the marvelous things about this world. There are so many opportunities for education, for enriching our inner selves. I firmly believe we should avail ourselves of every chance to do so. Don't you agree, Mr. Watson?''

Quint and his helpers had freed the assistant manager from his chains. It took all five of them to control the twisting, lunging Newcomer as they dragged him across the sand toward the surf. Despite the trouble they were having, Kipling did not offer his help. He remained next to Harcourt, just a suggestion of fear in his own cold eyes. Harcourt was talking to him; light banter, inconsequentialities. He didn't really hear what his boss was saying, though he nodded affirmatively when he thought it was required of him. He was too fascinated by the drama unfolding before him.

Watson kept digging his feet into the sand until two of Quint's people finally lifted his legs into the air. Blood appeared beneath his fingernails as he fought for a purchase in the beach, clutching at rocks and driftwood. The sand was too deep, the rocks and bits of flotsam too small.

Quint spoke to his newest recruit, who was having a tough time maintaining his grip on Watson's right leg.

"You never seen this before, have you, Billy? Oh, man, you ain't gonna believe it.''

"Believe what?'' the man wondered aloud. "What're we gonna do, stick his head under?''

Quint grinned nastily. "Somethin' like that. See, seawater is like battery acid to these guys. Not everybody knows about it. It ain't the sort of thing that shows up on the six o'clock news a lot. I don't know what it is that actually does it, myself. Some kinda chemical reaction. Mr. Harcourt, he says it has something to do with the kinds of salts and trace metals that are dissolved in the oceans, whatever the shit that means.'' He glanced down at the struggling, helpless Newcomer, mock concern in his voice.

"What do you think it is, Watson?'' A leg kicked free, thrashing wildly as two men fought to bring it back under control. "Whoa, hold him!''

They were below the high-tide line now, where the water polished the dark sand slick as new linoleum. A wave rolled in, foam crawling up the slight decline toward the approaching men.

"What I love about the surf," Quint mused aloud, "is that you can never tell how far up it's going to come until it—whoops, got a little wet there." A wavelet had broken over his shoes.

The second one barely touched Watson's lower legs as they waded into the water. He let out a piercing scream, a high-pitched howl that could not have come from any human throat. As he flailed madly one of his hands dipped below the roiling surface. He howled and yanked it clear. Water dripped from the exposed skin. Seconds later a thousand miniature droplets of purplish blood began to appear on the backs of his fingers, hand, and on his palm, oozing out through his pores as his body reacted to the touch of the seawater. The beads swelled and ran together. Watson was crying now, moaning and sobbing as the men halted.

The water sloshing around their hips, they began to swing the Newcomer back and forth, building up momentum.

"All together now," Quint urged his people. He sneered at the pitiful form of Watson. "Last call, sucker. What'll it be?" When the best the alien could produce was little more than a sucking sob, Quint raised his voice. "Ready? One—two—THREE!"

The five heaved simultaneously, flinging Watson far out into the water.

Harcourt and Kipling had crossed the beach until they stood close to the waterline. They stared out across the moonlit sea. Watson continued screaming awhile longer, then there was once more only the sound of the waves.

Quint and his men studied the placid surface, hesitating in case their efforts would be needed to finish the deed. They were not. Watson made no more sounds, nor did he appear above the surface even though the water was barely chest-deep where he'd landed.

Kipling had to fight down his unease. He was only partly successful. They were much too close to the water for his liking. Harcourt appeared unperturbed as he gazed out toward the horizon. He was no longer thinking about Watson. The assistant manager of the club was, so to speak, a dead issue.

The longer they stood there the more nervous Kipling became. He'd read about freak waves that slammed unexpectedly into otherwise calm beaches and sucked people out to sea. It was peaceful and calm and the surf was running less than a foot, but he was still uneasy. Maybe a word or two...

"When we picked him up," he told his boss, "he'd just finished talking to those two cops. The ones who tried to question you about Hubley. It was sheer luck we showed up when we did or we'd never have known."

That brought Harcourt out of his reverie. "You're sure about the cops? That they were the same two we encountered outside the hotel that night?"

"Absolutely. No way would I forget that ss'loka'."

The entrepreneur's expression was unreadable as he kicked lightly at the sand. "This is getting out of hand. I want you to deal with it. Immediately."

"Any suggestions, Mr. Harcourt?"

The Newcomer again favored his assistant with that unpleasant smile. "Use your imagination. That's what I pay you for. If I had any specifics in mind I'd use Quint. I value you for your independence of thought, Kipling. That's why you're my assistant. I can't do all the thinking and planning. I have too many far more important matters that require my limited attention."

Kipling came to attention. "Yes sir. I understand."

Amazing, Harcourt thought, how useful a little flattery could be when dealing with primitive types like Kipling.

A wave rushed up the beach toward them. The sun would be up in an hour and the tide was starting to come in. Kipling didn't like to think about things like tides, and waves. No Newcomer did. The world they'd been dumped upon was a difficult enough place to live without pondering the most discomfiting reality: the fact that three-quarters of its surface was covered with a deadly, caustic liquid. Dwelling on such things risked one's sanity. A healthy Newcomer couldn't even watch the smaller humans as they frolicked in the horrid stuff. It brought sickness to the stomach.

Instead of dying and retreating, the wave continued to rush

up the incline toward them. Kipling stood it as long as he could before jumping convulsively backward. Harcourt held his ground, gazing placidly at the onrushing fluid. The foam halted less than an inch from his highly polished, sand-encrusted dress loafer. He continued to watch with interest as the water sank harmlessly into the absorbent sand.

"We must learn, Kipling, to embrace that which we fear. From that we grow strong. Mental adaptation to a new world is as important to eventual success as is physical adaptation. Humans respect such things."

You adapt to this, Kipling thought. Not for the first time he wished fervently that the people had been settled somewhere like Kansas City or St. Louis instead of L.A. But Los Angeles was near where their ship had landed, and Los Angeles was where the most extensive immigration and resettlement facilities were located, so that's where most of them had settled.

Harcourt had no trouble with the city's proximity to the ocean. In that respect he was special. To Kipling's knowledge, no other Newcomer voluntarily went within a mile of the Pacific except on a dare from some friend or enemy. Newcomers did not enjoy family excursions to the horrible places called "beaches." They went to the desert and the mountains.

Maybe we can throw the next one off a cliff somewhere, he thought hopefully. Harcourt gave him a lot of leeway in his work. He would suggest it. The sooner they were away from this place the better. No matter when they departed he would still have to hear the agonizing roar of what Quint referred to as the "surf" for days to come. He knew he would dream about it.

Harcourt spun on his heel and started back toward the waiting limo. In passing he motioned at Strader's body. Quint and the others had emerged from the water to join the two Newcomers.

"There are signs posted everywhere here, Mr. Quint. We don't want to be seen breaking the law."

Quint frowned. "What law is that, Mr. Harcourt, sir?"

"Why, littering, of course." He gestured a second time at Strader's corpse.

Quint grinned. He enjoyed working for Harcourt. "I understand, sir. No littering." What a card, he thought. A Newcomer with a real sense of humor.

Together he and his men hefted the body and walked it toward the water. Harcourt didn't bother to turn and watch as they heaved the heavy corpse far out into the waves.

Francisco eyed the receiver of the wall phone with distaste. It was dirty and grease had collected in the cracks where the different parts of the phone were cemented together. He reluctantly placed it against his aural opening and dialed. As soon as the phone at the other end was picked up he began speaking quickly in his own language, having to bend slightly to clear the low ceiling in the kitchen alcove.

Sykes flipped on a second light, let his eyes flick through the kitchen. He opened the fridge and examined the contents, removing only the bottle of vodka and a tray of ice. While his partner earnestly addressed the phone, Sykes mixed booze and cubes in a tall glass.

Still on the phone, Franciso turned and watched his partner work. His gaze shifted to the still-open refrigerator, where his eyes came to rest on the carton of milk sitting on the bottom shelf. The last time it had been used it had not been properly closed at the top.

Bringing the receiver to the end of its cord as he listened to the voice on the other end, he leaned toward the fridge and sniffed. His eyes widened. He concluded the conversation, leaving his wife with an elaborate phrase that denoted both love and reassurance, and hung up. Sykes was taking a long pull on the vodka as Francisco came up beside him to peer into the refrigerator.

Eventually Sykes noticed his partner's intent expression. "You want something or what?"

Francisco reached in to extract the milk carton. He took a long whiff of the contents and sighed. "Would you mind?"

Sykes shrugged and found him a glass. Francisco filled it and took a long swallow. The odor that filled the tiny kitchen made the human grimace. He nodded toward the phone.

"So, she keeps you on a pretty short leash, does she?"

Francisco considered thoughtfully. "My wife? She worries about me. I find her concern reassuring. Your tone implies disapproval of the situation. I find it quite the opposite."

Sykes regarded a chair, chose instead to lean against the kitchen counter, cradling his glass in one hand. His tone was more weary than bitter.

"Yeah, I know the routine."

The Newcomer studied him closely. "You are married? You have never mentioned having a mate." He studied his surroundings. "I see no signs of a mate's presence."

"That's because she ain't here. Never was. That's the operative word, George. Was. I'm divorced."

"We mate always for life, though I am familiar with the relationship you describe. I was required to learn about it while at the Academy, as part of a course on dealing with domestic violence. Divorce is a strange concept for us. That kind of separation usually comes only with the death of one partner. To induce such a parting voluntarily is a new and difficult idea to grasp." He leaned forward. "What is the feeling like? Can you phrase it in terms that I might comprehend?"

"I dunno. Can you comprehend having an eleventh finger removed? It hurts like hell, but you realize later you never really needed the damn thing in the first place."

Francisco pondered this explanation, finally nodding even though he didn't understand. What was obvious was that it was important to Sykes that he *did* understand. So, he nodded. Sykes slugged down another shot as his partner sipped sour milk and examined the apartment in detail. The effects of the rotten cow juice were beginning to make themselves felt.

"Your home is quite disorganized. I thought perhaps you had been burglarized when I first walked in."

Sykes growled over the lip of the glass. "I appreciate your honesty, George. Tell me something: in that class on dealing with domestic violence, didn't they teach you anything about tact?"

"A great deal, which I memorized as carefully as everything else I was taught. Procedure."

"Yeah, you're a real shitkicker where procedure's concerned. So if you know all about tact, how can you say something like that about my beloved domicile?"

The Newcomer eyed him innocently. "I do not need to employ tack with you, Matthew. You are my partner."

Sykes made a face and nodded at nothing in particular. "Right. That explains it." He held his glass up and out. Francisco stared dumbly.

"What are you doing with your glass?"

"Making a toast, stupid. Haven't you ever seen a toast before?"

A bewildered, slightly hurt expression came over his partner's face. "There is neither bread present, nor a means for carbonizing it."

Sykes muttered something under his breath. "A toast is when you drink to each other. To your friend's health, to his future, his girlfriend, his dentist, whatever. Kind of a salute. You each have your own poison and you clink glasses together."

Francisco nodded. "Now I understand. You must be patient with me, Matt. With all of us. Our education was hasty and uneven. We acquired a lot of useless knowledge along with missing some important things." He touched his glass of old cold milk to Sykes's. Then they both drank.

It was a pleasant custom which Francisco found he both appreciated and enjoyed. They worked on the fine points all night. By the time the Newcomer had it down pat, Sykes had removed his wallet and was showing his partner a rumpled, dogeared photo that had been crumpled and restraightened too many times.

"Ignore the bitch on the left," he muttered across the table. "That's Edie. I call her Edie Amin."

"If you don't like her, why do you carry her picture around with you?" Francisco inquired curiously.

"Because I can't cut her out of the photo because she's

standing too close to Kristin and she's got her arm around her. Beauty and the Beast.'' He tapped the picture. ''That's Kristin there. My daughter. It's kinda an old picture, but you know how you get about old pictures. You always have this one special image of your kids, when they're a certain age, when they look a certain way. When you're seventy-five and they're fifty you'll still see 'em that same way.'' He stared moodily at the photo.

''Old picture. She's twenty now. Hard to believe, lookin' at this. Always hard to believe. Twenty. Geezus. Gettin' married, in fact.''

''When is the happy occasion?''

''Sunday. This Sunday.''

Francisco took the photo gently between his thick fingers and gazed at the fading color. As he did so he was swaying ever so slightly from side to side. Sykes didn't sway, but he no longer sat erect in his chair. Each sip of vodka bent him a little lower. Eventually his head would make contact with the top of the table and he could finally relax.

''Human children can be very beautiful, if one can manage to ignore the fur that distorts their skulls.'' He returned the picture. Sykes resumed his staring. ''Getting married, you say? Congratulations. A most important time. You will be taking Sunday off, then.''

His voice thick and uneasy, Sykes laid the picture down. ''Maybe. Maybe not. I don't know. I'm not sure I'm gonna go.'' His voice fell. ''She doesn't need her burnout of a father there. Lousy cop, never made Lieutenant, probably never will. Her fiancé's family's got money. Important people. They don't need me there either. Spoil the family portrait. Don't wanna embarrass nobody, 'specially Kristin. She says she wants me there, but that's just the way she is. Loves everybody. Even her bum of an old man.''

Francisco found himself staring at his partner, seeing something he never expected to see there: vulnerability. Any minute now, Sykes looked like he might start crying. That was something unexpected that Newcomers and humans had in common, perhaps one of the most important things. To break the mood, Francisco fumbled in his jacket until he located his own wallet. He was mildly surprised that it took him so long to find it.

"I must show you." He flipped open the leatherette case. Inside were four crisp, recent photos of an alien woman. Each pose was different. All had obviously been taken in a studio, with flat background and professional lighting.

"This is Susan, my wife."

Sykes hesitated, then peered curiously at the pictures in their plastic holders. "Yeah, I saw her the other day when I picked you up. Not bad."

His partner flipped through the plastic holders, past credit cards and various forms of identification, until he came to a series showing a young Newcomer male.

"And this is Richard. My son. He's three years old. We named him after one of the former presidents, Richard Nixon."

Sykes stared at the photos on the table. Gradually his glum expression was transformed into a grin. This became a wide smile, and then he was laughing out loud at Francisco. His partner gazed back confusedly, his face full of sincerity and puzzlement.

"Is there something wrong with naming a child after a prominent leader? Susan and I thought it was a common and respected custom."

Wiping at one eye, Sykes forced himself to quiet down. Samuel-George, Susan, and Richard. Ozzie and Harriet. The Martians next door. And now this. Damned if he wasn't starting to like the guy.

"You open to a piece of friendly advice, George?"

Francisco smiled pleasantly. "I am always receptive to good advice, Matthew. I believe it is one of our better qualities."

"Swell. Then if anybody happens to ask, you tell them you named your kid after Richard Burton, the actor."

"I do not understand the reason for such a deception."

Sykes was making calming gestures with his left hand. "Just take my word for it. Have I ever given you bad advice before?"

"Well, Matt, as long as the subject has come up, I should remind you . . ."

"Exactly," said Sykes, interrupting his partner. He raised his glass. Francisco did not hesitate to respond appropriately. He hadn't hesitated in some time. Vodka and milk slammed together.

Despite continued practice, Francisco was surprised to find that his new skill at toasting was growing progressively worse, not better. A couple of times he and his partner managed to miss each other's glass entirely. It required increased attention and concentration simply to place their glasses in proximity. It was also getting very late, but since Sykes chose not to comment on the time, Francisco felt it would be impolite of him to do so.

The Newcomer had doffed his jacket and tie, but it still struck him as too warm in the apartment. He was concentrating single-mindedly on what his partner was saying. Concentrating hard. This was imperative, because his ability to concentrate on anything at all was rapidly fading.

"And so," Sykes was saying enthusiastically, "and so the doctor says, 'If this is the thermometer, then where'd I leave my pen?' " He leaned back in his chair, laughing hysterically. Francisco gazed blankly across at him with the look of a man waiting for the train that left the station five minutes earlier. Sykes stopped laughing, frowned.

"You're not—you don't think that's funny. George, you've got to make an effort if you want to fit in. Work with me. I always get a laugh with that one. Even guys who've heard it before always laugh." He leaned over the table. "Look. If the doctor's got the thermometer in his hand, then where's his pen gotta be? Use a little logic on this one."

"The logic of it is clear," said Francisco evenly, if a little more slowly than usual. "The pen is in the other man's rectum."

Sykes starting guffawing all over again. "Sticking out of his ass, yeah, right! See, that's what makes it a joke. There's like a surprise, and your mind fills in the funny picture. Here's this guy with a pen stuck in his ass and he thinks it's a thermometer."

Francisco tried, but the best he could muster was a querulous blink. Sykes looked more saddened than disappointed.

"Nada, huh?"

Francisco shrugged apologetically. Sykes considered whether to give it another try, poured a fresh round instead. He was so far gone by now that the stench of spoiled milk no longer bothered him. He raised his glass in a gesture become automatic.

"Your health."

Francisco hefted his own glass. "Ta ss'trakyona'..."

Glasses clicked again. They swallowed.

They sat at the table and talked about small things suddenly become large, big things that no longer seemed half so important, and the debris of a person's life called memories. Eventually Sykes felt the need for a change of scenery, if only to get away from the refrigerator, and they moved into the living room. The couch no longer held its old appeal, however, and balancing in a chair was obviously out of the question. So they chose respective squares of carpet and arranged themselves tastefully around the coffee table.

Sykes was much quieter now, no longer in the mood to try out jokes simply to see what sort of reaction they might provoke from his partner. Could be that the thermometer gag would have gone over like a lead balloon in the Sudan, too. It wasn't Francisco's fault. He'd given it an honest college try.

"There is still so much to learn," he was saying. "So much our two peoples don't understand about each other."

"No shit, Holmes. I mean, we can't even get along with each other. So don't feel like you're being singled out, know what I mean?" Francisco nodded somberly whether he understood or not. It seemed the right thing to be doing. Sykes rambled on.

"We fight with other guys for all sorts of stupid reasons. Because we go to different churches. Because we speak different languages. Because we like different kinds of football, or the same kind of football but different teams, or the same team but different players. Hardly any wonder we're havin' a tough time gettin' along with you. You're only from another goddamn planet, for crissakes.''

Francisco sipped at his nearly empty glass of milk. The carton was empty and he was husbanding what remained.

"It works both ways, Matt. You humans are very strange to us. We try and try to make sense of your ways and always we fail.''

"Hey, what the hell, don't let it bug you, George. I mean, if *we* can't make sense of us, how the hell can you expect to do any better?''

"It is so contradictory. All of it. You invite us to live among you, in an atmosphere of equality we've never known before. The Masters would never allow such an arrangement. We are endlessly grateful. You lay before us a beautiful, benign green world, full of new freedoms and opportunities, and ask only that we conform to the rules of your society. Even then, you allow us to retain many of our own customs and ways and do not attempt to interfere with them. You give us ownershp of our lives for the first time in our history, and you ask no more of us than you do of yourselves: to live by the rules. Rules that are designed not to keep one people subordinate to another, but that exist to preserve equality. In many ways your world and your race is terribly immature. Yet you aspire to very high ideals.''

Sykes was staring mesmerized at his partner. This was more than Francisco had ever said at one time, a veritable dissertation spilling from the mouth of an individual Sykes had come to think of as congenitally close-mouthed. He hardly knew what to say.

"I aspired to Betty Ann Shirankis in the eleventh grade, but that's about it.''

Francisco ignored his quip, whether intentionally or because he was so wrapped up in what he had to say that he didn't hear. He wasn't finished. Amazing what changes a little spoiled milk hath wrought, Sykes thought.

"I hope you can understand how special your world is, Matt. How unique a people you human beings are. We recognized this soon after our arrival and awakening, when you treated us not as possible slaves or burdens but as refugees who had lost their way, and gave us help. So it is all the more painful and confusing to us that so few of you seem capable of living up to the ideals you set up for yourselves. You philosophize wonderfully and then ignore your own philosophy. It is an endless puzzlement.''

Sykes leaned back against the couch. ''Don't count on me, George. I never had any ideals.''

Francisco smiled at his partner. He was no expert at the arcane and still new Newcomer discipline of recognizing and sorting human truth from human lies, but he'd been a cop long enough to recognize bullshit when he heard it.

''We don't understand so many things about your people, Matthew. We don't understand your capacity for hatred and bigotry. You welcome us, teach us your language, give us access to all your civilization has to offer, and then as individuals you call us names and spit on us.

''But we must bear it. We cannot ever react in anger because our situation here is still very fragile. The Separationists would see us returned to the quarantine camps. The Fundamentalists say we are not made in the image of God and therefore have no souls. Others say we have no more rights than dogs or cats. The truly violent extremists would have all of us sterilized so that we might live out our lives harmlessly until the last of us, ancient and crippled, dies and leaves you alone in this world once more. But there is a truth in the universe that is the same as a truth in personal relationships, Matt.''

''Yeah? What's that?''

''It is not good to live alone.''

Sykes said nothing, let Francisco finish. The Newcomer was gazing off into the distance, fondling his milk glass. ''The prejudice we face here is so insignificant compared to the pain and isolation we've known before. That is why we are so grateful.''

Sykes had had about enough. ''Hey, lighten up already, man.''

''I'm sorry.'' The Newcomer sipped the last of his milk, swallowing slowly and with undisguised pleasure. ''These are things that needed to be said. At least, I need to say them.''

"Yeah, well, that's all very beautiful and well and good and all, except I did hear that you eat your dead.''

Francisco stared sleepily across the table at his partner. Their eyes locked and he said, perfectly deadpan, "Only on Fridays.''

The other detective gaped at him for about five seconds before exploding with laughter. He was choking and had to grab the end of the coffee table to keep from falling over.

"You son-of-a-bitch! You're okay.''

A strange expression spread across the Newcomer's face. Exerting himself, he succeeded in standing, stood swaying before the still seated Sykes. "No, I am not okay. I believe I have said all that I have to say, possibly for quite some time to come, Matthew. Now I am going home.'' He turned and started for the front door.

"Yeah,'' Sykes yelled after him. "Go home. Get some sleep. You do sleep, don't you? And if you don't sleep, say howdy to Susan for me. Good-lookin' babe, your wife.''

"Thank you.'' Francisco spoke gravely as he neared the door, making an effort to keep from stumbling. "I will convey your greeting.'' He waved once without turning around. Turning would have required an effort that might have defeated him. Somehow he found the door handle. Then he was gone.

Sykes turned back to his nearly empty glass, shaking his head and chuckling to himself. "What a wild man.'' He picked up the glass and headed for the kitchen. That was where the dirty glass belonged. On the other hand, the couch was much closer.

He allowed himself to tumble sideways onto the stained, thick cushions.

# IX

It was one of those spectacular, Chamber-of-Commerce–type L.A. mornings. The wind had shoved all the smog inland to San Bernardino, where there were never enough votes to shove it back. A mockingbird was faking a Stellar Jay in the lonesome aspen outside the apartment house. Dogs were on their way to work, yapping and pissing and looking for love.

The first flat hues of dawn streamed through the open window into Sykes's apartment where they were not welcomed. The detective was still passed out on the sofa. Sleep was too feeble a description of his condition.

Safe from dogs and confusion, a cat lay hunkered down beneath the comfortingly motionless mass of the slugmobile. A noise made it turn. When he saw what was coming his way, the stray tom took off, running fast and low like a halfback trying to turn the corner against the Redskins' defensive line.

The heavy-duty tow truck slowed as it came down the street. It parked several car lengths ahead of the slugmobile. The driver looked to his right, inspecting the building just behind him. Then he relaxed in his seat and kept his attention on the street ahead, his hands resting on the wheel.

His passenger exited. He wore a serviceman's coveralls complete to fully equipped work belt and matching cap. A tool kit dangled from one hand, a heavy paper sack from the other. The man's name was Quint, and it was not embroidered above his breast pocket.

Rapid examination indicated that the street was largely deserted. Too early for casual strollers. Anyone awake would be traveling straight from apartment to garage to car to work, never setting foot on the ribbonlike sidewalk. No cars coming or going at the moment either, which was just the way Quint wanted it.

The narrow steel tool he removed from his kit was known colloquially as a slimjim. In Quint's experienced hands it made short work of the slugmobile's lock. He opened the door and slid behind the wheel.

Working rapidly and easily, he dumped the contents of the sack on the seat next to him. These consisted of a packet of C-4 plastic explosive, a primer cap, and double lead wires whose ends had already been properly stripped. The naked copper sparkled in the morning light. With a grunt, he turned sideways on the seat and eased himself down to the floorboard, reaching up and back as necessary for the right tools and ingredients.

Just as he was getting comfortable with the car's wiring, a new face appeared above the back seat. Francisco blinked tiredly as his blanket slid off his head and shoulders. He'd been lying motionless in the back, covered from head to toe by Sykes's emergency "bed."

Now he rubbed his eyes and yawned, feeling out of tune with this or any other world.

Beneath the dash, the contented Quint began to whistle while he worked. It was not the wisest thing for him to do at that particular moment in time.

Francisco was sleepy, but the sound woke him fast. A puzzled expression on his face, he leaned forward over the back of the seat to see Quint working under the dash, screwdriver in hand. Quint saw him at about the same instant. Being fully awake, he had an advantage, which he used to the fullest, sitting up fast and throwing himself fist-first at his unexpected audience. Francisco was slammed backward. Quint was striking from an awkward position and it wasn't much of a punch, but it didn't have to be due to the condition of the detective's sinuses.

Yelling to his driver, Quint bailed out of the slugmobile like the last sailor off a sinking sub, tripping on the way out and leaving a trail of tools behind as he scrambled toward the tow truck. It took the startled driver a moment to gun the engine, get it in gear, and send them roaring away down the street. Tires squealed around the far corner as Francisco, clutching his throbbing face, stumbled out of the car.

Shoot, stop. The words were short but took a long time traveling from his brain to his arm. He whipped out his pistol and swung it around to aim. His arm had the message, but someone had forgotten to inform his fingers. The .38 went flying out of his hand, skidded to a stop against the curb.

Francisco stared helplessly as the backside of the tow truck vanished. Then he sagged against the slugmobile, muttering to himself in his own tongue. A good linguist would have blushed at some of the phrases.

Sykes lay as he'd fallen the previous night. A distant pounding in his ears finally woke him. As his eyes opened against the intrusive light he became aware that the pounding wasn't all that far away. It came, in fact, from the other side of his front door.

"This better be good news or money," he mumbled. He found his feet, was mildly surprised to discover that they were still attached to his ankles, and stumbled toward the door, yawning and scratching his crotch. "I'm coming, I'm coming. Give it a rest, already!"

The door opened to reveal his partner standing, or rather swaying, on the other side. His face looked like hell. In his right hand he held the C-4 charge, neatly packaged in a clean handkerchief. This the detective passed to a bemused Sykes.

"Hold this." He stumbled in, bumping Sykes out of the way as he made a beeline for the kitchen sink. "I believe that I am feeling extremely horrible. No, correct that. I am certain of it."

Sykes watched him bend over the sink and run the cold

water, then turned his attention to the handful Francisco had passed to him. Even in his still swozzled state he recognized it for what it was. Examining it respectfully, he turned and walked back to join his partner. Francisco was running cold water over his mottled pate.

"Where'd you get this?"

The Newcomer winced. "Please, Matt. Not so loud. Would you have a towel?"

"A towel. Yeah, sure." Sykes found a dishrag, tossed it at his partner. "You want bubble bath and shampoo? Well, bubble bath, anyway."

Francisco straightened as he mopped his skull. "No, thank you. Under the circumstances the plain water was quite sufficient. As to your question, a man, a human, was wiring that to your car, beneath the dash. I am certain his intention was to connect it to the ignition."

"Naw," said Sykes sarcastically as he turned the C-4 over in his hands, "he was gonna wrap it and put 'do not open 'til Christmas' on it."

"I didn't get a good look at him." Francisco blinked at the window and suddenly panicked. "The sun is up! It's daytime!"

Sykes stared at his partner. "I guess that's why they jumped you to Detective. Unsurpassed powers of observation."

The sarcasm was lost on the frantic Francisco. "I must call my wife! Where is the telephone?" He looked around wildly.

"Where you left it last night," Sykes told him evenly. "On the wall." As the Newcomer hurried to the phone, Sykes took note of the position of the hands on the battery-powered wall clock above the stove. "Make it fast. We're late clocking in."

For the first time since they'd started working together, Sykes was the better-looking of the two as they entered the precinct house. While his partner had babbled none too coherently on the phone, Sykes had taken the time to shower and change. Francisco entered still clad in the rumpled suit he'd slept in, his underwear a day old and the taste in his mouth considerably older despite elephantine doses of Sykes's mouthwash. Apparently the chemicals in human mouthwash didn't do anything but irrigate the flora in a Newcomer's mouth. The result was that at close range, Francisco's breath reeked of sour milk.

They neared Sykes's desk. The expression on his partner's face would have done justice to a retiring mortician. The desk was as well organized as Sykes's apartment. As he'd explained on more than one occasion to inquiring passersby, this condition was maintained deliberately. It prevented anyone from stealing from him, since absolutely nothing atop the desk was arranged in any kind of order. No potential thief could find what he was looking for. Neither could Sykes, but that never slowed him down.

"She's going to divorce me." Francisco was inconsolable.

"George," Sykes said patiently, "she's not gonna divorce you. You mate for life, remember?"

His partner refused to be mollified. "She's very progressive. I'm certain she's considering it. She watches television all the time, and not just the Newcomer channel. She's taken up flower arranging in her spare time. If she can pick up a human habit as bizarre as that, why not also divorce?"

Sykes started to reply, frowned instead. "What's bizarre about flower arranging?"

"Flowers are arranged by nature. They do not need to be repositioned according to some obscure aesthetic."

"I think you're wife's interested in the artificial kind of flowers."

Francisco looked thoughtful. "Oh. I had not considered that. The duplications of the natural world that your people consistently manufacture are a source of confusion as well as wonderment to us. We see nothing wrong with the original world, and no need to reproduce it in plastic. I am convinced it is but a short step from flower arranging to divorce."

Sykes had had about enough. "And I'm convinced your brain needs rearranging."

The uniformed clerk passing out phone memoranda spotted the ill-matched pair and hustled to intercept Sykes.

"You guys are looking for somebody named Strader, right?"

"Yeah." Sykes eyed her in surprise. "You know where we might find him?"

"Not me." She showed him the relevant record. "Fedorchuk and Alterez just phoned in. They found him. Or apparently what's left of him, washed up on the beach at Zuma."

Francisco reacted sharply, leaned over his partner. "This 'Zuma beach.' It is on the ocean and not a lake or river?"

"That's right."

The Newcomer straightened and looked solemn but did not comment further. Meanwhile Sykes was studying the phone-record printout. "Not a helluva lot of detail."

"They're still out there if you wanna try and catch 'em. From the volume of calls going back and forth I'd say they'll probably be there awhile." She glanced surreptitiously at the towering Francisco. Engrossed in reading over Sykes's shoulder, he missed her stare. "Isn't every day you find a dead Newcomer in a public park." She turned and continued her distribution.

"Well, let's roll, George." Sykes headed for the exit. Francisco followed, holding back.

"To the—to the beach?"

Sykes looked back over his shoulder. "No, man. To Disneyland, to check out the new rides. Come one, let's go, dude. Surf's up!" So was Sykes's adrenaline as he headed fast for the door.

Francisco stayed close but behind, so that his partner could not see the look on his face.

Sykes drove while Francisco monitored the radio. The Newcomer seemed to be spending a lot of time checking and rechecking their position as Sykes drove up the coast, even though Zuma was impossible to miss. When Sykes questioned him about it Francisco replied that he wanted to be certain they didn't drive too far. Actually, he kept talking with the dispatcher because it helped to keep his mind off their destination.

Then they turned onto the Pacific Coast Highway, leaving the Santa Monica Freeway behind, and Francisco couldn't ignore the view to their left anymore. He looked the other direction as much as possible, trying to concentrate on the sandy, collapsing cliffs or the traffic that swirled around them. But there was no way he could totally ignore the surging, stinking ocean.

Only a comparatively thin stir of granulated rock separated the paved roadbed from the hungry sea. A sudden storm could send waves crashing onto the highway, though he knew from the morning weather report that this was unlikely. It wasn't enough to keep the images out of his mind. And what of the tsunamis he'd read about? Didn't they strike without warning, without giving people a chance to escape to higher ground? If one hit now they'd be trapped beneath the cliffs.

Sykes was mulling different possibilities, so he didn't notice the strain on his partner's face.

Eventually the roadbed climbed the first bluffs and Francisco could relax a little as they cruised through Malibu. But then the pavement dipped again, as if the road had been designed to torment him. Trees appeared on their left, screening the lower beaches from view.

Finally Sykes pulled off onto an access road that led down to a parking lot and beach.

"Stop the car," Francisco told him abruptly.

Sykes frowned at him. "Why?"

"Please. I must get out here."

"Come on," Sykes chided him, "you won't have to get near the water."

"This is already too near the water. *Stop the car.*" The fear in his voice was unmistakable. Sykes might have been driving down to Hell.

Halfway to the parking lot he abused the brake. The slugmobile rolled to a stop in a cloud of dust. "All right, okay! Keep your pantyhose on. Geez, when in doubt, freak out, for crissake."

The Newcomer body odor was sharp in the confines of the car. His hands were trembling and suddenly the huge, powerful form looked fragile. Sykes's attitude changed.

"It's all right, George, it's cool. You don't have to talk

about it and I won't mention it again, okay?'' His tone had softened considerably. "Just wait here. I'll be back in a coupla minutes, soon as I get what we need. Then we'll get the hell out of here and back inland, okay? I'll even drive back the long way, through the Valley.''

The big detective relaxed a little. ''Thank you, Matt. I do not mean to make trouble.''

''I said it was all right.''

The slugmobile had halted facing the water. Francisco had his head down and his eyes closed. His fingers worked nervously against each other. The poor guy was an emotional basketcase, Sykes decided. He resolved to finish their business here as quickly as possible.

''You gonna be okay?''

Francisco nodded. Taking a deep breath, he exited the car. Sykes saw he was standing in the middle of the access road.

''You stay there like that, you're liable to get run over.''

Francisco forced himself to walk in front of the car until he was standing against the railing overlooking the parking lot. He forced himself to open his eyes and look out at the beach, at the ocean, much as an acrophobe forces himself to look out the window of a plane.

''I'll be okay, Matt. But I hold you to your promise. Don't linger.''

Sykes nodded, put the car back in gear, and drove down to the beach, aiming for the cluster of vehicles parking at the edge of the sand. There was a sheriff's black-and-white (they were beyond L.A. jurisdiction here: this was strictly county), a coroner's wagon, and an unmarked sedan he recognized as belonging to Fedorchuk.

One of the coroner's assistants waved absently at him as he climbed out of the slugmobile and ambled over. He waved back, his eyes on the object lying on the sand surrounded by onlookers. It had the general shape of a person: head, torso, arms, legs, but like your basic Detroit wheels, all the customizing was missing from the chassis. There was nothing but a person-shaped pile of yuck that might easily have been extruded by a passing street-paving machine. Streamers of kelp and seagrass were wrapped like green and brown wire around different parts of the corpse. It looked like it would fall apart in sections if anyone tried to pick it up, which might be why it was still lying untouched on the sand.

A coroner's technician was bent over the loathsome flotsam, examining it through a studyscope. Sykes wondered if he was finding anything distinctive in the mass of dark goo. From his vantage point he could see nothing that might be called a distinguishing feature. Fragments of an expensive silk suit clung to parts of the body.

Fedorchuk acknowledged Sykes's arrival with a glance and nod. He was unusually quiet. Remembering something, he reached inside his jacket and removed a plastic bag.

"Found his wallet in his jacket pocket. Joshua Strader, big as life. Well, not as big as life anymore, I guess."

The tech straightened, clicked off his scope as he stared disgustedly at the thing buried in the sand. "Jesus, what a mess. It's gonna be a bear to try to make positive identification."

"Give it a try," Fedorchuk urged him. "If you mess up I'll see you still get your birthday present."

The tech made a face, gazed thoughtfully at the corpse. "It's tough going in there. Everything keeps melting and crumbling around the probes. But if I had to make a guess I'd say he was shot before being tossed in the drink. At least twice." He tapped his own chest to show where the alien hearts were located. "Here, and here."

Sykes stored and filed the information as he eased over to Alterez. He had no desire to go poking around inside Strader's corpus himself. Fedorchuk had found the wallet, and that was ID enough.

"How're you two doing on Tuggle's killer?"

Alterez spoke up importantly. "The store owner's son is in a street gang, so now we're thinking maybe it's gang related."

Sykes nodded approvingly. "Yeah, that's real good. Me, I never woulda thought of that." He shook his head in amazement. "It just goes to show: sometimes the answer'll be right in front of your face and you'll be too blind to see it. You guys must be on the right track, all right. You follow up on that for a coupla months.''

"We'll do that. Just make sure you stay out of it. You heard what the Captain said.''

"Hey." Sykes raised both hands defensively. "I swear I won't go near the store again, and if I talk to any gang types in the neighborhood you guys can have my car.''

"Who'd want it?" Fedorchuk snorted. His eyes went to the access road that led down to the beach and a smile spread across his face. "Speaking of not wanting something, look at your dildo partner. He's too scared even to come down on the sand." Cupping his hands to his mouth, he shouted toward the solitary figure standing alone on the road above.

"You're not gonna get wet standing down here, moron!"

Sykes growled a response. "I'd like to see how you'd react standing next to a sea of hydrochloric acid, Fedorchuk. See how much surfin' you'd want to do.''

Alterez had his Polaroid out and was shooting a full-length of the body. As soon as the picture emerged from the camera's mouth, Sykes grabbed it and headed back toward his car. Instead of arguing or commenting, Alterez turned away and covered his mouth with his free hand. Fedorchuk flipped the retreating detective the bird, watched with a smile on his face as the other detective rounded his car.

It was hard to miss. Someone had used a yellow liquid chalk marker to paint a big star on the door. Beneath it were the still damp letters "E.T.P.D." Sykes spun. Fedorchuk and the others were standing close together, looking everywhere but in his direction. Occasionally a suggestion of muffled laughter escaped from the group.

"Cute," he muttered. "Real cute." Ignoring the paint job, he got in and backed up fast, climbing the access road recklessly.

Francisco was waiting for him. "Find out anything?"

"It was Strader, all right." Sykes slid out of the slugmobile, popped the trunk, and hunted around until he found an old rag and a half-full bottle of solvent. Francisco was close behind as he made his way back to the driver's side of the car.

"Dead, I would assume."

"Worse than dead. Dissolved would be more like it."

Francisco's gaze rose to the placid sea glistening beneath them. "A most unpleasant way for one of us to die."

"Sure makes a mess." Splashing solvent on the slugmobile's flank, Sykes started scrubbing with the rag. Fortunately, the yellow marker was still damp.

Seeing what he was doing, Francisco read the letters and frowned. "E.T.P.D. What does that mean?"

"Nothing. Forget it. A bad joke. It doesn't have anything to do with you."

"Oh." Francisco straightened and peered down toward the parking lot. "Detective Fedorchuk and Alterez are approaching."

"Swell." Sykes leaned harder into his work.

Fedorchuk slowed his car and leaned out to yell at the Newcomer. "Well, if it isn't *Detective* Francisco. How come you didn't join the party down there? You forget your hip waders, big guy?"

Sykes glanced up from his job. "Lay off, asshole."

Fedorchuk grinned down at him. "I may be an asshole, but at least I'm a real detective, not some outer space shit thing who got rank because he looks good in somebody's PR brochure."

His expression neutral, Sykes put the rag carefully aside and sauntered over to Fedorchuk's side of the car. "Yeah? You mean you're a real honest-to-God detective?"

Reaching in, he grabbed the back of Fedorchuk's head and slammed it into the steering wheel. It bounced nicely, but he was sorry he'd done it because he hurt his hand again. He turned away, wincing and holding his wrist.

"Damn! Should've used the other one." He shook the reinjured member while reaching into the car. Before a startled Alterez could react, Sykes yanked out the keys.

Turning, he used his good hand to hurl the keys over the side of the bluff below the access road. They landed somewhere in the dense ground cover.

"Detect these!"

Holding his bloody nose, Fedorchuk recovered just in time to see the keys go sailing out in a high arc to vanish somewhere far below. Francisco had just climbed into the slugmobile when the keys were launched. He observed the rest of the inexplicable episode in silence, wondering what strange manifestation of human behavior it signified.

Fedorchuk was leaning out his window, trying to open the door, and hold his nose together while simultaneously hurling epithets at Sykes. Alterez had to hang on to his partner to keep him in the car.

"You son-of-a-bitch, Sykes! You're dead meat, you understand? You hear me, Sykes? I don't give a shit what the Captain says. The next time I catch you alone you're mine!"

"I always knew you had the hots for me, Chuckie." Sykes slid behind the wheel of the slugmobile and slammed the door, flinched as his aching hand locked on the wheel. Clutching it gingerly, he threw the car in gear and rooster-tailed dirt as he roared up the road toward the highway. Francisco turned for a last look in the direction of the still hysterical Fedorchuk before eyeing his partner curiously.

"What was all that about?"

"Nothing," Sykes snapped, embarrassed and confused over what he'd done.

"A lot of violence for nothing."

"You think that was violence? You oughta be in the squad room some day when Warner's passing out commendations and some paper-pusher from upstairs walks off with all the brownie points."

"Detective Fedorchuk appeared extremely distressed with you."

"Fedorchuk was born distressed. Don't sweat it."

Francisco would have continued save for the fact that something in his partner's tone suggested that this was not the best time to analyze this particular sociology lesson. The Newcomer squared himself to the windshield, looking thoughtfully as Sykes goosed the slugmobile back toward L.A.

They ate at a different burger stand that night, though the

menu was little different from the other. Only the cutesy-pie names had been changed to protect the copyright. Dead meat was still dead meat.

Sykes reminded himself repeatedly that fast-food burgers were actually wholesome meals, if you discounted the fact that most of them were fried. A burger with everything contained protein, carbohydrates, vitamins and minerals, vegetable bulk and fats. It was also tasty when it wasn't dried out.

The night was mellow and the two detectives sat across from each other as they dined. A young couple smooched nearby, shakes and fries languishing amidst whispers and sly little kisses. The kid looked to be about twenty-three, the girl a year or so younger. He kept trying to slip his hand between her thighs and she kept giggling and trapping his fingers, which was what he had in mind in the first place. It was all so innocent.

Hell, Sykes thought suddenly. You start thinking of a guy of twenty-three as a kid, that's a sure sign you're getting old. You start watching kids feeling each other up, that's a sure sign you've been alone too long. Tough to go from being married to waking up by yourself in an empty bed. Shit.

Francisco was demolishing his mole strips with unabashed gusto. This time Sykes knew what to expect and didn't let the sight bother him. He'd been on the force a lot of years, seen a lot of street scenes as gruesome as the one on the beach this morning, and dead mole shouldn't make him queasy. Hadn't he known a guy who used to tell a favorite 'Nam story about surviving in the jungle on rats and snakes? Better to eat a mole than a snake. What did moles eat, anyway?

And what did it matter? He'd eaten shark plenty of times, found it delicious, and sharks were the garbage scows of the sea. Since the Newcomer couldn't handle saltwater, he found himself wondering if they could eat saltwater fish. Would they want to? He could've asked his partner, but found his mind turning back to business.

You accumulate enough seemingly unrelated facts, he

mused, and toss 'em all in the pot together, and pretty soon they start matching up out of sheer number.

"So we've got three guys dead," he heard himself saying thoughtfully. "All Newcomers, all killed the same way. Execution style. Unless you want to give credence to the theory that Strader went nuts and decided to take a late-night swim."

"There are neater ways of committing suicide," Francisco assured him. "Even an insane Newcomer would retain enough sense to keep clear of the ocean."

"All murdered, then. What else we got?"

"Not a great deal, I should say." Francisco ticked off what they knew on his thick fingers. "Warren Hubley was in middle management at a refinery, Joshua Strader was the prosperous operator of a bar and nightclub . . ."

"And Porter ran a piece-of-shit mom-and-pop minimart." Sykes swallowed chocolate shake. "What the hell's our connection?"

"I do not know and cannot imagine." Francisco looked discouraged. "I fear I am not a very good detective."

Sykes was instantly sympathetic. "The hell you ain't. We put puzzles together, that's all. Any such thing as an alien crystal ball?"

"A what?" his partner wondered curiously.

"Guess not. Too bad." The detective masticated a mouthful of burger. "You know, when you guys first landed here everyone expected extraordinary things from you. Supersecrets of the stars, and all that crap."

"Unreasonable expectations." Francisco daintily ticked a loose fragment of mole into the corner of his mouth.

"No shit. Imagine the disappointment when everybody realized you were just a bunch of dumb joes stuck on a one-way barge you didn't even know how to operate. I hear it's gonna take decades, maybe centuries for our scientists to even start to figure out how the engine on your ship works."

"None of us knows," Francisco explained unnecessarily. Newcomer ignorance of their own science was common knowledge. "We were only passengers. When you get on a plane all you have to know how to do to reach your destination is how to buy a ticket. No one expects you to fuel the plane, check it for damage, and navigate it.''

"Yeah. Still, I suppose that U.N. team tearing the guts out of your ship will get a few money-making patents out of it sooner or later. Hey," he said brightly, "maybe it's a good thing you folks weren't any better than you turned out to be, huh?''

"That is probably the truth," Francisco said carefully.

# X

Except for Winter the pathology lab was deserted. He was seated behind his desk, demolishing cold takeout chicken and avidly scanning a very peculiar magazine when Sykes and Francisco entered without knocking. He hurriedly slid the magazine into an open desk drawer and smiled up at them, his mouth full of cholesterol.

Sykes didn't waste time. "You guys finished the postmortem on Strader yet?"

Winter mumbled around his chicken. "You mean the Blob? They're finishing up now."

Francisco was staring past Winter, at the open door leading to the main lab and beyond. "Is Bentner here? I must speak with him."

"He went home early," Winter informed him. "His kid was sick, so I told him to take some time off. Slow day anyhow. All the excitement was Strader, and when we finished with that, no new business came in. So I'm not missing him."

The Newcomer frowned, at which point Winter put down his chicken. "Hang on, though. He left something for you."

Wiping his greasy fingers on a napkin, he searched the top of his crowded desk until he found what he was looking for. Francisco took the envelope and tore it open, scanned the alien script as Winter watched him closely.

"Does this have something to do with the test he ran that

he wouldn't tell me about? I mean, he doesn't have to tell me everything he does. Nobody here does. We all do our own work and try to stay out of the other guy's way, but there isn't a whole lot of call for privacy when you're working on somebody's insides.''

Francisco ignored the technician as he read on, his expression turning stricken as he neared the end. Sykes was watching all the time, finally turned back to Winter.

"What kind of test?"

Winter shrugged. "Looking for some foreign compound in the blood of that alien you dropped the other day.''

"Did he find anything?"

The lab tech shrugged again, nodding toward the message Francisco was perusing so intently. Sykes held off until he couldn't stand it any longer.

"Well?"

His partner glanced sharply at him, then folded the paper and placed it in his coat pocket. Seeing that Sykes was still staring at him, he hastened to look elsewhere.

"Answer me, man.''

"It is nothing." The Newcomer detective turned to depart. "It is useless to remain here where nothing further may be learned." He headed rapidly up the hall.

"Thanks, Winter,'' Sykes said quickly.

"Hey, no problem." The tech returned to his chicken, frowned at a new thought. "You'll let me know if Bentner found anything out, won't you?'' But Sykes didn't hear him.

Francisco was moving fast and Sykes had to hurry to catch him at the elevators. The Newcomer jabbed one of the buttons with his thumb, made a show of following the indicator arrows as the car descended. Anything to avoid meeting Sykes's gaze.

His partner came right around in front of him. "Now what's this 'nothing' shit? It wasn't nothing yesterday when you asked this guy Bentner to run that test and he looked like he was about to shit peach pits, and it's not nothing now. Don't lie to me, George, you're bad at it.''

"All right." Francisco's voice was quiet. "There was something."

Sykes relaxed slightly. "That's more like it. So tell me what it was. Anything important?"

The Newcomer sounded very far away, as though by whispering he could put space between himself and his partner. "You must leave me alone on this, Matt. It is not something you would understand."

"Try me. I'm a good listener."

"No. I cannot explain."

The elevator stopped at their floor and he entered. Sykes followed, waited while his companion hit the button that would take them down to the parking level.

"You still don't understand how this works, do you, George? You don't ask me to leave you alone, I don't leave you alone. I'm your *partner*. I don't work that way. Tug didn't work that way. I don't care what kind of alien crapola your buddy Bentner dug out of that thug. If it has anything to do with what we're working on, I need to know. Whatever it is won't shake me. I've been on the street too long, and believe me, nothing from another world can shake me any worse than some of the stuff I've had to deal with downtown or over in Hollywood."

Francisco did not reply, concentrated instead with single-minded intensity on the colored green light that was illuminating one floor after another. They were nearly at bottom when a frustrated Sykes slammed his palm against the red emergency stop button. Both men stumbled as the car lurched to a halt between floors. Sykes turned angrily on the baffled Francisco.

"No secrets, goddamnit! You don't hold back from me. Whatever is going on, you're gonna tell me now!" He reached up and grabbed the Newcomer by the lapels, an action more significant as a gesture than a real threat. His partner could have dislodged him easily.

This time Francisco's voice was agonized. He refused to meet Sykes's eyes. "No. I cannot involve you. This is not your concern."

"The hell it isn't, when somebody wires up enough C-4

to my car to turn me into pink mist!'' His expression narrowed as he shoved his face closer to his partner's. "That Slag was on something, and no sour milk, either. Am I right? Go on, tell me I've got it all wrong." By now he'd backed the Newcomer up against the back wall of the elevator cab. "Tell me! What is it?"

Francisco sighed deeply. It was an acknowledgment of resignation, and Sykes promptly let loose of his partner's suit, took a step backward.

"It is called ss'jabroka'. To us it is a potent narcotic."

Sykes felt vindicated. "About time. See, I ain't comin' apart at the seams from the shock. How potent?"

"It is difficult to draw anything like an exact analogy because of the differences in our physiological makeup. We react to ss'jabroka' much the same as you do to your cocaine, but the manner in which our systems deal with the combination of molecules involved is very different. To all outward appearances the effect may seem similar, but internally our bodies are doing different things."

"Sounds like strong stuff."

"It is precisely that. The 'high' lasts for several hours, varying according to the tolerance of the individual. But no one is immune to the effects. We would receive small amounts of it as a reward for our labor, for good behavior, for a number of reasons. It was a reward we could have done without, for it was a means for keeping us under control as well as satisfied."

"*We?* You're telling me you've taken it?"

"We all did, in our previous existences." Despite the obvious pain the confession cost him Francisco confronted his partner as squarely as he had the question.

Sykes was shaking his head dubiously. "That doesn't make sense. Where did the stiff get the stuff? Was there some of it on the ship, maybe tucked away somewhere to provide future 'rewards' for the right sort of performance by selected individuals?"

"No." Francisco shook his head. "I am sure not. It was a clean ship. I can remember when the checks were run. It was a necessary part of the departure and flight procedure.

That is why I am so concerned. If our dead holdup man had it in his system, and the test Bentner ran appears conclusive, then someone must now be producing the drug here. Even if it had come from the ship its effects would long since have faded, unless it was held in the medical section where the proper long-term storage facilities were available. And I *know* that was impossible. That was the most heavily guarded and frequently inspected part of the ship.

"Besides, no one was conscious during the journey. Ship's records can prove that. But that is not what has me so puzzled and worried. None of my people knows how to make the drug. It was always given to us in its finished state. The process of manufacture was carefully guarded by the Masters, for obvious reasons."

The enormity of what his partner was telling him was still sinking into Sykes's overloaded brain.

"Jesus, this is major. Why didn't you tell me sooner? Why'd you hold out on me? Did you really think I couldn't handle it? Hell's bells, George, I've been dealing with narcotics my whole career. It's nothing new to me."

"I know that, Matt. I realized from the start that you would have no difficulty in comprehending the problem. That is not why I kept silent for so long."

"So then tell me, why?"

"Because your people are ignorant of this part of our past. In the main they see us as not very bright innocents, big and strong but otherwise comparatively harmless, and willing to adopt and hew to your own moral codes even when that code is not applied fairly to us. I have watched your popular media and learned much from it. Can you imagine the headlines if this news becomes known? 'Alien Dope Fiends Run Amok,' or something like that. You see, I know how your society reacts to such things, and it is usually not with understanding.

"If this were to become common knowledge it would threaten our entire existence here. At the very least there would be new restrictions just when we are beginning to integrate effectively. At worst it would mean a return to the quarantine camps and a lifetime of surveillance by your medical specialists. It must be kept a secret or we are lost. Our future here will come to a dead end, and presently things are going much too well for me to allow that to happen. Tell me that you understand, Matt. I need to hear you say it.''

As he listened to his partner Sykes had calmed down completely. When Francisco had finished, the senior detective spoke calmly but with great force, looking him straight in the eye.

''George, I've got just one thing to say to you. Don't you ever lie to me again. No matter what. Ever.''

''I must trust you, Matthew.'' Francisco was staring at the ceiling of the cab. ''I suppose I would have had to tell you sooner or later. Now that it is out I feel better for having explained. I wanted to choose the right time, but you are an impossible man to say no to. Believe me, Matt. I cannot stop this without you. And stop it we must before it can spread and before the news becomes public. Understand me clearly: no one else can know of this but you and me. It must not go beyond this place.''

Sykes nodded curtly, then hit the emergency stop a second time. They descended the rest of the way to the parking level in silence, each lost in his own thoughts.

It was dark outside as they made their way back to the slugmobile. Sykes reached for the handle and winced as the fingers of his injured hand sought to grip the metal. The son-of-a-bitch still hurt like hell. He'd just have to manage. A thought struck him as Francisco opened the door on the other side.

He didn't have to manage.

''George?'' The Newcomer peered over the top of the car at him. ''How about you drive?''

Francisco didn't say anything. He didn't have to. His expression said it all for him as he reacted to the small but welcome vote of confidence. The two detectives switched places.

Sykes always liked to relax by listening to dispatch when he was concentrating on another case. It soothed him to know that someone else was responsible for checking out reports of homicides and burglaries, rapes and break-ins, vice busts and vandalism.

But listening didn't help tonight. What had been a fairly straightforward case made important by Tug's death had exploded into something infinitely more complex. If Francisco was to be believed, his people's whole future stood at risk. The responsibility was one Sykes hadn't asked for, didn't want, and would have put aside if possible. Couldn't do that now. Thanks to his dedication to his old partner's memory and his damnable curiosity, he was involved up to his neck.

George continued to insist that the ss'jabroka, or whatever the hell it was, had no effect on human beings. How the hell could he be sure? He'd covered up everything he'd known about the stuff ever since he'd suspected its presence because mere knowledge of it was so dangerous. Suppose he was covering up something else as well? Suppose he'd decided to give his partner the minimum amount of information concerning the situation so they could proceed? What if the stuff did have some kind of dangerous effect on humans? That would be reason enough to keep things secret. If that was the case, then widespread knowledge of the drug's existence and origin would be far more damaging to the Newcomer cause than anything that merely affected them.

He glanced sideways. Francisco was driving silently, professionally, a clean-cut graduate of Academy driving school, both hands firmly on the wheel and eyes concentrating on the traffic. He would've taken pursuit class too, Sykes knew. Was he telling his good buddy Matt Sykes everything he knew, or was he still holding back? No way to tell.

Just go with the flow, Sykes told himself, and keep an ear out for any obvious slip of the tongue. And watch his face, he reminded himself. The Newcomers were lousy poker players.

How many hands were being played here?

He tried to put it out of his mind. He was after Tug's murderer. Concentrate on that. It was why he'd fought so hard to get this case, why he'd volunteered to work with a damn dumb Slag. Think about Tug. Let George worry about possibly dangerous Newcomer narcotics. Take him at his word that the junk is not dangerous to human beings.

Until something else proves otherwise.

They pulled into the parking lot outside the government building in West L.A. The night guard acknowledged their ID with a smile and a wave. Little traffic here this time of night.

Sykes spoke briefly to the watchman stationed in the lobby, who directed them to the proper floor. The elevator dropped them off halfway up the tower. The corridor ahead was deserted, the lighting turned down but not off.

"There's gotta be some other connection," he mumbled as they walked.

Francisco looked down at him. "What?"

"Nothin', nothin'. Forget it, George. Sometimes I just like to talk out loud, okay? It helps me see things."

The Newcomer sighed. "Another astonishing human behavior."

Sykes eyed him irritably. "What is?"

"Talking to oneself. A difficult concept to fathom."

"You think so? Fathom this." Sykes flipped him the bird, a gesture Francisco was familiar with. He tried to connect it to what his partner had just said and failed. Let it slide, he told himself. You had to do that with humans a lot. Otherwise you put your sanity at risk.

## BUREAU OF NEWCOMER AFFAIRS

Sykes eyed the lettering on the door, wondering if his partner had spent time here previously, but said nothing. The door was unlocked. No reason to secure it, he mused as he entered the room beyond. No one made it this far without passing lobby security.

A maze of partitioned cubicles stretched out before them.

Francisco's gaze swept the room. "Nobody here."

"Got to be somebody," Sykes argued. "The guard downstairs said the place was operational. Somebody's got the lights on for a reason. Let's have a look around."

They pushed into the maze. Each cubicle was decorated to individual taste, a warren of posters and family portraits and silk flowers. Each cubicle boasted a computer and printer.

"Maybe we don't need anybody. Can you run any of this stuff?"

Francisco shook his head. "I can handle the basic machine, but I have no access to authorization codes."

"Who needs code authorization?"

The voice stopped them at an intersection between cubicles. The woman standing there was young, black, and wary. "Who are you guys and what are you doin' up here this time of night?"

Sykes handled the intro. "Detectives Sykes and Francisco, ma'am. LAPD, homicide division."

She studied the badge Sykes proferred, looked satisfied. Her gaze kept returning to Francisco. It was possible she'd been the one to process him after the ship's arrival.

"We could use a little help," Sykes told her.

"Couldn't we all. Why you think I'm working this late?" She sighed. "Homicide, huh? That's more interesting than the stats I'm totaling. Come on. I was going to get some coffee, but it can wait."

"You give us a hand," Sykes said encouragingly, "and I'll buy the coffee."

She smiled. Had a pretty smile, Sykes thought, from somebody who spent all day in a six-by-six cubicle running records across a glass screen. Never define somebody by their job. Who the hell had told him that?

Her cubicle was adorned with photo blowups of high white mountains and grassy valleys. One showed a castle in some unidentified European country. Travel agency stuff. She sat down in her chair and glanced up at them as she brought the screen in front of her to life.

"What do you want to know?"

"Recently deceased alien individual name of Warren Hubley," Sykes told her. "We know a few things about him. Not enough."

She nodded and her fingers danced on the keyboard. "Let's see what we can find."

Information scrolled past too fast for either detective to follow, braking automatically at the name HUBLEY, WARREN. She thumbed a switch and shifted the name to the top of the screen. Information in profusion appeared below. Too many abbreviations for Sykes's taste.

"Here's Hubley," she informed them.

"I can't read it." Sykes peered over her left shoulder. "Bureaucratese. How about interpreting?"

"Too much information too spread out," the operator explained. She translated from the screen. "Warren Hubley. Left quarantine on November thirtieth, relocated first to Riverside, then moved to Los Angeles early in February the following year. Field of expertise: chemical manufacturing. Did work with the alien ship when it was being prepared for departure, helped with the awakening from deepsleep on arrival. Was one of the first Newcomers out of suspension, according to his preprogramming. So he could help with the setup for the others, I guess."

Francisco's eyes were glued to the screen. "Makes sense."

She went on. "Was officially debriefed by US Army Chemical Engineering. Looking for information on ship's functions. Apparently he couldn't help them there. All he'd been trained in was maintenance and closedown of the ship's sleep facilities. His other education was to be utilized on arrival. He didn't know anything about the operation of the ship itself."

"None of us did," Francisco murmured. "We were not even passengers. We were cargo."

Sykes didn't comment. "What happened to him after he was let out of quarantine?"

The operator enlarged the print slightly. Working at night was a strain. "He was a lot better off than many Newcomers. Apparently he didn't have too much trouble adapting his specialized knowledge to useful jobs here on Earth. He must've known he'd do okay here, too."

"What makes you say that?"

She tapped the screen with a fingernail. "Says here that he passed up several other better-paying jobs waiting for one at a particular refinery in Torrance. Not many Newcomers could afford to pick and choose like that. I guess it was just the kind of work he wanted to do.''

Sykes and Francisco exchanged a look. Squinting at the screen, the senior detective tried to separate any useful information from the lines of statistics and history. It all looked like personal stuff: known addresses, physical characteristics, relationships, and movements. That wasn't what they were after.

"That's enough Hubley. Try a Joshua Strader, will ya, darlin'?"

"For you, anything." She gave him a lewd wink. "Is that Strader with an 'a' or an 'ay'?"

"S-t-r-a-d-e-r," Francisco spelled helpfully.

She nodded and punched in the request. Information filled the screen almost immediately. Sykes didn't know much about computers, but he knew that when a query was answered that fast there was some awesome CD RAM behind it.

The operator leaned slightly forward. "Released on November twenty-ninth. Came right to L.A. Specialist in interpersonal analysis and personnel management."

"That figures," Sykes muttered.

"Ten weeks after arriving," she went on, "he took over an abandoned nightclub on the edge of the Los Angeles Newcomer District, oversaw its renovation and refurbishment thanks to a substantial loan from the Federal Newcomer Small Business Bureau, and renamed the place 'Encounters.' "

"That's all?" Francisco asked.

"It's followed by the same standard personal information and vital stats. Apparently he was doing well financially, paying back his loan on time and taking out a decent profit besides."

Sykes found himself digressing. "I didn't think the government would loan money for a project like that. A nightclub. I thought the idea was to help 'elevate' the Newcomers' status. You get elevated in that joint, but it ain't your status that goes up."

The operator was grinning. "The government loaned money to any Newcomer they thought could learn to support himself and create jobs for others. The only kind of elevation the Bureau is after involves full employment and getting everybody off welfare.''

The detective shrugged. ''Hey, somebody's showing some sense, anyway.''

Francisco gestured to the screen. ''Enough about Mr. Strader. Now I think we should inquire about the gentleman who first provoked our curiosity. Could you please research a store owner named Cecil Porter, please.''

She entered the name and once more the information materialized almost instantly.

''Released December first,'' she drawled. ''Married, unlike your first two. Took a more roundabout route finding his way to L.A., too. He and his wife first went to Modesto, but they got themselves caught up in the Hmong race riots there and had to get out. Went to Coalinga next, wherever the hell that is.''

''Up on the west side of the Central Valley,'' Francisco informed her softly, ''near nothing else.''

She grunted a response. ''Settled in L.A. in April. Field of expertise is organic chemical engineering. Looks like he first tried to hook up with one of the big agribiz outfits in Modesto, same thing in Coalinga, and finally gave up and moved down here to Newcomer country. Took out a loan to buy the store. He and his wife have one son.'' She smiled back at Francisco. But then, Sykes reminded himself, she has to work with Newcomers and their problems every day.

''You folks tend to have children later in life.''

The Newcomer didn't bat an eye. ''Our women reach the equivalent of menopause at a later stage in their physical development.''

''I don't know whether to envy them or feel sorry for them.'' She chuckled, turned her attention back to the computer. ''You want details on the boy?''

''Naw, we already met him,'' Sykes said conversationally. ''Wonderful kid. Close personal friend of George's here.''

''Hey, I know it's none of my business, but why the interest in these three?'' She swiveled in her chair. ''I can't imagine three more different personalities. Are they supposed to have something in common that involves homicide? They in some kind of trouble?''

"Yeah, you could say that.'' Sykes was looking past her, past the giant wall photo of the fairy-tale castle that dominated the back wall of her cubicle. An idea was forming, slow as the first life to emerge on land, crawling painfully up from the oleaginous depths of his brain. It was what he was best at, why Warner overlooked his many other faults. Somehow Sykes had the ability to pull seemingly unrelated bits of matter together from the vast reservoir of garbage that drifted loosely in his skull, to turn nonsense into logic and nothingness into reality.

It wasn't much of an idea. Not something any of his colleagues would have considered. He stood there silently mulling it over, his expression that of a man who'd just swallowed something sour. It took another minute to assimilate it all.

If he hadn't been working with George it might never have occurred to him, but he was doing a lot of thinking about Newcomers lately, learning a great deal about them. Things you didn't get in the supplementary alien classes everyone was required to take.

Or as the Porter kid had said to him, "Didn't they teach you anything about us?" They did, but some stuff you didn't pick up in class, and a lot of what went through your mind at the time never crossed it again. Well, Sykes found himself wondering about some of that now, thinking long and hard.

His eyes widened suddenly. "Holy shit." He looked sharply at Francisco. "Look what we're staring at. No wonder we're not getting anywhere. Three Newcomers with nothing in common, right? Or so it appears. What if it's just *one* other guy who's killed these three?" He was so excited he didn't realize that for the first time since they'd taken on the case he wasn't thinking about Bill Tuggle.

Francisco eyed him uncomprehendingly. "I do not see where you are going with this line of thought, Matthew.''

"Gimme a minute. You will. Think about it, George. Three dead. Three and one make four. Four Newcomers, three dead, one still alive somewhere who's responsible for the deaths of the other three. All four from 'totally different' backgrounds.''

His partner shook his head doubtfully. "I still fail to recognize a useful connection.''

Sykes was so excited now he was all but hopping up and down. "C'mon, man! You're the one who gave me the glue to put it all together.''

"Me?'' Francisco looked honestly surprised.

"Yeah, you. What you told me earlier. You and the store owner's son, that damn punker.''

"But we had already decided he had nothing to do with these murders.''

"He doesn't, damnit! You and him, two Newcomers also of utterly different backgrounds, but you still had something in common. One thing. Remember what it was?''

"No, there was nothing, besides the fact that we are both of the same . . .'' The detective straightened. "Quarantine.''

Sykes nodded vigorously, turned back to the operator. "Can you dig up quarantine records on this thing?''

"For the three guys we just reviewed?'' Sykes nodded again. "Sure, just a minute.'' She turned back to her console. "I'll have to run a cross-reference layout so you can see all three sets of records simultaneously. What were those first two names again?''

"Warren Hubley. Joshua Strader,'' Sykes reminded her impatiently.

She ran the crossref and scrolled old man Porter to the top of the screen. "Your market owner was in Lodge Seven Seven Two. I'll make a run with that.''

It took a little longer for the computer to process the request. Quarantine information was sensitive and access to it restricted. A moment later the info flashed on the screen.

OCCUPANTS, QUARANTINE LODGE 772: HUBLEY, WARREN—STRADER, JOSHUA—Sykes and Francisco looked anxiously at the screen—PORTER, CECIL . . .

The fourth name now. The answer to all their questions, asked and not yet thought of—*if* Sykes was right, and the names appearing on the screen offered incontrovertible proof of that.

It took forever for the machine to print it out.

—HARCOURT, WILLIAM—

Man and Newcomer exchanged a last look. Words were unnecessary.

# XI

Nobody had a chance to open the door for Harcourt this time. He was in a hurry as he stepped out of the limo.

The Encounters sign illuminated the entrance to the club, but the rest of the garish exterior lighting was turned off. The place was closed tonight, the parking lot out front was deserted, the driveway empty except for the limo and the van parked in front of it. The rear bumper of the van was badly scratched and rife with small dents as if metal had been pulled violently and repeatedly across its otherwise shiny surface.

Harcourt took a moment to study the entrance to the club. Then the noise of the van doors opening turned him in that direction. Kipling was just exiting the passenger side and Quint the driver's seat.

His assistant slid open the van's side door. Reaching inside, he extracted a large black suitcase, then turned to confront his boss. Harcourt nodded once. Together they strolled into the club. Quint trailed a respectful distance behind, hands jammed in his pockets. He would have whistled except that he'd learned early on many Newcomer's didn't like that. Something to do with the frequencies humans sometimes hit. Personally he didn't see how it could bother them since they didn't have any ears anyway. Just those dumb openings in the sides of their heads.

Not that it was any of his business, he reflected.

The chairs had been stacked neatly atop the tables. The lights in the booths were dark. Feeble illumination turned the bottles of liquor ranked behind the bar to crystalline teeth, imparting to the labels and shapes a magical softness they didn't deserve. Harcourt led his men toward the back, then up the stairs to the second floor.

Cassandra was waiting for them. She produced a weak, strained smile by way of greeting. Her eyes never left Harcourt. The dress she wore was too modest for a performance, too extreme for a church. She was doing her best to be friendly, but it wasn't easy. Harcourt made her very uncomfortable.

Kipling and Quint walked right past her, heading for the door to the main office and conference room. Harcourt slowed, stopped to smile back at the female. One hand rose and the fingers drifted easily over the neckline of her dress, slid possessively down into the depths of the cleavage displayed there. Cassandra shivered but didn't pull away. She'd already learned that much about Harcourt.

"Quite lovely," he whispered. "What was your name again?"

She fought to keep from flinching. "Cassandra."

Harcourt smiled, and it was neither the smile he reserved for his adoring public nor the one he'd bestowed on the absent Watson. In its fashion it was more chilling than either.

"I am sorry not to have remembered that. I will not forget again."

Withdrawing his hand, he continued on to the office. Cassandra watched him go. She was shaking and angry at herself for doing so.

The refinery functioned around the clock, but with a reduced crew at night. Computers made that possible even as they kept the highly volatile products of the plant from igniting to destroy half of Torrance.

The slugmobile skidded to a stop outside the loading dock. Sykes and Francisco checked the ID numbers above the platform to assure themselves they were at the right spot, then climbed out and started up the stairs. The interior of the building beyond the dock was brightly lit.

The few nightworkers didn't even look in their direction as the two detectives strode purposefully toward the back. Francisco was moving fast, but Sykes was so up he had no trouble keeping pace.

The Newcomer detective was talking almost as fast as he was walking. "It all seems so obvious now."

"Easy once you make the connection," his partner agreed tersely.

"Yes. They had many months in quarantine with nothing else to talk about. They must have discussed this plan early on and in great detail. With his chemistry background, Porter would supply the formula for ss'jabroka. I cannot imagine how he originally obtained it, but a resourceful person with enough drive and intelligence can accomplish seemingly impossible things. He was such an unprepossessing type. Those are the people who can slip past Security where a more forceful personality would immediately be suspected and detained.

"Hubley, with his contacts in the city, would provide the means for manufacturing. It took me a moment to imagine what Strader's contribution might be, but now it is clear that he was to establish a distribution network which would use the club as its base. It would provide a place to conduct business with privacy, a means for making contact with the human underworld and a useful way of laundering large sums of money. They had it worked out so well. And of course Harcourt..."

Sykes finished for him. "Harcourt was the brain who brought it all together and provided the start-up funds. Listen to me good, now, George. If we want it all we gotta play this real smart."

"If the drug is here, we must destroy it."

"No, George. You're missing the point. I know how you feel about this junk and how worried you are, but you can't let yourself get involved on a personal level. That's bad police work. Poor procedure." The irony of his little speech escaped him.

"The drug is *evidence*. We need to have evidence, ya know? Otherwise we've got nothing on these guys but your say-so. Bentner's test report won't mean squat without the real thing. You remember what they taught you about evidence, don't you?"

It was a measure of how far their friendship had advanced that Francisco didn't try to mitigate the coldness of his reply. "I was not promoted to the rank of Detective entirely for public relations purposes, Sergeant Sykes. I have some small knowledge of what sort of material prosecutors require."

"So sue me. Half the time I can't keep track of what *I* know and don't know. The main thing to remember is that we need something concrete, something the D.A. can hold up in court and shake at the jury. A signed deposition from you ain't gonna put anybody behind bars, you follow?"

"I follow," Francisco said evenly.

"Great. So let's not do anything stupid, no matter how much righteous anger we got flowing through us today, okay?"

The Newcomer spoke without looking at his partner. "Okay."

Since they'd first entered the complex Sykes's eyes had been working overtime, searching the floor ahead, the cat-walks above, and the jungle-gym network of pipes and conduits that comprised the business end of the refinery.

"I don't see the guy."

"Nor do I," said Francisco, "but the guard told us he had registered for duty and had clocked in tonight."

"Doesn't mean he's still here. He could've been tipped off, could've split by now."

"You are worrying unnecessarily, Matt. I do not see how he could have been contacted so quickly."

"Bad news travels fast, George. George?"

Francisco didn't reply. His attention was on the upper-level door that led to the methane section. He pointed. Sykes glanced along the line of his partner's arm and nodded.

"Yeah, that's O'Neal."

They managed to get close before the section manager

recognized them. This time he didn't wait to answer questions, didn't come to meet them with his hand outstretched. Maybe it was the expression on the Newcomer's face, maybe something in Sykes's stride, or maybe he'd been warned to keep an eye out for possible trouble. Whatever the reason, as soon as he spotted the two detectives approaching he ducked through the open refrigeration door and started to pull it shut behind him.

Sykes reacted by accelerating like a halfback taking a quick pitchout. His hand landed on the door handle an instant before O'Neal could latch it from the other side. Despite the technician putting his weight against it, the detective slowly shoved it open. Four O'Neals couldn't have pulled it tight against Sykes that night.

The technician was backing away from the portal as Sykes entered. The detective grabbed him by the collar, smiling mirthlessly, and unceremoniously hauled him deeper into the deserted chamber. It was soundproofed and solid, and O'Neal couldn't help but wonder if maybe he should've made a run for it instead of trying to lock himself inside.

Retreat having failed, he tried courage.

"Hey, what are you, crazy? You can't come in here like this! *Hey!* Lighten up, will you?" Sykes continued to drag him toward the back of the room.

A second door stood slightly ajar at the rear of the chamber. Light poured through the opening, illuminating Sykes's path.

"Where's your authorization? This section of the plant is off-limits to anyone not having proper authorization!"

"You want authorization?" Sykes's fingers had a death lock on the man's collar. "Read my lips." He mouthed a few choice words. O'Neal did not require elaboration.

When they finally reached the rear door Sykes gave it a push with his right foot. It swung aside on heavy hinges. He stared at what stood revealed, and grunted with satisfaction.

"So much for playing it smart."

O'Neal's feet barely touched the floor as Sykes hauled him inside. The detective kept a firm grip on his prisoner as he studied the racks of tubes and beakers, the carefully hand-welded copper tubing, the stainless steel tankards and reducers and piles of cannibalized plastic plumbing. Funny how certain setups gave off a feel all their own. He knew little about chemistry and nothing about alien organics, but no one would mistake this Tinkertoy setup for anything other than what it was.

Francisco had followed closely and was now conducting his own inspection. Reaching a stainless steel tub, he bent to run a finger along the gleaming interior. Holding it up to the light, he examined the sticky residue he'd recovered. In the dim light it was the color of azurite.

He stared at his finger, mesmerized. So close to his lips, just a little of it. Not enough to hold for evidence anyway. What a waste it would be to wash it down some human sink. A trace that couldn't punch you in the hearts, just barely enough to tingle, to thrill, to stimulate . . .

Sykes was gazing curiously at the blue stain on his partner's finger. It looked harmless as gel toothpaste.

"That's it?"

Francisco gazed a moment longer at his finger, then whirled sharply on his partner, his eyes wide, his expression tense. Turning back to the drug-still, he went a little crazy. Having never seen his partner act under anything less than complete control except for the night when they'd gotten quietly and harmlessly smashed together, Sykes didn't know how to react. So he simply stood off to one side and hung on to the gaping O'Neal.

The Newcomer swept a rack of equipment off a worktable. Glass shattered against floor and walls. Metal containers flew like grenade fragments. Sykes had to duck once.

It must have finally occurred to Francisco that the drug-manufacturing equipment was evidence as important as the drug itself, because he stopped as abruptly as he'd begun, breathing hard and staring at the still largely intact miniplant before him.

Then he spun and ripped O'Neal out of Sykes's grasp. One massive fist bunched the hapless technician's shirt front up beneath his chin as he was lifted off the floor. The

Newcomer slammed him against the nearest wall, moderating the gesture just in time.

Sykes came up behind him. "Uh, George."

Francisco ignored him. His face was very close to O'Neal's, all vestiges of the polite, courteous cop a recent memory now. "Where is the drug? Where have they taken it?"

O'Neal was gasping and choking, his feet treading air. Both hands wrestled with the detective's wrist, trying to break his grip.

"What drug?" he wheezed as he tried to suck air through a suddenly narrowed windpipe. "This is an oil refinery, you goddamn Slag pig!"

Sykes's expression turned thoughtful. " 'Slag pig.' That's tight. I like that. I hadn't heard that one."

Ignoring his partner, Francisco tightened his grip, feeling the man's esophagus beginning to flatten beneath his fingers. "WHERE?"

The bug-eyed technician's voice had been reduced to a pained whisper. "You—can't—do—this!"

Sykes reached up to tap his partner politely on the shoulder. "George, I'm sorry to interrupt your fun, but you're gonna break his little neck bones. Not that I care one way or the other." He smiled disarmingly at the panicky O'Neal. "But it wouldn't look good on the report, and I know what a stickler you are for proper procedure. Besides, if you kill him too soon we'll never get an answer out of him."

"Stay out of this, Matthew." The Newcomer's eyes burned into O'Neal's. His voice was as cold as a mugger in a rest home. "Tell me where the drug has been taken *right now* or I will crush your lungs against this wall."

"You heard him," the technician murmured weakly. "If you kill me you won't learn a damn thing."

"Then we will ask someone else. It will not matter to you because you will be dead."

Maybe it was something in the alien's voice, or something O'Neal saw in his eyes. Whatever the reason, he began to feel real fear for the first time.

"Or maybe I do not have to kill you." Francisco eased up

on the pressure a little, letting O'Neal breathe. "Perhaps I will just break all of your bones, one at a time."

Seeing that there was no way he was going to be able to dissuade his partner from his chosen course of inquiry, Sykes decided he might as well back him all the way. Since Francisco had chosen the role of heavy, Sykes figured he ought to play the other. Good-cop bad-cop was no kid's game.

"Don't piss him off, O'Neal." Sykes adopted his most serious mien. "When he gets like this I can't control him. These Newcomers, they don't get excited real often, but when they come close to the edge like this you can't do anything with 'em short of bringing in a SWAT team. Might as well write off anybody they take a dislike to. I've seen him like this before. Got his adrenaline or whatever the hell they've got inside them all pumped up. I saw him jerk a guy's spine out and show it to him. Nothin' I could do. I hadda go throw up. I mean, it was the most gruesome, sickening thing you'd ever imagine you could . . ."

Now it was fear and not Francisco's grip that made it difficult for O'Neal to talk.

"They took the stuff out, all of it, this afternoon."

"How much?" Francisco demanded to know.

"Jesus, I can't tell you guys everything. If any of this gets out, I'm a dead man."

The Newcomer put a little of his great weight behind the arm pinning the technician to the wall. "You may be a dead man anyway."

"All right, all right!" O'Neal took a deep breath. "About fifty kilos." The detective went numb inside. Mistaking his expression, the technician rushed ahead. "Concentrate mostly, some street grade already tubed. You figure it out. Me, I'd guess they had to run up some samples to give the dealers."

O'Neal would never know how lucky he was at that moment. Francisco came within a hair's breadth of actually breaking the man's neck. Seeing the look that came over his friend's face, Sykes steeled himself for a jump onto his partner's back. But somehow the Newcomer restrained himself.

"Where have they taken it?"

"Encoun—Encounters Club."

Francisco maintained the pressure for another moment, then abruptly let go. Gasping for air and clutching his bruised throat, O'Neal slid to the floor. Sykes stared down at him.

"If I were you, chum, I'd find my bank's nearest night-teller and make a big withdrawal. It's definitely overdue vacation time for a certain methane engineer. By the time you come back from wherever you have the good sense to get off to, we'll have this all wrapped and packaged for Christmas and nobody'll remember you had shit to do with it. If anything goes awry I'm gonna assume you blew the whistle on us. Then I'll have my partner here pay you a visit, no matter what beach your ass is on.

"But I don't think you're that stupid. Guys running this kind of operation don't like employees with big mouths, even if the babbling ain't their fault. You try to warn your Slag friends that we're on to them, all they're gonna think is that you told us how to find them. They'll tell you thanks a million, man. Then one week you'll find yourself swimming off Catalina with a concrete aqualung. Understand?"

Still coughing and choking, O'Neal managed a feeble nod.

"That's peachy. Don't forget it. Let's go, George."

They abandoned the technician inside the refrigeration chamber, still rubbing his damaged throat, the drug-manufacturing apparatus glistening uselessly around him.

This time Sykes had to run to keep pace with his partner. Eyes locked straight ahead, Francisco was heading for the car, a runaway juggernaut. Brain locked too, Sykes thought. Got to try and change that.

"Don't worry about O'Neal. The guy's no moron. He's not gonna run to the nearest phone and ring up Harcourt and say, 'Hey Bill, a coupla cops were just here and I had to tell 'em where you took the junk but don't be sore at me, okay?' He'll be on the next plane south."

"I am not worried about O'Neal." Francisco's gaze did not deviate from the path that led out of the refining complex and back to the loading dock.

Sykes found himself having to run for a few yards, then falling back as he walked only to have to jog anew to keep up. "George, c'mon, take it easy. It's a beauty of a case. Don't sweat it. We got him by the short hairs. He ain't gonna make any more of this shit. Nobody is."

"The fifty kilos, Matthew," Francisco rumbled. "I have to find it. I can't let it get out on the street."

Sykes was confused. "What's the big goddamn deal? Even if the stuff's already being pushed it can't hurt too many people. There's no more supply if Harcourt and his bunch get put away. And they're going to, for a helluva long time. There's not enough stuff going out to get anybody serious hooked, especially if it's spread around. Hell, if I knew somebody was bringing in fifty kilos of coke paste but that it was the *last* coke paste in existence I'd escort him over the border myself just to get it over with. Are you listening to me, George? It's no big deal. When this batch of junk is gone, it's all gone."

They reached the loading dock. Francisco easily made the leap to the ground and headed for the car. Sykes had to scramble to follow.

"George, pay attention. You destroy the fifty kilos, you blow our whole case!" His partner was already sliding behind the wheel. Sykes rushed to put a restraining hand on the Newcomer's shoulder. It calmed him slightly.

"We've got to have some solid evidence besides O'Neal's word that Harcourt is involved. The stuff that gal at the Bureau dug out for us isn't enough. It's coincidental. Sure we can stop the operation, but we want Harcourt, remember? So we've got to have something linking him to the operation besides hearsay. Otherwise, we got no case. Don't blow the whole thing now by ignoring procedure."

Francisco leaned out the window as he shook off his partner's palm. "*Fuck* procedure."

And to Sykes's shock, he threw the slugmobile into gear and peeled off toward the exit.

"Hey!" Sykes stood inhaling exhaust and gaping at the receding vehicle.

The Newcomer accelerated as he approached the plant

Security kiosk. The guard stationed inside glanced up from his magazine. His eyes grew wide as he jumped out, waving his arms and yelling. Francisco ignored him. The slugmobile splintered the yellow-and-black wooden barricade.

Sykes was racing toward the gate, screaming at the top of his lungs. "GEORGE—GODDAMNIT!"

He slowed as he reached the shattered barrier. A few splinters were still settling to earth. No partner and now no car. He felt like a complete idiot.

The sound of an approaching engine turned him to his right, in time to see a battered pickup truck ambling toward him. Its driver, a lineman just going offshift, saw the obliterated barricade and slowed. As he did so Sykes jumped in front of him, waving his badge in the glare of the headlights. The pickup skidded to a halt inches from the detective's belly.

Sykes raced around to the driver's side, flashing his badge like a talisman. "Police business, emergency! Get out. I need this thing *now*." He grabbed the door handle and yanked. "Out!"

The bewildered occupant of the pickup bailed out, barely missing Sykes as the detective scrambled behind the wheel and threw the truck into drive. The transmission howled in protest. Years and miles and plenty of work lay behind it. It was no yuppiemobile and hardly intended for quick pursuit. Sykes cursed the lack of horsepower as he floored the accelerator and crawled slowly toward the gate.

# XII

Cassandra greeted the dealers at the door of the club. They surveyed the darkened interior uneasily, relaxing only slightly as they followed her swaying shape across the deserted dance floor. Two of the visitors were Newcomer, the third human.

She led them up the stairs to the office, opening the door for them and flashing her best professional smile. Only one of them bothered to acknowledge it. Intent as they were on the business before them, they were not the kind of individuals to allow themselves to be distracted by a pretty face.

When the last had entered she prepared to follow. A huge hand emerged from the darkness to grab her from behind. It covered her mouth completely. The other hand went around her waist. Wide-eyed and trying to scream, she found herself being hauled backward down the dark hallway.

Francisco dragged her to the back end. There he turned her around so she could see him while he pinned her against the wall, keeping his hand over her mouth. Only when she recognized her abductor did she cease struggling, slumping against the paint.

"I am here to take Harcourt," he whispered to her. "We have all the evidence we need to put him and his cronies away permanently. Where is he? I will find him eventually myself, so you have nothing to lose by cooperating with me, and may have much to gain."

She hesitated briefly, then nodded toward the office doorway. He slowly removed his hand from her mouth. "You'd hear him anyway. He's in there, with the others."

He looked to his left as he pulled his service revolver. "How do I know I can trust you?"

She shrugged tiredly. "Go and look for yourself."

"Not good enough. You show me."

She was suddenly scared. "Oh, no. Leave me out of it. They'll kill me."

The detective showed her the gun. "I came up behind you, silenced you, forced you to talk by pointing this at your head. No one will blame you."

She studied his face for a long moment, then nodded once and started back down the hall.

The introductions being performed in the office were perfunctory. Everyone in the room knew his neighbor by name, profession, or both. They had not gathered for small talk.

Everyone focused on the large black suitcase which Kipling set in the center of the conference table. The visitors eyed it curiously, wondering what it might contain. They'd come because of Harcourt and Harcourt's reputation and so far had been shown nothing. However, it was known that William Harcourt did not waste his time or that of others, so it could be presumed that the luggage sitting so prominently before them held something of interest as well as of value.

One of the Newcomer visitors spoke up, utilizing English for the benefit of his human colleague and also because he enjoyed showing off his diction.

"So what's the deal, Bill? Why drag us to this dump in the middle of the night?"

"I could explain, but it's all self-explanatory, so why waste the time?" Harcourt approached the table, Kipling flanking him closely. Quint had stationed himself in the shadows, just in case. Harcourt trusted the three he'd invited as much as he trusted anyone, which was to say not at all.

Track lighting illuminated the conference room, creating alternating pools of light and darkness. Harcourt now entered the beam which happened to be aimed at the suitcase. His fingers nudged the double combination locks, then flipped the twin latches. He opened it slowly, making his audience wait, heightening their curiosity. Despite their best attempts to appear indifferent, all three visitors found themselves staring at the black bag.

The track light shone directly down on fifty carefully arrayed one-kilo glass tubes, each resting in its individual padded slot. Each tube was filled to within a centimeter of its stopper with a deep blue gel.

Several small plastic containers lay in the bottom of the case, below the ranked tubes. Harcourt removed one of the glass cylinders and held it up to the light, eyeing it like a proud father studying his firstborn. The light shined through the translucent gel, sparkled off the lab-quality glassware. After a suitably theatrical pause he placed it back in the case, next to its siblings.

The eyes of the two Newcomer visitors had grown wide as they realized what the contents of the suitcase might be. Only their human colleague sat with a puzzled expression on his face, wondering what all the silent excitement was about.

"What is it?" he finally asked.

Harcourt smiled lazily. "A sweet indulgence from our past, resurrected for our future. A delight we thought had been lost to us forever, a simple pleasure once allowed us only on another's whim. Something for which we hungered daily and over which we now can exert control. Our own destiny in a test tube, if you will."

He observed the expressions on the faces of the two Newcomer dealers, knew what they were going through. They weren't strong enough to handle something like this. No one was strong enough except for him. That was why he had control. That was why he was the one in charge. That was why he would always be the one with the power.

He let them stare, let them drink as much as they could with their eyes, knowing that wouldn't be enough. When he thought they couldn't stand it any longer, he graciously spared them the indignity of having to ask. Removing one of the plastic dispensers from the case, he slid it across the table.

"Please feel free to sample the quality. The experience will be everything you remember it to be. So that there can be no doubt in your minds, I have gone to the expense of doubling the active ingredients in this particular dispenser. Therefore, a small amount will be sufficient to bring back memories, physical as well as mental. For those who are on top, only the best, yes?

"If anything, I believe this product to be of higher quality than what we were used to receiving prior to our journey, because it was produced by *us* and for us and not by the Masters. You would be surprised to learn, as they would themselves, of the skill of these humans at chemical engineering. Some of the ingredients are not readily available here, but that is only a matter of money. The necessary equipment is easily obtained and the manufacturing process surprisingly simple." He grinned by way of reminder.

"None of which matters unless one has access to the formula and concomitant methodology. That remains secure with me."

"If you're telling the truth, Harcourt. If you're telling *half* the truth . . ." The alien dealer nearest the dispenser picked it up and put it to his lips, squeezing out a tab of the blue gel. His companion tried not to display his anxiousness as he waited his turn, occupying the interval with conversation.

"Where'd you get it, Harcourt? The formula and the methodology?"

Harcourt reminisced. "I arranged to spend some time with three very resourceful people. I had made the necessary inquiries, forbidden of course, before we were placed in deepsleep, and sought them out subsequent to our arrival here. I did not expect anything to come of my inquiries, so you can imagine my surprise when my contacts suggested there might actually be one among the Travelers who had some knowledge of the supposedly forbidden formula. With a certain amount of coaxing, he was indeed able to reconstitute it for me.

"Mere access to the formula was not sufficient, of course.

Our touchdown on a world of comparative freedom and relative scientific sophistication was an unexpected bonus, as I did not have to try and steal equipment or improvise it from the ship's stores. But there was still a great deal of work to do. Funds had to be acquired according to this world's laws, and the team I was putting together had to be kept secret.

"I have worked very hard, gentlemen, and made something of a success of myself. I ingratiated myself to our hosts, whom I could naturally not ask for help in this matter (both Newcomer dealers chuckled knowingly) and achieved wealth and notoriety among them. They believe such things to be adequate ends unto themselves. They could not imagine I was doing all that I had done merely to achieve a means to a much greater end.

"My three associates worked well together. Unfortunately they are no longer with us, but I was lucky enough to reap the benefit of their endeavors."

No one inquired as to why Harcourt's three associates were no longer around. It would have been impolite.

By this time the first alien Dealer was swaying gently in his chair as he experienced the indescribable rush the drug produced. His companion took the dispenser and squeezed out a hit for himself. The rush swept through him even faster than it had his colleague. No fool, the human dealer grabbed the plastic container and blued his own tongue.

"Let me try some!" As soon as the taste reached the back of his mouth he spun to his left and spat. Only after he'd cleared his palate did he look disgustedly at Harcourt. "Jesus! This crap tastes like detergent."

Harcourt was grinning at the man's reaction. "And it will affect you about as strongly. It may even clean your mouth out—it has certain interesting side-effects—but there are mouthwashes available for human use at considerably less cost. Your physiology is not attuned to it."

The man was still spitting, wiped the the back of his mouth with the sleeve of his silk coat. "You can say that again."

"I am no chemist, though I have been forced by recent

developments to acquire some small knowledge of that branch of science. As I understand it, human physiology is so different from ours that there is no possibility of this having any effect, benign or detrimental, on any human being. Not even on a child. This will prove useful since humans are reluctant to interfere when their interests are not directly at stake. I have learned that much about human society. You are a very self-centered people.''

"As opposed to altruists like yourself, right, Harcourt?" The human dealer displayed a greater command of the language than Harcourt would have given him credit for.

"I am merely pointing out some of the advantages of the mutual enterprise in which I think you will desire to participate. When my fellow Newcomers learn they can obtain this drug, they will work very hard to make as much money as they can, to give it to *me*. If necessary, they will lower themselves to the kind of work which is to our particular advantage, much as do human addicts. This drug represents much more than money, my friend. It is power."

"You haven't told him all of it." The voice came from the shadows near the door that led to the adjoining office.

Harcourt crouched slightly as he reacted. Everyone else spun in the direction of the pronouncement. Caught off guard and resting, Quint jumped to his feet while Kipling's hand edged toward his shoulder holster.

A silhouette appeared in the door and resolved itself as it entered the room. Cassandra, with Francisco right behind her.

Quint had his gun out and was starting to take aim when his eyes widened as he caught sight of what the detective carried cradled in his right hand. The bundle was compact and familiar: the plastic explosive he'd intended to connect to the ignition wires of a certain human detective's automobile. The wires had been properly run from the explosive pack to the detonation switch, an uncomplicated pressure-release button. You squeezed it tight and when the ignition was turned, it let the switch bounce upward and . . .

Francisco held the switch depressed, his thumb heavy on the sensitive trigger.

"He's got the C-4 charge!" Quint yelled, incriminating himself while warning his companions. Kipling's hand hesitated and Harcourt lost the rest of his smile.

"What is a C-4 charge?" one of the Newcomer dealers inquired through the haze induced in his brain by the drug he'd just ingested.

"Human plastic explosive." Quint's eyes were locked on Francisco's right hand. "Primitive but impressive stuff. That's a real bomb he's carrying there. And the way he's got it set, if he moves his thumb it's gonna go off real easy."

The dealer started to rise. Francisco turned on him, holding out the charge. The Newcomer got the idea fast and sat back down.

Francisco was sweating profusely and the room rapidly filled with the odor of alien perspiration as the others joined him. He advanced by nudging Cassandra gently ahead, keeping her where he could see her. Despite what she'd already done for him, he didn't trust her. Right now he didn't trust anyone. He couldn't afford to.

Quint had slowly put his pistol away and was making reassuring motions with both hands. "Just take it easy, buddy. Nobody here's gonna do anything stupid. Keep your finger on that button and don't do nothin' squirrelly. Whatever you want, I'm sure we can talk about it, right?"

The detective nodded slightly. "Right. We'll talk."

Harcourt was watching the intruder, not the lethal device in his hand. It was the detective they had to disarm, not the bomb. The detective who had to be rendered harmless.

"If you release that button," he said as he gestured toward the depressed detonation switch, "you will not only kill us, but yourself as well."

"That's for sure." Francisco's expression was grim, his tone unwavering. "This will not merely demolish this room, it will level the entire floor of this building."

"No joke," the edgy Quint said confirmingly. "There's enough stuff there to bring the whole place down."

"That does not make any sense," Harcourt observed softly.

"No," Francisco shot back, "it makes perfect sense, since you're the only one who knows how to make the ss'jabroka. To finish you, and that," and he nodded in the direction of the open suitcase and its gleaming contents, "I would do it."

As he spoke he stared straight at the Newcomer entrepreneur, and Harcourt knew he wasn't bluffing.

"Everyone up against that wall." When Francisco gestured with the C-4 everyone moved. "Slowly." They rose from their chairs and walked in slow motion. Quint moved more slowly than anyone. "Except you."

Complying with the order, Harcourt halted behind the conference table. Her face alight with fear, Cassandra remained where she was, watching the others as they lined up against the wall. Kipling was having an especially tough time. His pistol hung heavy against his shoulder, within easy reach yet untouchable. He wanted to break the detective's face. Slowly. But the thumb depressing the trigger controlled them all. He glanced in the direction of his boss, saw that Harcourt was not giving any signals, and decided quite correctly that now was not the time for improvisation. Wait.

Trying to watch all of them at once, Francisco approached the table. He picked up the sample dispenser and tossed it back into the open suitcase. With his free hand he succeeded in closing the case and latching it tight.

Harcourt watched him silently, his emotions seething inside him. He experienced actual physical pain as he watched the detective pick up the suitcase on which so much effort had been lavished.

"One small matter seems to have escaped your attention, sir." Harcourt nodded at the luggage. "Just as it has escaped the attention of my friends here. What you hold in you hand is not listed on any human law books as a controlled substance. Legally it might as well be fifty kilos of grape jelly."

Francisco shook the suitcase and Harcourt stiffened as he heard the precious glass cylinders clinking inside.

"This? The ss'jabroka is a bonus, an extra. The charge against you, Harcourt, isn't dealing. It's murder and conspiracy to commit. Hubley, Porter, Strader, probably others. You got to the top too fast, Harcourt. You should have shown more patience, should not have been so ready to kill. Murder makes human police angry and persistent. I've learned what that means. It is an ethical thing with them. So they will not show you any compassion simply because you are a Newcomer who has murdered only other Newcomers. That's the wonderful thing about their system of justice. Once you join their society you find yourself subject to their laws even if you try to maintain your own. You have to live up to their standards even if they fail to themselves.''

For the first time a glimmer of concern showed behind Harcourt's icy blue eyes. Meanwhile Cassandra had joined the detective in staring hard at the Newcomer entrepreneur, but for a different reason. Francisco's diatribe had contained an unexpected shock.

''You—you killed Strader?'' With both hands full Francisco couldn't prevent her from rushing forward to grab Harcourt by his jacket. ''Where's Todd? Did you do something to Todd?''

Harcourt gazed down at her in irritation. ''Todd? Who is this Todd?'' Then he remembered, and smiled ever so slightly. ''Ah yes, Todd. The unfortunate Mr. Watson.''

Cassandra's eyes widened in horror as she made the obvious connections. Meanwhile Francisco had come around the table and was nudging Harcourt with the suitcase. Together they started for the door. Cassandra watched them for a moment, then darted to her left. With his attention focused on Harcourt and the detective, Quint didn't see her coming. She moved with a dancer's speed and assurance to snatch the .357 from his holster. She let out an unintelligible shriek as she aimed the pistol in Harcourt's direction.

Francisco let out a violent ''No!'' as he saw her intention and lunged for the weapon, striking it with the suitcase as she fired. The bullet slammed into the wall behind the flinching Harcourt.

It took only a couple of seconds, but that was all the time the waiting Kipling required. Striking with both hands, he grabbed the lead wires on the C-4 bomb and tore them free of the plastic. Quint shut his eyes and swallowed his heart, but nothing happened.

"Got it!" Kipling yelled triumphantly before throwing himself at Francisco. The two Newcomers crashed to the floor. Quint moved on Cassandra as she pointed the gun at Harcourt a second time, yanking the Magnum from her hand and slamming her across the side of her head. As she dropped to her knees he hit her a second time.

Francisco was fighting to get back on his feet. As he started to rise, Kipling hit him hard beneath the right arm, folding the detective instantly. Taking his time and savoring the experience, Harcourt's assistant then brought his knee up into the detective's face, blasting him backward. Breathing hard, he lifted him bodily and slammed him face-first into the wall, pinning him in place.

Harcourt was as calm as ever as he straightened his suit. "Kill them both."

Kipling looked uncertain. "Here?"

"Do it!" the entrepreneur said sharply. "If you try taking them somewhere they're liable to get away. Do it here, now. We'll worry about the cleanup later."

Stepping close and raising his gun, Quint placed the muzzle against the base of Cassandra's skull and squeezed the trigger. The explosion was loud in the enclosed office, but it didn't come from Quint's weapon. Cassandra flinched, then looked up in surprise as Harcourt's henchman staggered away from her.

Sykes stood in the doorway, the Casull smoking in his right fist.

Quint stumbled hard into the window overlooking the back alley and went through, propelled by the force of the heavy slug. After that everything happened very quickly.

Before Quint hit the ground outside, Kipling had shoved Francisco aside and drawn his own weapon. Sykes saw him just in time and dove for cover inside the adjoining office. Newcomer and human alike, the three visiting drug dealers tried to press themselves into the carpet. This was not their fight.

Harcourt grabbed the suitcase and made a dash for the

door that led to the office on the other side of the conference room. Kipling covered his retreat, firing rapidly and pinning Sykes down until the two Newcomers could escape to the hallway.

Still unsteady on his feet, Francisco rose and took off after Harcourt and Kipling.

"George, wait!" Francisco ignored him, as Sykes suspected he would. Until the drug had been recovered again the detective knew his partner was unlikely to listen to him or anyone else.

Straight-arming the Casull back into the conference room, he saw the three dealers slowly rising behind the table. They had their arms in the air and the expressions on their faces were sufficient for Sykes to write them off as potential threats.

"Don't shoot, man—we're unarmed—look!"

Sykes already had turned his attention to Cassandra. She was leaning against the conference table, supporting herself with one arm and holding the side of her head where Quint had socked her.

"You okay?"

"Yes—I think so."

Sykes left her to her own devices as he rushed out into the hall.

Harcourt was pounding down the fire escape, the dim light giving him no trouble. Kipling was right on his heels with Francisco barely ten feet behind and Sykes bringing up the rear. All of them could hear the approaching police sirens.

The first cruiser pulled up outside the club and disgorged two officers who sprinted for the back door, guns drawn. The car sat empty, its lights circling lazily in the night. The uniforms burst inside just as Harcourt and Kipling were abandoning the fire escape. Harcourt saw the idling cruiser and grinned. The luck that had sustained him ever since he'd regained consciousness on this world was still with him. He beckoned to his assistant.

"Here!" Kipling saw, and followed.

Throwing the suitcase into the back seat, Harcourt slid in

on the passenger side while Kipling climbed behind the wheel, put the car in gear, and thromped the accelerator, burning rubber as he pulled away from the curb.

Sykes saw them fleeing as he caught up to Francisco. The Casull shattered one taillight and put a couple of holes in the trunk, but his aim was too low. The car kept going.

"This way!" Francisco headed for the slugmobile.

This time Sykes made sure he reached the car first, got behind the wheel. Another police unit screamed past them as they pulled out of the club lot. A cursing Sykes scraped brick as he squeezed by.

They were maybe three-quarters of a block behind Harcourt. Not bad, Sykes thought with grim satisfaction, considering the head start their quarry had taken on them.

Kipling swerved wildly around a slow-moving car in the lane ahead, swearing in his own language. Staring through the rear window, Harcourt could see the slugmobile dogging their tail.

"They're right behind us. Lose them."

"I can't! There's too much traffic!" his assistant yelled.

"We can fix that." Harcourt was as composed as ever, though there was tension in his face. Leaning forward, the entrepreneur began flipping switches on the dash until he hit the right one. The siren wailed and the roof lights came to life. Harcourt leaned back and smiled contentedly as the traffic in front of them compliantly moved to the curbs, making Kipling's task much easier.

"You see?" he explained to his assistant. "All organized societies are the same. It is simply a matter of knowing which buttons to push."

"How did they find us?" Kipling spoke without taking his attention from the road and the rearview mirror.

"I do not know. When this is over I will find out, and that particular lesion in our enterprise will be excised."

Kipling looked over at his boss in astonishment. "You still believe we can go on with this?"

"Certainly!" Harcourt was feeling much better. They'd gained another quarter block on the pursuing vehicle. "We have the drug and the formula. We will find new means of distribution and a new base of operations. We can still work through one of the other human tribes where dealings of the type we intend are common. With the kind of money our initial sales will generate we will have enough power to do anything we want."

"But what about them?" Kipling indicated the rearview, where the slugmobile clung relentlessly. "What if we go to jail?"

"First they must catch us. If we can lose these two I can get out of the country for a while. I have escape routes planned for just such an eventuality. You will come with me. Everything else I can leave behind. Much of it will run itself in my absence, and human communications are good. I will be able to keep in touch and supervise.

"As for the legal aspects of our present small predicament, I have contacts in the community I can work through. I have studied some human law. Unless the humans can bring me to trial for specific crimes within a certain time, and present evidence, the case will be dropped. I have good human lawyers and excellent character references. Without the ss'jabroka to prove their claims and without witnesses to other incidents, their legal process will forget us. I can have the particular interfering officers retired or transferred somewhere where they will not trouble us further."

Kipling's thoughts were churning. Sometimes it was hard to keep up with his boss. Harcourt was always two steps ahead of everyone else, human as well as Newcomer.

"What about the murder charges, like that damn cop said?"

"Once we are in a place of safety I can make certain no one with any knowledge harmful to us is capable of informing on us. Don't worry about that. Such things are surprisingly simple to take care of. Silence one potential talker and it serves as a sufficient object lesson to any others.

"And remember that the formula is always safely with us because I carry it here." He tapped his forehead. "That is the key to everything. As long as the formula exists, its owner has power." His gaze rose to the rearview. "But we need time to reorganize. We must not be taken by these stupid police. They know too much, can make too many connections if we are taken into their custody. Once safely away I will see they are taken care of.''

''Won't eliminating them make their superiors suspicious?''

''Suspicions count for naught in a human court. You must be able to prove things. I will arrange it so that nothing can be proved.'' He smiled contentedly at his assistant. Yes, he was feeling much better now. ''Everything is going to work out in spite of this little setback.'

His confidence was contagious. Kipling found himself beginning to smile as he worked with the wheel. His boss was going to see to it that the two cops who'd caused all the trouble were eliminated. If everything worked out well, perhaps Harcourt would allow him to be a part of that.

Francisco focused on the oncoming traffic, patiently pointing out potential trouble spots to Sykes, letting his partner do the driving while scouting ahead for him as he'd been taught to do at Academy. No matter how close they came to another car or truck, the Newcomer's voice never changed. Cool, Sykes thought, then corrected himself. No, not cool. Relentless.

''Slow traffic coming up on the right,'' Francisco announced evenly. ''You're clear at the left rear. Careful, red light ahead, but you can make it.'' Sykes shot through the intersection, toying with the changing light and the squalling horns of oncoming drivers. ''Big rig at three o'clock.'' The sergeant made sure to avoid the eighteen-wheeler.

With his partner's help, Sykes diced his way through the cross-traffic without so much as scraping a single civilian paint job. It was easy to keep track of their quarry since they'd been thoughtful enough to turn on their siren and lights. The reason for doing so was clear, just as it was clear that Harcourt didn't realize running the siren would have done the job just as well without making himself half so visible. Sykes wasn't about to pick up the radio and inform the Newcomer of his mistake.

Kipling was having an easier time of it now that he believed they were running to something and not merely away from the pursuing cops. In the rearview he saw to his delight that the same traffic which had swung over to let the wailing police cruiser pass was edging back out into the street and making pursuit increasingly difficult. They were going to make it with ease, lose their pursuit and then abandon the police vehicle before others could join in the chase. After that Harcourt would see that they slipped safely out of the country. Harcourt was smarter than the humans. Harcourt was unstoppable. Kipling knew that swearing allegiance to the entrepreneur was the smartest move he'd ever made.

Sykes clung grimly to the wheel, using his horn frequently to clear a path through the converging, obstructing traffic ahead. Francisco continued to serve as copilot.

"Yellow light ahead turning red, oncoming traffic both directions." Sykes ignored the instructions this time and floored the accelerator. The police cruiser was getting too far ahead.

Francisco abruptly lost his cool. "Red light, *red light!*"

Sykes swung around the merging traffic and cut through the intersection to continue the chase. Oncoming cars let loose with their horns, scattering in all directions as the detective sliced across lanes and barriers. The slugmobile bashed across concrete dividers and kept going. Sykes patted the wheel. She was as tough as she was ugly.

The wild ride finally brought them parallel to the cruiser, but in the wrong lane. Sykes kept one hand on the wheel and drew the Casull with the other, bringing it up and around to ping through the passenger-side window. Francisco tried to shove himself into the back seat as Sykes fought to balance the huge pistol a few inches from the Newcomer's nose.

Kipling happened to glance to his left. His eyes widened at the sight of the huge bore bobbing in his direction.

That's when Francisco reacted to something he saw beyond the barrel of the gun. "Green light, Matthew." Sykes was fighting to steady the heavy weapon and didn't respond. *"Green light!"*

Finally Sykes glanced ahead, in time to see a row of

waiting cars leaving the intersection in front of them. None of which would have mattered if they hadn't been in the wrong lane.

"Shit!" Sykes locked up the brakes and fought the wheel, slewing the slugmobile sideways in front of the braking oncoming traffic. Kipling veered around one slow truck ambling through the intersection and accelerated westward.

There was no time to check maps. The side street directly ahead was the only course left open that didn't involve retreat. Sykes floored the gas and rocketed into the double alley. Garbage cans went flying, banging like ball bearings in a pinball machine off walls and pavement. Sacks of heavy-gauge plastic tore under the slugmobile's impact and showered the windshield with debris. Sykes cursed, turned the wipers on High, and kept going.

The slugmobile emerged into the next main street and wheeled to the west. At the first avenue, Sykes ripped back out into traffic.

"Anything?" he asked hopefully.

Francisco stared hard, straight ahead. "Nothing, Matt."

"Goddamnit! They must've turned up Washington." He started searching for a place to turn right.

"No, wait! There they are, two blocks ahead of us in front of that bus."

"Nice try, you bastards." Sykes leaned back in his seat. Moments later he was able to pull in close behind the fleeing police unit.

It immediately ascended an overpass. Two cars pulled in right behind it, cutting Sykes off. Pounding on the wheel in frustration, the detective sped along beneath the overpass until he saw the next onramp approaching.

Francisco saw it too. "Matthew, please don't do anything foolish. I have a wife and young child."

"Yeah. Cute, too." Sykes floored the pedal, sent the slugmobile racing up the onramp. Francisco shut his eyes as well as his mouth.

The car went flying over the edge, just missing the curve that led onto the freeway, and slammed back to the pavement only a few yards behind the police cruiser's bumper. Sykes apologized absently to his partner, who had been bounced off the slugmobile's roof, and concentrated on hanging tough.

The police unit hung a sharp right, cutting through a parking lot with the slugmobile in close pursuit. Following Harcourt's directions, Kipling turned right into the Second Street tunnel, clipping a sedan in passing. The driver of the oncoming car hit his brakes and sent his vehicle into a wild skid. Traffic piled up behind him.

Sykes screeched to a halt behind the congestion and leaned out his window, trying to make himself heard over the babble of angry horns and drivers.

"Forget it, move it! Move your goddamn cars!"

No one was paying any attention to him. Dazed drivers were climbing out of their vehicles, checking themselves for cuts and bruises, inspecting their cars while trying to decide which of their equally bewildered fellow drivers to exchange insurance numbers with. A swearing Sykes slid back behind the wheel and sent the slugmobile forward until he made contact with the rear bumper of the first car in front of him. The slugmobile's engine raced and the temperature gauge rose alarmingly as Sykes began to push the stalled coupe out of the way.

A young man saw what was going on, abandoned the woman he'd been arguing with, and rushed toward the slugmobile, waving both arms madly.

"Hey, man, that's real chrome! What the hell you think you're doing?"

"Sorry." Sykes spared him the briefest possible smile. "Police business." He rolled up his window and continued to push, ignoring the gesticulating driver who paced the slugmobile, pounding on the glass as he strove to get Sykes's attention.

He made room before the slugmobile's radiator blew, scraped paint and chrome as he accelerated up the tunnel.

Kipling took the police cruiser up the first freeway onramp. Harcourt had been gazing out the back window. Now he settled back into his seat.

"There now. That wasn't so difficult." He worked the dash controls that switched off the siren and lights. "No need for these any longer."

"I was beginning to worry," Kipling confessed.

"No need to. You do the driving and I will do the worrying for both of us." Harcourt reached into the back seat, picked up the suitcase, and put it on his lap. He indicated the speedometer. "They really had no chance of catching us. Even though this is an official vehicle, there is no need to draw attention to us. Reduce your velocity to the speed limit." Kipling nodded and promptly slowed down to sixty.

Sykes was picking his way through the freeway traffic like Andretti at Indianapolis, weaving around cars and pickups until his partner sat up straight and let out a shout.

"There! Straight ahead of us, in the slow lane!"

"Don't worry," Sykes told him. "I got 'em."

He eased off the accelerator. Francisco eyed him quizzically but said nothing, which was just as well because his partner wasn't in the mood to explain. The van on their right made an excellent blind. It was traveling slightly faster than the cruiser. Sykes watched the van, the traffic ahead and behind, the freeway itself. Calculating.

Offramp coming up soon. He'd have to time it just right because he knew Harcourt wouldn't give him a second chance. Sykes had begun to respect the Newcomer as much as he'd come to hate him.

*Now!* The slugmobile fell behind the van, changing lanes quickly. Sykes found himself parallel to the police unit. Kipling drove unconcernedly, convinced they'd lost their pursuers miles back in the Second Street tunnel. By the time he glanced to his left the slugmobile was turning hard right to slam into the cruiser's flank. Kipling struggled to correct, only to discover the maneuver had forced him onto the offramp immediately ahead.

Door to door, the two vehicles went squealing and slewing to the right. Kipling thumped the pedal and broke out in front with Sykes clinging determinedly to his back bumper. Both cars roared off the ramp and up onto the Vincent Thomas Bridge that crossed Long Beach Harbor.

Traffic was blessedly light. At eighty miles an hour Sykes had no time for sightseeing, but Francisco couldn't keep himself from gazing out the window and down at the inky bay they were traversing. Not all his thoughts were on their quarry. Humans built sturdy bridges, but they had been known to collapse. Then there was the matter of side barriers, which *looked* high and sturdy, but at the speed they were going . . .

He was immensely relieved when both cars thundered off the far end of the bridge and skidded out onto Henry Ford Boulevard.

The two-lane straightaway ran parallel to the sea. Sykes pushed the slugmobile to its limits as he pulled out one more time alongside the police unit. His car still hadn't recovered from bulldozing a path through the pileup back in the tunnel and the temp gauge continued to flirt with the red zone. Sykes knew he could hang on for as long as it was going to take. He wasn't as confident about his vehicle. The engine sounded lousy, but at ninety miles per he kept slamming into the side of the fleeing police cruiser.

Kipling finally got the idea, realized he could push as well as take. He raked over the front of the slugmobile, turning its nose slightly. Metal screamed. Sykes found himself speeding along the dangerous dirt shoulder and was forced to drop back. Rolling himself wouldn't catch their quarry.

Kipling grinned into the rearview mirror as he pulled far out in front, turned back to the road barely in time to see the barrier ahead coming up fast in the cruiser's headlights. Harcourt was bellowing at him as he slammed on the brakes.

A chain-link fence marked the end of the road. Kipling had halted maybe a couple of yards in front of the barrier. On the other side of the fence, pavement led to ocean and an abandoned drawbridge. Except for the bridge, all was dark water. He found himself sweating. If he hadn't turned in time, hadn't stopped before crashing through . . .

"Turn it around, turn us around!" Harcourt was yelling at

him. Startled, he spun the wheel and headed back the way they'd come.

To find the slugmobile heading straight for them. At the last possible instant, ignorant as he was of Newcomer attitudes toward suicide, Sykes yanked the wheel over and sent the car sliding sideways. The passenger side rammed into the police unit, the nose of the black-and-white smashing into the rear door of the slugmobile. Locked in a twisted metallic embrace, both cars did a pair of screeching pirouettes before coming to a stop. Fire erupted beneath the hood of the cruiser.

Though he'd braced himself for the impact, Sykes was still stunned. Disoriented but aware, the first thing he saw when he looked up was the unconscious Francisco. The Newcomer was bleeding from a gash across his forehead. Sykes leaned over. The head wound was messy but not serious. There was more blood than damage.

Then he noticed the blaze flaring merrily beneath the hood of the other vehicle. Its front end was locked into the slugmobile's rear seat and trunk. Near the gas tank.

Sykes wrestled with his seat harness until he freed himself, then stumbled outside and around the front of the car. Dragging the door on the passenger side open, he grabbed two handfuls of Francisco and hauled him out of the ruined vehicle.

As he was struggling with his partner's bulk he saw Harcourt squeezing himself through the police cruiser's broken windshield. Bruised, bleeding, and no longer confident, the Newcomer entrepreneur reached back inside to extract the priceless suitcase. He jumped to the pavement and started running.

Sykes forced himself to keep dragging Francisco until he was certain he'd removed his partner to a safe distance. Then he drew the Casull and put his legs in gear as he headed off in pursuit of Harcourt. With each stride he could feel himself loosening up, felt the pain of the collision fading from his muscles.

How fast could a Newcomer run? They were big but not particularly quick, but how did they hold up over the long haul? Maybe he should have paid more attention to the Newcomer section of the sports pages.

He reminded himself that this race wouldn't go to the swiftest. Don't sprint, he told himself. Keep it steady, keep it even, and he'd have Harcourt under the gun in a few minutes.

The Newcomer wasn't far ahead. Harcourt was older than Kipling and he looked tired. Once he stumbled and Sykes found himself grinning. They were big, but they had their own weaknesses.

Harcourt reached the chain-link fence at the end of the road, heaved the suitcase over the top, and started climbing. The drawbridge loomed ahead. He wasn't climbing too well, either. The crash had obviously affected him.

Sykes lumbered past the burning police cruiser. A glance in its direction showed Kipling still behind the wheel, his head slumped forward on the dented plastic. The detective was ten yards beyond when both gas tanks went, one after the other. Hoods, door panels, engine parts, and glass went flying in every direction. So did Kipling.

Sykes felt something hot and hard strike his back. He didn't slow down to check it out or even to feel if his coat might be on fire. It was a chilly evening. A small blaze would be welcome.

As for Kipling, Sykes was warmed by the knowledge that he'd been able to spare the taxpayer one more court cost. But Kipling was nothing; a loose screw, a cog in the wheel. The wheel himself was up ahead, fighting to clear the top of a ten-foot-tall fence.

Harcourt fell to the pavement on the other side, struggled to his feet, and recovered the suitcase. He stumbled toward the dark silhouette of the drawbridge. With great satisfaction the detective observed that the Newcomer was now limping.

Reaching the fence, he paused briefly to aim the Casull with both hands, blowing the lock to scrap. A single kick opened the gate.

The bridge's roadbed hung frozen in the open position, a massive dark slab of steel and asphalt stabbing the night sky. Harcourt ran through alternating pools of moonlight and shadow as he approached the towering structure. Black seawater drifted past him. He ignored it as he concentrated on the way ahead, the only path remaining open to him. Once, his foot slipped and he almost went over the edge. He was panting hard now.

Sykes pounded along close behind, trying to regulate his breathing the way he'd learned on the street. If the other guy doesn't have a car waiting or a ready hole to bolt into, you take your time and wear him down. Don't kill yourself trying to catch up to him. Wait until he collapses from exhaustion. Then you pick him up and read him his rights.

A pity Miranda had been extended to cover Newcomers. The Casull weighed heavily in his fist.

Harcourt finally ran out of protective shadows near the beginning of the bridge. He turned a slow circle, his gaze intent on his surroundings, but there was nowhere else to run. The leap from the crest of the drawbridge to the other side was too much for any Newcomer, even had he been able to negotiate the steep climb to the top. There was ocean on both sides, and the relentless human detective hardly a few strides behind. He might conceal himself for a minute or two and then make a dash back to the main roadway, but his leg was hurting and the human appeared intact.

Though it was too late, he now realized how badly he'd underestimated the seemingly ignorant, foul-mouthed, poorly educated cop. Not that he wasn't ignorant, foul-mouthed, and poorly educated, but he knew his job. Harcourt realized he would have no chance to flee back to the road. The man would hunt him down, checking each hiding place until he had Harcourt cornered. If by some miracle he managed to elude the detective momentarily, there was still the matter of the enormous handgun the man was carrying. Even with a limp he might outrun the tired human, but he could not outrun a steel slug.

It was intolerable.

A great calm came over him. When there is nothing else left, you do the last thing. Flipping the double latches on the suitcase, he slowly opened it to reveal the precious contents. Tube after gleaming glass tube, each brimming with blue ecstasy. The culmination of a lifetime's dreams, of endless hard work and planning. All worthless now. Worthless, but not useless.

Sykes slowed as he neared the buildings. Several minutes had passed since he'd last seen Harcourt, and there were places here where even an outsized Newcomer could conceal himself. He wasn't as worried about Harcourt as he'd been about his bodyguard Kipling, but the entrepreneur was still an alien: big, strong, and desperate.

Something moved in the darkness on his right and he brought the Casull to bear on it. It moved again—and flew away. A nesting gull, disturbed by all the activity. Taking a deep breath, he walked on, his finger tense on the Casull's trigger as he studied the night.

More movement, there to his left. Up came the big gun again. Despite the chill he found he was perspiring, and not just from exhaustion. He found himself wishing for the backup that wasn't there.

"Come on out, Harcourt," he said tensely. "It's all history. Kipling's dead, your people are scattered, and we found your lab. You're history, too." A drop of sweat stung his eye. He ignored it.

No reaction from the shadows, and then Harcourt stepped into the moonlight. His expression was composed, relaxed. The smile was back on his face, the glint of superiority in his eye. He held his hands out from his sides, palms facing upward, in a gesture of surrender.

Sykes advanced cautiously. Harcourt stared back at him, unmoving, reading the conflict in the detective's face. He wanted Harcourt to try for the gun, to run, to give him an excuse. How disappointed he must be at my compliance, Harcourt thought amusedly.

"Here I am, Officer. As you can see, I am unarmed."

"Yeah, I can see. Move a finger, Harcourt, and you're history for sure. Tug— I wish he was here, wish he was the one holding this. But he ain't, so I'll have to do."

"Each of us does what we have to do, Sergeant. But you are wrong. History is not involved here. Eternity is."

Sykes's eyes fell as he saw what Harcourt had been carrying concealed in the crook of one arm: one of the kilo-size cylinders of the blue drug. Ss'jabroka. The glass gleamed in the moonlight. As he looked on, the still grinning entrepreneur quickly lifted the tube to his mouth and swallowed. A full kilo of pure concentrate poured down his throat, dribbling like runaway jello down his chin as his mouth filled to overflowing. He chugalugged the tube's contents before Sykes could react.

Tossing the empty cylinder aside, he gazed defiantly back at the detective. It hit within seconds. His face contorted in agony as his whole body convulsed from the effects of the massive overdose. A gaping Sykes lowered the muzzle of the Casull and stared as the Newcomer collapsed on the ground, his body in the grasp of a massive, violent seizure. Limbs hammered against the earth and his back arched spasmodically.

It took all of ten seconds, maybe twelve. Then Harcourt lay still.

It took Sykes longer than that to recover enough to move. Still holding firmly to the Casull, he slowly approached the motionless form and took its pulse the way he'd watched his partner do it. There was nothing. No indication of life whatsoever.

The gun dangling heavy and cold in his fingers, Sykes rose. Espying the suitcase lying nearby, he latched it shut and hefted it in his free hand. Then he turned back to the still blazing cars.

Francisco lay where his partner had left him. Sykes picked up his pace a little as he came within sight of the prone detective. His mind was still full of what he'd just seen, so it wasn't surprising that he failed to notice that the door on the driver's side of the police cruiser was standing open.

The weight hit him hard and heavy, knocking him down. The suitcase went flying and the Casull skittered noisily across the pavement. Sykes rolled, found himself staring up at the singed, badly burned and still bleeding nightmare shape of Kipling. As the Newcomer reached for the suitcase, Sykes heard the sound again, a sound as distinctive as the tarnished silvery bracelet the Newcomer wore. The sound of Bill Tuggle's killer.

He'd hit the ground hard, bouncing his head, and though he struggled hard he was unable to stand. Nothing from his eyes to his toes was working right. Kipling raised the heavy case preparatory to bringing it down on the detective's skull.

Somewhere in the distance a gun roared. A huge hole appeared in Kipling's chest. He stood tottering over Sykes's prone form, the suitcase held high overhead. The detective rolled to his right, saw Francisco sitting up and holding the smoking Casull in his right hand as he tried to steady himself with the other.

Kipling came on again, wielding the suitcase like a club. Francisco fired a second time, kept firing until he'd emptied the cylinder. The fusillade drove Kipling backward, back into the molten inferno that had once been two vehicles.

Rising painfully, Sykes stumbled to his partner's side. Francisco let the weight of the handgun carry his hand back to the ground as the sergeant knelt beside him. Gently he took the hot Casull from the thick, alien fingers.

They stayed like that, resting together, ignoring the crackling, stinking blaze behind them as sirens began to wail against the night.

# XIII

After the first cruiser arrived to check out the reports of a fire, things moved quickly. Sykes got on the radio and exhaustedly ran through the events of the evening, leaving out only what he thought was unnecessary. Ordinarily he would have been full of piss and vinegar, swearing at the dispatcher, boasting of his own accomplishments, cursing the entire department for not moving fast enough to help and for not reading his mind. But not this time. Not tonight. He was too tired, and still stunned from what he'd witnessed.

The mop-up was winding down. The blazing cars had long since been doused and the fire department people were rewinding their hoses and washing up. Cop cars formed a black and white halo around the scene of destruction. The coroner's wagon had parked close by. Two techs were studying Kipling's remains, marveling at the size of the holes Sykes's nonregulation pistol had put in the Newcomer body. Radios crackled, disembodied voices speaking to the living across miles of metropolis.

Having completed their preliminary reports and concluded their interviews, the two detectives were finally left alone. They sat side by side on a curb, staring out at the harbor. A ship was heading slowly to Somewhere Else, its lights moving at right angles to the horizon like computerized fireflies.

Francisco held his knees up close to his chin, his fingers locked. Now he turned to regard his partner.

"With Harcourt and Kipling dead and this business concluded to your satisfaction, I would assume you will be requesting reassignment now. You've obtained what you wanted."

"It'd be for your own good," Sykes mumbled without meeting the Newcomer's eyes. "I'm not just shitting you. I mean it. I think you'd be better off with a partner who's a little more," and he couldn't keep himself from smiling, "by the book. In tune with procedure. Like you said, you've got a wife and kids. You're the first Newcomer detective. With luck you might become the first Newcomer lieutenant, maybe even captain someday. You'll never do that hangin' around with me. I'm strictly street, George. I break too many rules, step on too many toes. You, you're not the toe-steppin' type."

"You could find yourself in line for a promotion out of this as well, Matthew," his partner reminded him.

Sykes shook his head. "Administration doesn't appeal to me. You know, I never really wanted to make Lieutenant. Got to kiss too many boots, get dressed up and go to the right kinds of places. Functions like where we first ran into Harcourt. That means dealing with and being nice to people like Harcourt. That's not my style. I'm a duty cop, George, even if somebody did lose his mind and make me a detective. That's what I do. I like doing it.

"You, you're admin material. You give good speeches. I don't talk so good. And you sure dress a helluva lot better than me."

"My wife," he declared with a shrug. "I can get by."

"You sure can. I gotta tell you, George, for a quiet guy, you're sure hell on wheels when you make up your mind to get goin'. I'd kinda hate to miss your *next* two days as a detective."

The Newcomer smiled, glancing up as red and blue lights approached. Sykes recognized the uniform who was driving, a solid uniform named Whiltey. He rolled down his window and leaned out.

"You guys want, I'll give you a lift back to the station. They're waiting there to take your statements on the shootings."

"We've already done that," Sykes told him.

Whiltey shook his head and looked apologetic. "You know the routine. Where shootings are involved, all field reports have to be followed by formal debriefings. You're gonna have to go through it all again, Sykes." His eyes shifted uncertainly to Francisco. "You too."

"I am aware of the procedure," the Newcomer informed him blandly. "I thought we might have some time to rest."

"Don't look like it. Hop in."

Sykes started to rise. "Let's go, partner." He looked back at Whiltey. "Oh, and it's shooting. Singular."

The cop frowned. "They said there were two."

Sykes was shaking his head as he started around the front of the patrol car. "Nope. I guess some joe just assumed. I didn't shoot Harcourt. He OD'd."

Since he was walking ahead of his partner, Sykes didn't see the look that came over Francisco's face.

The coroner's wagon was jouncing along the side road, the driver in no hurry to make it to the freeway. Why rush? Their stiff passengers never went anywhere and nobody was getting paid by the hour. So they took their time. To keep from bruising the bodies, the official reports always insisted. Made the work of trying to tell which bruises were induced by blunt objects and which by the long ride in the wagon much easier.

The driver handled the wheel with one hand. His assistant leaned against the door and gazed at the dark street in front of them. He was looking forward to the relaxing drive back to the morgue. Night duty was a delight. Oh, it played hell with your social life, but anything was worth not having to fight L.A. traffic during the day.

"So it's just me and her left in the hot tub, right?" the driver was saying as he cruised through a green light.

"You and the blonde?" the other man asked.

"No, man, the redhead." The driver kept his attention on the road ahead. "The blonde's in the house with some other guy. But a few minutes later she comes back alone, when me and the redhead are going at it fast and furious in the tub, ya know? And she sees us, and she climbs right in with us.''

The assistant made a face. ''You're full of shit.''

An expression of outraged innocence came over the driver's face. ''I swear it! If I'm lyin', I'm dyin'.''

The argument kept them too busy to see the hand that ripped through the tough material of the body bag secured in the back of the wagon. The hand was not human.

It was not even Newcomer.

Francisco rode up front with Whiltey. Sykes sat on the edge of the rear seat as he nervously scanned the road ahead. His partner was trying to look every direction at once, wishing for eyes in the sides of his head. His stomach was twisting itself slowly around an invisible steel bar.

''You are certain this is the route they would have taken?''

Whiltey frowned. ''I ain't positive. Sometimes those meat wagon guys do funny things. I wouldn't want 'em truckin' my corpus around. They might've stopped off for a quickie somewhere, or a burger, or to see somebody's mother, without reporting it in. But if I were drivin' and heading straight for the morgue, this is the way I'd go.''

Sykes couldn't stand it anymore. ''What's this all about, George? I know that look.''

Francisco started to reply, instead spotted something out his window and began gesturing wildly. His usual calm had deserted him. ''There! Go back. Down that side street.''

Whiltey obediently braked, backed up, and made a left turn. There was little enough traffic on the main drag, but down here by the docks it was utterly deserted this time of night.

Deserted, but not empty. They found the coroner's wagon halted in the middle of the intersection. Headlights and roof lights were still on, cutting through the blackness. The back doors stood ajar. There was also a patrol car, parked on the other side of the wagon. Sykes searched for signs of life, found none.

Whiltey approached the eerie scene slowly. The wagon

and car looked like abandoned props from a film waiting for cast and crew to return and bring them back to life. His eyes were as big as saucers as he reached for the radio mike. A huge hand quickly covered the pickup.

"No!" Both Sykes and the uniform gaped at Francisco. From the looks on their faces he knew more than action was required. "We must do this alone."

"Do *what*?" Sykes was at the end of his always short mental rope. One minute they were taking it easy preparing to head back to the station, then George was going crazy, insisting they take off in mad pursuit of the coroner's wagon. What the hell was going on, anyway?

When asked, Francisco responded by exiting the patrol car. Sykes and Whiltey had little choice but to follow. Not if they wanted answers.

They reached the van. Sykes took a flashlight from Whiltey and shined it through the open back doors. They had not been opened in the manufacturer's approved fashion. Both were bent outward, smashed half off their hinges.

He played the light around the interior until it came to rest on the split body bag. The rotating blue and red lights atop the deserted patrol car filled the wagon with garish carnival colors.

Francisco took one look and sprinted for the patrol car. There was no sign of the occupants. One door had been torn off and lay like a dead scallop in the middle of the street. The front windshield was completely gone, smashed in, pulverized. Shattered glass filled the front seat.

It was Whiltey who reached the other side of the car first. "Oh, God . . ."

The two detectives joined him, saw what had brought their companion officer up short. The bodies of the coroner wagon driver and his assistant lay stretched out on the asphalt, battered and crushed. Twisted and bent like mistreated children's toys, the two uniforms who'd arrived in the freeway cruiser lay in a heap not far away.

Whiltey held a hand to his mouth as he backed away from the corpses.

"That's it. I'm calling for backup, now."

Francisco took a step toward him. "Whiltey, *no*."

The cop wasn't in the mood to listen to anyone, much less a Newcomer. Trying to follow, the detective found himself caught and spun around by an angry and frustrated Sykes.

"Okay, George, I've had enough. I want an explanation." He nodded tersely in the direction of the four bodies. "You've got an idea what happened here, I want to know what you know. What is this, George? What the hell's going on here?"

Francisco licked his lips, his attention on the far end of the avenue where warehouses marked the boundary between docks and street. He kept his voice low so Whiltey wouldn't hear, though given his current state of mind it was doubtful the duty cop could concentrate on anything except the image of the four executed men lying on the pavement nearby.

"It's Harcourt."

Sykes made a face. "Harcourt is dead."

"No, he's not."

Sykes had prepared himself for any of several replies. That wasn't one of them. "George, what the hell do you mean he's not dead? I checked him myself. Cold, no pulse, nada. If that ain't dead, then what is?"

Francisco tried to explain. "If he overdosed on ss'jabroka as you describe, then he did not die. Small quantities of the drug generate great pleasure. An overdose can induce violent seizures which sometimes result in death from double heart failure and so forth. But when ingested, an amount on the order you describe does something entirely different to us. Sufficiently massive amounts can trigger a—a change. Do you have any idea what a physiocatalytic enzyme can do?"

"No. Should I?"

"I suppose not, since insofar as I am aware there are no human analogs. It involves the hidden nature of the drug. Your body functions seize up, the hearts stop, and you appear to be dead, but it's really a state of incubation. The enzyme affects the entire system. Our cellular structure is far more malleable than yours. It has to do with the way we were engineered to cope with dangerous environments.'' He gestured down at himself.

''This is the preferred mode, both for ourselves and for those we once served. But they designed us very carefully, so that in a last-chance case, on a world more hostile than anyone could imagine, we would still have a chance to survive with the aid of the drug-enzyme. We would be capable of little else but survival. As I said, the enzyme was to be employed only as a last resort.

''After you ingest that much of the drug you lie very still for a short time until the metamorphosis is complete. When you recover you're . . .''

Sykes was staring at the four bodies sprawled on the pavement. ''Tell me about it.'' He took a deep breath. ''So what do you want to do, once you've been metamorphosed or incubated or microwaved or whatever the hell it is that happens to you? What would Harcourt do?''

Francisco was studying the silent warehouses. ''He would not run far. It is much too soon, *after*. The process of internal change takes days to solidify. Other changes require rest in order to strengthen properly, much as a newly emerged butterfly needs time to exercise its wings before it tries to fly. He must wait for the process to finish. Then . . .'' He glanced back toward the patrol car. ''We must explain some of this to this man Whiltey.''

Sykes looked in the direction of the idling cruiser. ''I'll leave that to you. I ain't sure I understand it all myself.''

''Very well. Afterward we must do what we can.''

Whiltey didn't take the explanation very well, but the four bodies in the street lent emphasis to Francisco's vague commentary. The cop had questions, decided to ask them later. They had no trouble convincing him to drive the car. He was glad of the protection it offered.

With Whiltey manipulating the door-mounted spotlight, the three of them started toward the warehouse complex. As the uniform played the intense light over buildings and shadows, Sykes and Francisco walked alongside the slowly coasting car. Guns drawn and ready, their eyes flicked over every alcove, every possible hiding place. Only the Newcomer knew what they were really searching for. His companions, he reflected, were the fortunate ones. Sometimes a little ignorance is a good thing.

Sykes kept his voice down as he talked across the hood of the cruiser. "I never thought I'd say this, but for once in my life I think I'm willing to wait for backup. You sure we're goin' about this the best way, George?" The image of the four dead men lying on the pavement behind them was still fresh in his mind, not to mention the bent and torn back doors of the coroner's wagon.

"We can't let him get away," Francisco muttered from the other side of the slowly advancing patrol car.

Sykes squinted across at his partner. "Why the hell are you so dead set against having backup?"

It was a while before the Newcomer replied. "Because—because of what might happen if humans see what we are capable of becoming."

"But there's no more drug, and Harcourt's the only one who knows the formula. You don't have to worry about that. You know he'd never entrust it to anybody else. Maybe his boy Kipling, but that boy's dead for real."

"*You* understand that, Matthew. But how many others will? How much sympathy can we expect if this becomes widespread knowledge?" He stared hard at his partner. "How much sympathy would *you* have had if you'd learned all this by reading about it in a newspaper a few weeks ago?"

Sykes started to reply, shut his mouth as he found himself thinking realistic but unflattering thoughts. Just then Whiltey detected movement cutting the far end of his spotlight beam some fifty yards in front of them. Whatever it was ducked through an open warehouse door.

"There he is!" the cop shouted excitedly. "We got him!" Before either of the detectives could stop him he floored the accelerator and kicked the patrol car toward the target. Sykes and Francisco stood stunned and abandoned in his wake.

"Whiltey!" Francisco howled. He and Sykes took off in pursuit.

The cop sent the cruiser screeching to the left, barreled through the gaping warehouse doorway. Both detectives came running after. They reached the portal in time to hear the car's brakes locking up somewhere deep inside the cavernous structure.

They finally caught up to it at the far end of the building. It was idling softly and kicking out fumes. There was no sign of its driver. Slowing cautiously, the two detectives edged around to the front of the vehicle. Liquid was dripping from the front bumper. It was too thick to be coming from a punctured radiator.

Whiltey's severed head sat on the front of the car, a grotesque and unexpected hood ornament. Sykes was relieved the eyes were closed. The body lay in a heap beneath the bumper.

Both men spun, their eyes hunting the shadows for the source of the cop's quick death. Sykes found himself wondering what sort of thing could have managed such a quick decapitation. He was shaking inside.

The old building creaked and groaned as intermittent wind assaulted it from off the harbor. Water dripped from ill-maintained and rusty pipes. Two hallways led away from the central parking area where the car and its gruesome burden sat. Neither corridor was well lit.

Francisco searched the patrol cruiser until he found the standard-issue riot gun, began grabbing shells from their box. He was loading while Sykes checked the Casull. They exchanged a last, silent look of understanding before they split up. Sykes took the path to the left, Francisco hurried off silently up the other corridor.

Turning the first corner, Sykes froze at the sound of a voice. Several voices, unexpectedly amused. He eased forward around an open doorway and found himself staring at an unoccupied table and chair. The mini-television on the table was tuned to some late-night talk show. Sharing the tabletop with the TV was a Thermos, a steaming cup of coffee, and a half-eaten Twinkie.

Night watchman or guard's duty station, he told himself. Hanging on the chair was a jacket with the word SECURI-

TY stenciled across the back. Its owner was nowhere to be seen.

Sykes entered the room carefully, glad of the bright overhead light but uneasy at the silence. A quick inspection turned up nothing. He resumed his hike up the corridor.

The purpose of the building stood revealed in the next room, which was far larger than the guard's office. Fish nets of every size hung from the ceiling, blocking his path as they dried in the cool night air. Trying to keep the Casull in front of him at all times, he began pushing his way through. He couldn't see the far side of the drying room. It was like a House of Mirrors at an old-time amusement park, only without any reflections. He had only one hand to pull at the nets with since he didn't dare risk entangling his gun.

He wasn't expecting the face when it leaped out at him.

Stumbling backward, he let out a cry and found himself caught in the nets. The gun whipped around wildly as he tried to bring it to bear—on the eyes of an old wooden figurehead lifted from God only knew what worn-out sailing ship eighty years or more ago. It was worm-eaten and decaying but still of value to someone.

Sykes cursed nonstop as he extricated himself, wishing that someday he might meet the owner of the paralyzing sculpture in a dark alley. His heart was pounding against his chest. That was okay. Much better than the alternative. He resumed his advance, forcing himself to move each net aside before continuing forward.

Having cleared the net-drying chamber, he found himself in an empty storage room. An intersecting hallway lay beyond. As he headed toward the junction, a faint clinking sound caught his attention. He paused to listen before turning toward the sound.

It was a double strand of heavy ship's chain, rattling in the wind. With a sigh he reached out to steady the metal. Then it occurred to him that the links were awfully heavy to have been moved by a stiff breeze. The alternative was that something else had set them in motion. Backing away from the chain, he tightened his grip on the Casull.

Something else in the room with him. He felt it, street-smart senses in high gear now, internal alarms blaring. His nostrils flared though he smelled nothing. His ears were cold though he heard nothing. He whirled, and saw nothing.

But he could *feel* it.

He spun a second time, and there it was, stepping out of the shadows behind him. Harcourt. No, not Harcourt. What had once been Harcourt but was now Something Else. He was breathing hard and fast, mesmerized by what he was seeing. Thank God for the solidity of the Casull.

Harcourt still, but transformed. Altered, changed—how had Francisco described it? Metamorphosed. Bigger and more powerful, the skin scaly and hard, neck muscles corded, skull swollen, eyes sunken and burning—but still William Harcourt. The intelligence still shone behind the altered eyes, but it was a different kind of intelligence, no longer concerned with the subtleties of civilized behavior, no longer interested in anything except surviving, at any cost.

His next question was answered. The creature was still capable of speech. Somewhere deep inside the monstrosity sounded the voice of William Harcourt.

"Looking for me, Sergeant? Well, now you've found me. What do you think?" Massive, muscular arms stretched lazily toward the ceiling. "This is on your head, you know. You forced me to take this step. I didn't want to. There are consequences as well as compensations. The last resort. You forced it on me. The fault is yours."

Sykes didn't even try to respond. He stumbled backward as he fired, nearly losing his balance and going head over heels. The report of the Casull was thunderous in the enclosed room. The heavy slug caught Harcourt in the right shoulder, twisting him around.

It took him only a moment to recover from the impact. To his horror, Sykes saw that while the disheveled and torn shirt was shredded and powder-burned, the bullet had failed to pierce Harcourt's transformed, armored hide. Grinning to display razor-sharp fangs, the Newcomer started toward the wide-eyed detective.

Scared shitless and unashamed to admit it, Sykes

backpedaled fast, firing until the Casull clicked empty. One shot missed completely, exploding a crate close to Harcourt's head. The other four caught him full on. Each slug made him jerk reflexively. None penetrated. They slowed Harcourt up but they didn't come close to stopping him.

Sykes turned to flee and the Newcomer pounced on him, moving with preternatural speed. One hand grabbed the detective's gun hand and pulled. Sykes screamed as his shoulder was dislocated and the pistol fell out of his trembling fingers.

Picking him up with one hand, Harcourt carried him to the edge of a stairwell and contemptuously tossed him forward. Sykes hit the stairs halfway down, rolled the rest of the way. The pain in his shoulder nearly rendered him unconscious.

At the bottom he somehow struggled erect, turned to flee. The thing that Harcourt had become simply vaulted the rail and dropped the last fifteen feet to the ground, cutting off the detective's retreat. Sykes still tried to break free, but a clawed hand grabbed him by the shoulder. He felt himself being propelled through a back door, toward the docks.

Out front, Whiltey's legacy took the shape of two black-and-whites. They pulled up next to the coroner's wagon as other units, sirens wailing, arrived one at a time. Their occupants rushed the warehouses.

Sykes heard the sirens. Exerting all that remained of his strength, he managed to slip Harcourt's grasp and went stumbling along the edge of the dock. The Newcomer followed, in no hurry.

The fishing boat was old. Nets trailed behind it as it cleared the jetty at a knot or two. Sykes spotted it and broke into a dazed run. Still in no rush but increasing his pace slightly, Harcourt followed.

Francisco emerged at the top of the stairs, hunting frantically for some sign of his partner. He'd heard the Casull roar and had followed the echoes to this spot, picking his way as best he could through the mazelike warehouse. Now he saw the two figures making their way along the concrete path atop the harbor jetty. Sykes was in front, making the best speed he could. Harcourt was right behind and closing fast.

With an apprehensive glance at the dark water, Francisco started down the nearest stairs.

Sykes felt his legs going. His dislocated shoulder was throbbing painfully. By the time he reached the end of the jetty the fishing boat had just cleared the point. He was out of room by a few feet. With no other choice left to him he leaped, pushing off on his right leg the way he'd been taught to do in high school. He'd always hated that coach. Now he could have kissed him.

He didn't gain much altitude, but the end of the jetty was higher than the stern of the boat. It made the difference.

He landed hard on a coil of net in the back of the craft, yelling in pain as his ankle twisted beneath him. But he'd made it. The boat continued out to sea, out to safety. He lay on the stinking ropes, clutching his shoulder and breathing raggedly.

Harcourt had delayed a moment too long, had once more been a bit too overconfident. By the time he reached the spot where Sykes had taken off, the boat had traveled beyond even his jumping range. But there was a fishing platform next to the jetty, and another longer jetty protruding from it into the water. He grinned, fangs shining in the moonlight. What was it humans said? A hop, a skip, and a jump?

He made the leap to the platform without straining, raced down the next jetty. The boat was rounding the far point, farther than any human could have jumped, but Harcourt knew he could make the distance. He felt no pity for the poor, dumb human cop who doubtless thought he'd made it to safety. In his new form Harcourt felt no pity for anything.

Sykes saw the massive shape land high up on the boat near the central cabin. Nowhere else to run to now. The little craft continued chugging up the access channel toward the open sea, leaving the harbor behind.

Francisco reached the end of the first jetty, breathing hard. He'd seen it all. A bright light made him blink and he found himself squinting up into the intense beam of a police helicopter sungun. It was coming in low over the docks, searching, probing. In hunting for quarry, it had found only another cop.

Francisco fumbled for his badge and began waving it frantically at the hovering chopper, trying to signal it down. The pilot saw the metallic flash, hesitated at the sight of the big Newcomer, then descended.

"Go, up!" The pilot gaped at his passenger, was reassured by the sight of the detective's badge, then nodded and leaned on the stick. As they rose into the night a whole squad of uniforms materialized on the dock, minutes too late to help. Francisco gestured anxiously seaward, leaning toward the glass and trying to penetrate the darkness.

"On that boat, out there!"

The pilot indicated his understanding. Tilting forward, the copter shot out over the water. Francisco tried to find the fishing boat and avoided looking straight down.

Moving painfully on all fours, Sykes crawled his way up fishing net toward the stern. Harcourt dropped from the roof of the cabin. A taloned hand touched the detective's leg and Sykes jerked clear, bellowing as the sharp claws ripped through his pants into the flesh beneath. He continued to climb the net, however inelegantly.

It was draped over a dinghy slung from the boat's stern. He succeeded in pulling himself over the railing, felt the tiny craft rock as he tumbled in. Then the Harcourt-thing was smiling at him over the gunwales. The dinghy was the end.

Sweat poured from Francisco's face as he forced himself to look down at the ocean racing past beneath the copter. They reached the slow-moving boat and the pilot turned the sungun onto the deck, searching for movement. The light quickly located Sykes and Harcourt, pinned both of them in its glare.

The pounding old diesel had muffled the sounds of Sykes's desperate flight and Harcourt's arrival, but now the ship's owner reacted to the presence of the police helicopter hovering overhead. Frowning, he turned to see what the light was focused on, and got his first glimpse of Harcourt. His hair stiffened and he let out an involuntary shout.

Momentarily distracted from finishing off his prey, the altered Newcomer turned to see the Captain gaping at him from the open bridge above. A wood-handled fishing gaff was slung beneath the railing nearby. Breaking the clips that held it to the wood, Harcourt threw it like a javelin. It went right through the Captain's chest.

Face frozen in shock, the man gripped the gaff protruding from his ribs and staggered backward. He was unconscious before he fell against the throttle. The boat leaped ahead as the engine revved noisily.

The sudden burst of speed threw Harcourt into the dinghy with Sykes. As the alien started to recover, the desperate detective spotted the release for the dinghy's ropes. Lunging forward, throwing himself at the safety release more than reaching for it, he managed to hit the switch. Both lines began to play out and the dinghy dropped neatly into the water.

The tie line was maybe ten feet long. When it had run out, the dinghy lurched ahead, slapping along in the wake of the runaway fishing boat. Ignoring everything else, Harcourt fought to regain his balance as he clawed his way relentlessly toward his quarry.

Water came splashing in over the transom. Never meant to be used in so rough a fashion, the ancient wooden dinghy was already leaking. Harcourt grabbed the detective's leg and began pulling Sykes toward him, his grip unbreakable. Sykes found himself dragged across the bottom of the dinghy as he fought desperately for a handhold. His fingers locked around one of the stern cleats. Harcourt grinned contemptuously, his expression especially horrifying because despite the fangs and distorted face and transformed skull he was still Harcourt, still the same suave, predatory, amoral Newcomer behind the hellish transformation.

He yanked the detective free with ease, breaking his frantic hold on the brass cleat.

As he was pulled toward the bow, Sykes kicked madly in the direction of the ratchet release. Harcourt was very close now, fangs gleaming brightly. In a moment it would all be over.

The detective's shoe connected hard with the ratchet lever. It flipped up and the tie line instantly snaked through the pulley in the bow, freeing the dinghy from the fishing boat. Caught in the grasp of the waves, the tiny craft rocked madly in the wake of the receding boat. Harcourt stumbled, fought for balance.

A wave splashed over the gunwale. Some of the seawater struck Harcourt, who let out an unearthly howl and released his grasp on Sykes. Hearing the copter close by, the detective tried to scramble over the side, only to have the Newcomer grab him a second time. Sykes flailed at the water. His weight on the side of the dinghy tilted it dangerously. More water sloshed in. They were starting to sink.

The drops continued to batter the moaning Newcomer. Thick blood began to bead up on his armored skin, showing where the sea had struck. Sykes was swept up in a desperate bear hug, felt the breath squeezed out of him as Harcourt's massive arms contracted. The pressure was agonizing.

He shoved backward with his feet, knocking the alien off balance. Harcourt lost his grip and staggered, fear showing on his face for the first time. He tried to recover, but it was impossible to stand up and stay stable in the wildly rocking dinghy. In the small boat, all his great size and strength worked against him.

He took a step toward the cringing Sykes, overcompensated to the left as the boat rocked right, tried to correct, and fell. The dinghy overturned, dumping its occupants into the sea.

Gasping for air and kicking madly, Sykes broke the surface. Using his one good arm, he fought for a grip on the smooth back of the capsized dinghy. Around him all was silent except for the lap of the waves, the receding moan of the fishing boat, and the *whup-whup* of the copter circling somewhere overhead.

Until Harcourt burst from the water behind him, body and face partly melted, and dragged him below.

Leaning out the open door of the copter, Francisco watched

helplessly from above, knowing there was nothing he could do to help.

Harcourt's slowly dissolving but still massive body clinging to him, Sykes broke the surface a moment later. He was utterly, completely exhausted. His shoulder had frozen up and he could no longer feel the ankle he'd sprained on his leap into the stern of the fishing boat. With no strength left and only one arm and one leg functioning properly, he could no longer stay afloat in the choppy sea. A wave swept over his head and saltwater went down his throat. He coughed weakly, went under, bobbed back to the surface. With his free hand he tried to beckon for help. He was drowning.

A Newcomer would not last long enough to drown, but Francisco knew what it meant for a human. He turned desperately to the pilot. "What about Air-Sea Rescue? We called in. Where *are* they?"

The pilot looked over at him and shrugged helplessly. "It takes time to get out here from the base! They might be another couple of minutes."

The Newcomer gazed back down at the roiling sea. "Haven't got a couple of minutes." He took the longest, deepest breath of his adult. "Take it down. *Take it down!*"

Nodding, the pilot slowly let the chopper fall toward the turbulent water below. The sungun turned the sea to boiling silver. Locking the fingers of his left hand around the nearest solid grip, Francisco forced himself to lean out and over. The thick, briny odor of the saltwater was ripe in his nostrils, making him dizzy and faint. The surface of the sea was an unstable, sparkling blue beneath him.

Sykes's head appeared in the middle of it, sank back below the surface. The pilot was doing some miracle flying, keeping the chopper's landing skids a scant yard above the water. Still too far away.

Francisco looked back and bellowed loud enough to make himself heard above the whirling blades. "ALL THE WAY!"

"I CAN'T!" the pilot screamed back at him. "IT'LL DITCH!"

Sykes appeared again. His head rolled back and he must have seen the copter, because one hand stretched feebly upward. Too far away. No telling how much longer the pilot could hold their present position.

Francisco could see that if his partner went down one more time, he wouldn't come back up. Trying not to think, not to feel, fighting to stifle every instinct in his body, the Newcomer detective proceeded to do the bravest thing he'd ever had to do in his life.

Hanging on tightly, he abandoned the chopper's cabin and stepped out onto the narrow landing skid. Locking one leg around the metal strut, he let himself dangle freely as he reached for Sykes's groping fingers.

Their fingertips met, slid apart. Feeling the strain in his leg, Francisco made himself stretch another inch, another two. Then he had his partner's hand in his, the grip firm. With success some of his strength returned. There was saltwater on his friend's palm and he winced from the pain as it penetrated his fingers. Ignoring it, he began lifting. Slowly, now wanting, not daring to lose contact.

Harcourt's head exploded from the water a foot in front of Sykes's face. The eye sockets were empty, the soft flesh there having dissolved away almost instantly. Most of the skin was gone, along with much of the underlying muscle. The nearly skeletal body threw itself back onto Sykes, the weight breaking his partner's grip. Sykes and the near-corpse sank beneath the waves.

There was nothing else Francisco could do, nothing more except . . .

Leaning out as far as possible, his face a foot above the surface, he took a deep breath to steel himself and screamed to block the pain he knew would be forthcoming as he shoved his lightly clad arm into the water.

The pain came immediately, racing up his arm toward his shoulder and setting his brain afire. His fingers felt nothing— and then a lump, bobbing just beneath the surface. Feeling around, he got ahold of the object and pulled. His hand emerged from the water, clutching his partner's wrist. The rest of Sykes followed, coughing and sputtering.

His arm feeling like a log in a fireplace, Francisco turned to shout. "Take it up!"

The pilot waved and the copter rose slowly. His wrist locked in Francisco's grip, Sykes began to rise clear of the waves—as Harcourt's arm rocketed upward to clutch the detective's dripping ankle. Sykes looked down in horror at the thing clinging to him as the chopper continued to ascend.

The rest of Harcourt's body broke the surface, the nearly skeletal arm ripped from off the dissolving torso, and the weight fell harmlessly away into the ocean. Trembling uncontrollably, Sykes managed to dislodge the still dangling severed arm from his leg. It spun back into the churning water below.

Francisco continued to pull, careful and steady, until he could slip both arms beneath his partner's. Then Sykes was safely inside the chopper. The pilot headed back toward land. The detective was soaked, battered, barely conscious as he sat on the floor clutching his injured arm. Wincing from the lingering pain, Francisco removed his jacket and wrapped the dry part around his own damaged hand.

As they turned, the pilot stared down at the circle of water where the rescue had taken place. "I was too busy trying to keep us from ditching to see much, but what the hell was that down there? It was *weird*."

Francisco hesitated, then turned meaningfully to his partner, waiting to hear what Sykes would say. The two men stared at each other for a long moment. Then Sykes shrugged painfully.

"Looked like every other damn Slag to me. Just plain ugly."

The pilot's look of uncertainty lingered a few seconds longer, then he grinned at his instruments, reassured. "Yeah, right. That was it."

Despite the pain that was roaring through his right hand, Francisco smiled.

# XIV

Not too much smog this morning, Sykes thought as he did battle with his clothing in the church anteroom. He was having a hell of a time trying to fasten the tuxedo tie with one arm in a sling.

A pair of alien hands appeared to help. One of them was also bandaged and in a sling. Beneath the bandages was one of the most peculiar resin casts Sykes had ever seen. It ran all the way up Francisco's shoulder. If anything, he was less mobile than his partner.

He looked out of place in his oversized tux, like a Chicago Bears linebacker suddenly plopped down in the midst of some royal coronation. Come to think of it, Sykes decided, that was a fitting description of the day's activities to come.

After finally beating the tie into submission, the detective turned sideways and struck a bodybuilder's pose in the mirror. The sling ruined the effect.

"How do I look?"

Francisco took a long look, nodded approvingly. His wife had dressed him. "You look very good."

A knock at the door made both of them turn. Sykes opened it, to reveal his daughter. She looked radiant in her wedding gown. Behind Kristin the interior of the church was swarming with assembled guests. Towering above all the

women and many of the men was Mrs. Francisco. Her son
darted through the crowd, playing with several human boys.

Sykes gazed at his daughter, remembering the little girl
with the perpetually dirty pigtails who was always getting
herself stuck in the tree house outside their Valley home.
What had happened to her? Who was this blinding light,
this cover girl, this movie star standing before him?

She reminded him with very few words.

"Ready, Daddy . . . ?"

Something inside him melted. He was going to take his
time escorting her up the aisle, was going to savor every
second of it. This time he wouldn't need a tape to help him
remember.

One more thing to do before that. The music was beginning outside and the guests were hurrying to take their seats.

"George, uh—I want to apologize now, in advance, for
all the rotten things I'm going to say to you over the years."
He let his daughter slip her arm through his.

The Newcomer smiled down at them. "That is all right,
Matthew. After all, you're only human."

Caught off guard, Sykes paused, then started chuckling as
Kristin led him out of the dressing room into the brightly lit
church. Half of Los Angeles seemed to be sitting in the
pews, and all of them were looking at him and his daughter,
and smiling.

"What a wild man," he murmured fondly. "Never know
what he's gonna say next."

His daughter was pulling slightly, but a moment later he
was matching her stride for stride.